# The Notorious Scarl of Edendal(

### A Clean Regency Romance Novel

## Martha Barwood

Copyright © 2022 by Martha Barwood
All Rights Reserved.
This book may not be reproduced or transmitted in any form without the written permission of the publisher. In no way is it legal to reproduce, duplicate, or transmit any part of this document in either electronic means or in printed format. Recording of this publication is strictly prohibited and any storage of this document is not allowed unless with written permission from the publisher.

*Emerson Lake*
*Kate Cooper*

## Table Of Contents

Prologue ..................................................................... 4
Chapter One ............................................................... 8
Chapter Two .............................................................. 17
Chapter Three ............................................................ 22
Chapter Four .............................................................. 27
Chapter Five ............................................................... 31
Chapter Six ................................................................. 39
Chapter Seven ............................................................ 44
Chapter Eight ............................................................. 50
Chapter Nine .............................................................. 57
Chapter Ten ................................................................ 63
Chapter Eleven ........................................................... 70
Chapter Twelve .......................................................... 80
Chapter Thirteen ........................................................ 85
Chapter Fourteen ....................................................... 96
Chapter Fifteen ......................................................... 102
Chapter Sixteen ........................................................ 112
Chapter Seventeen ................................................... 117
Chapter Eighteen ...................................................... 124
Chapter Nineteen ..................................................... 130
Chapter Twenty ........................................................ 140
Chapter Twenty-One ................................................ 148
Chapter Twenty-Two ................................................ 156
Chapter Twenty-Three ............................................. 163
Chapter Twenty-Four ............................................... 168
Chapter Twenty-Five ................................................ 171
Chapter Twenty-Six .................................................. 176
Chapter Twenty-Seven ............................................. 183
Chapter Twenty-Eight .............................................. 192
Chapter Twenty-Nine ............................................... 200
Chapter Thirty .......................................................... 205

Chapter Thirty-One ...................................................211
Epilogue ....................................................216
Extended Epilogue ....................................................220

# Prologue

*Angelfield House, Edendale, 1815*

The smoke had long since dispersed. That horrible crackling sound of wood being consumed by flames was no longer, an eerie quiet settling all around. It should have felt peaceful after the chaos that had ensued not too long ago, but Emerson felt as if those flames had taken all peace with them. Nothing but turbulent horror remained within him, slowly eating away at him.

The cold was slowly beginning to seep through his trousers. Snow crunched under the weight of his body as he sank closer to the ground, his knees already numb. The pristine white of the landscape before him was now marred with black soot and the remains of the once towering manor that had occupied the space. Now, there was nothing left. Nothing at all.

Emerson wanted to cry. His throat grew painfully raw, his body shaking. Whether it was from the chill of the wintery air or the horror he felt at the sight before him, he didn't know. But those tears would not come, no matter how hard he willed it. With painstakingly dry eyes, he could not look away from the carnage.

"My lord ...." Behind him, his butler called out to him. John Sparkes, or Sparkes as Emerson preferred to refer to him, sounded concerned. Emerson could feel his presence over his shoulder, hovering.

He didn't respond to him. He had no words.

*It all happened so fast. So, so fast.*

"My lord, perhaps it is best to get you out of those clothes," came another voice. His valet, Francis. "It is torn and blackened. It will not protect you against the cold."

Emerson ignored him as well. They were the only two servants who had remained. The others had left at Sparkes' behest, even though they had been the ones to put out the raging fire. They would be rewarded for their efforts, Sparkes had reassured them, but for now, it was time they returned to their families. Emerson envied them. He had no more family.

The family he once had now laid before him, deceased. If only he had been here when it started. If only he had arrived back home in time to save them all. If only that wooden beam hadn't fallen over him while he had been trying to save his mother. If only … if only ….

But nothing would bring them back. Slowly, Emerson let his gaze lower from the grey sky above him to the two bodies that lay a short distance away. The fire had not torn at their flesh, but the smoke had seized their lungs until they breathed no more. It was almost as bad.

Every bit of his body wished to move towards them. His mother's nightdress was black and burnt, her legs bare for all the world to see. The midnight black hair Emerson had inherited was fanned out behind her, an inky stain against the white snow. Alive, Lucy Lake, the Dowager Duchess of Edendale, always wore a slight frown of either worry or consternation. In death, she looked at peace.

Next to her laid his brother, His Grace Jeremy Lake, the recent Duke of Edendale. He was young, though his youth was marred by the wrinkles on his brow. Within the two years he had been duke, stress had bore down on him like a charging bull he could not escape. Emerson had not envied his brother and his responsibilities, but now he wished he had been in his place when the fire struck up.

At least perhaps then, Emerson would not be suffering now, knowing that he was the only one left.

"My lord," his butler broached again. This time, Emerson heard the crunch of snow, indicating that he was coming closer. "We should go to the nearest inn and—my lord!"

Suddenly, Sparkes was next to him, his beaten, worried face crumpled with distress. Emerson paid him no mind. He continued to stare at all he had lost, letting the pain consume him.

"Fetch Mr. Renner and bring him to the inn!" he ordered Francis frantically, and the telltale sound of pounding feet signified his order being carried out. Turning back to Emerson, he said, "My lord, please, we must get out of the cold and somewhere warm. You are injured. It would be best to find a bed and have Mr. Renner check your wounds."

Emerson blinked slowly. His head beginning to ache, he slowly turned to look at the dear butler. Sparkes had been with his family for as long as he could remember, and seeing him now should have provided some solace. All it did was make the hole in his heart grow larger.

The blankness in Emerson's eyes clearly frightened the older man even more. He hurried to his feet and gently coaxed Emerson to his. "Come," Sparkes said firmly.

"No." Emerson pushed him away weakly. The moment he did, he sank back to his knees, his strength leaving him. Now, he could feel it. The pain running throughout his body was not only emotional but physical. His hands, his arms, his legs, and, oh God, his face. His face felt as if it was on fire. Emerson didn't dare to wonder what was wrong with him. He only welcomed the torture. It was what he deserved after failing so miserably, after all.

Sparkes sighed heavily, hanging his head in dejection. A part of Emerson felt bad for worrying the butler so, but nothing could be done about it. Right now, it felt as if his life was ending.

*This is the second time.*

Shame rushed through him as he recalled that day two years ago. The day Jeremy found out that he was to be the new Duke of Edendale. They had stood together in the study as his brother read aloud the letter he'd received from their mother from Rome.

Their father was dead, driven to an early grave by a fever. He'd enjoyed his last moments in Rome, his mother had consoled them in her letter, but all Emerson could think at the time was that he'd failed them. He should have been there. His mother had begged him, after all, to come with them. If he had listened to her pleas, none of that would have happened. His father would still be alive, though still pestered by his heart problems, and the family estate would still be standing before him.

Once again, because of his selfishness, his family suffered.

Finally, the tears came, spilling over his dirty cheeks. Emerson didn't wipe at them, but he heaved, letting the sobs seize him completely. He sank his face into the snow as the tears soaked into them, the coolness pressed against his burning cheeks.

He cried until there were no more tears left. He cried until his body could no longer handle it, and he slipped into a deep sleep. And he was certain that when he woke again, there would be more tears to shed.

But once the crying was over, only one truth remained. With all that was lost, he'd gained one thing. A title. A dukedom.

What a cruel joke.

# Chapter One

*The Dower House, Angelfield Estate, 1817*

"Heavens, I think I have had enough now."

Kate quickly stopped reading, lifting her gaze to the elderly woman sitting across from her. She watched, slightly amused, as the woman lifted a cup of steaming tea to her lips and grimaced. Silence filled the dining space as the elderly woman became the center of attention, sipping the too-hot tea and realizing that she was scalding her tongue.

"Is it that good?" said the man to her left, his crinkled eyes filled with mirth. He, too, had a cup of tea sitting before him, but he had enough self-control to blow gently on it before sipping.

The elderly woman shot him a baleful glance, which made the man grin. "It is lovely," she said. "You know how Kate makes wonderful cups of tea."

"But perhaps you should slow down, Mrs. Bellmore," Kate said gently, hiding her own smile. "Drinking tea that is too hot cannot be good for you. I'm sure you will savour it all the more once it has cooled."

"Hmph." Mrs. Bellmore grumbled something under her breath, but she heeded Kate's advice, setting the cup back on its saucer.

Kate smiled. "Have you had enough of today's *Times*?" she asked.

Mrs. Hester Bellmore nodded her round head. The grey curls at her temples hardly moved, the rest of her silky hair tucked into a chignon at the nape of her neck. Kate had done it herself earlier this morning and was still pleased with her work. Mrs. Bellmore had certainly been a beauty in her younger years, and much of that held up today, her green eyes vibrant and her skin nearly wrinkle-free.

"Yes," she answered Kate. "I'm afraid the news of late is far too much for an old woman like myself. I think I would much prefer hearing you read something else to me."

"Would you like for me to fetch a book of poems then?"

"No, no, it is quite fine. It will soon be time for our nap, won't it, Thomas?"

Mr. Bellmore nodded in agreement with his wife. Kate assumed that he, too, had been rather handsome in his youth, but age had bore down on him far harder than it had his wife. Lines aged his face past his five-and-sixty years, and he walked with a cane. Still, he was as full of life as his wife. "Yes, my dear. Though I cannot think of a single thing I would hate more than to listen to poems."

"That is because you are classless," Mrs. Bellmore stated.

"And you are far too romantic," her husband shot back.

"Is that so bad?"

"No." Despite the slight squabble, Mr. Bellmore grinned. "It is how I managed to make you fall in love with me after all."

Kate watched, still smiling, as Mrs. Bellmore blushed furiously. She had only been with the elderly couple for a few months and was still quite taken with their love for each other. Mrs. Bellmore wasn't as open with her affection as her husband was, but there was still no denying that their love had stood the test of time. Mr. Bellmore grinned at his wife, sensing that she was going to either snap at him for saying such a thing in front of company or ignore him altogether.

She chose the latter, fixing her green eyes on Kate. "Kate, my dear, I am sorry."

"There is no need to apologise, Mrs. Bellmore," Kate said quickly. "I admire the affection you two have for each other greatly."

"And when will you be seeking such affection for yourself?"

The question caught her off guard. "Pardon?"

Mrs. Bellmore, despite her earlier decision, sipped her tea again. Since she did not wince, Kate assumed it had cooled enough. "You are only twenty years old, my dear. You are still young enough to be married. And an earl's daughter, no less!"

"Mrs. Bellmore!" Kate quickly looked around, even though they were alone in the dining room. The other servants were busy, she knew, but she couldn't help but worry that someone might overhear.

"Oh, don't worry," Mr. Bellmore chimed in. "You know your secret is safe with us. We shan't tell a soul. But what my wife says is true. I do think it is time that you think about finding yourself a husband. You are a lovely girl, after all, with many great qualities. It shan't be too difficult."

"I do not wish to be married," Kate said softly.

Mrs. Bellmore looked slightly concerned at that. "Don't you wish to bear children?"

Kate shook her head. She took a few moments to think about what to say next, folding the *London Times* still in her hands. One of the footmen would go into London early just to collect the daily newspaper, as well as any other mail the Bellmores may have. She lay it on the table and met their eyes. "I am quite happy being unmarried. And so what if I am an earl's daughter? That has done nothing for me, and I do not think it will help me find a husband, even if I wished to. I do not want anyone to know the truth of my lineage either, in any case."

Mrs. Bellmore sighed. "Well, there seems there is simply no convincing her, Thomas."

"No, there is no convincing her at all," Mr. Bellmore agreed, mimicking the sigh.

Kate smiled. "I appreciate your concern, however. But please, do not worry yourself over such matters any longer."

"I suppose I shan't." Mrs. Bellmore left her half-drunken tea and rose. "And I am afraid your wonderful tea has sapped all my remaining strength. Thomas, are you ready for our nap?"

"Just a moment." Mr. Bellmore picked up his tea and drank it with gusto. Kate giggled at the look on Mrs. Bellmore's face.

"Goodness, what am I to do with you?" the older woman murmured under her breath.

Mr. Bellmore set his cup down and shot her a wink. "You shall continue spending the rest of your life with me, I suppose."

She rolled her eyes in response, but there was no hiding the smile playing around her lips. "I suppose," she mumbled.

Kate watched with amusement and admiration as Mr. Bellmore grasped his cane and got to his feet. Before he turned to leave, he looked at Kate and asked, "And what shall you do while we are sleeping?"

"I think I might go for a walk," Kate answered. "It is a lovely day outside, after all."

"Well, don't wander too far," Mrs. Bellmore told her before grasping her husband's elbow and leading him out of the room. Kate watched them go, her heart panging with an unidentifiable emotion.

She shoved the feeling aside and rose as well to clear the plates. She brought them to the kitchen, where the cook and the scullery maid gave her their thanks, before she made her way to her bedchamber. The Dower House was quite large, as Mr. Bellmore had worked tirelessly in the army when he was younger. He'd been successful enough to afford this luxurious home for them to rent for the summer, as well as afford the servants they'd taken with them. Kate felt a well of gratitude within her as she meandered down the hallway to her chambers. It reminded her of her old home, the home of an earl who had let every pound he made slip through his fingers.

But it had been so long ago that Kate could not even remember her bedchamber. She stepped into the one she had now and sighed with contentment. It was the grandest bedchamber she'd ever slept in, and every time she laid eyes on it, it brought back to memory her previous hard times working with Mrs. King.

Mean, old Mrs. King who had done nothing but complain and curse at her all day long. She'd been Mrs. King's lady companion in London but had received such horrible treatment that Kate couldn't help but feel a twinge of relief when she'd passed away. That relief was always quickly followed by guilt, however.

But with the Bellmores, Kate truly felt like a part of the family. The fact that they knew that she was the daughter of an earl showed how much faith she put in them. Mrs. King would never have been able to get that bit of information out of her.

Kate wandered past her bed to the open window on the other side of the room, a gentle breeze brushing past the curtains. The view was immaculate, overlooking the lovely garden that the Bellmores had allowed to become overgrown. They had brought their gardener with them, who was working there now, snipping flowers to fill the house with. Kate watched her for a while, barely moving when someone came in.

"Oh, heavens, why do I even bother?" Mary, the housemaid, sighed heavily. "I shall stop coming to your room, Kate. It makes no sense. You leave everything so clean and tidy that there isn't any work for me to do!"

Kate smiled over her shoulder at her. Mary actually looked bothered, hands on her hips, her brown hair slipping out from under her cap. She was one of the few servants the Bellmores had brought with them to Dower House, the rest having already been employed by the house. "I like to do things myself," Kate explained. "It's an old habit, I'm afraid."

"Well, stop it right now. I don't want Mr. and Mrs. Bellmore tossing me aside when they learn I barely do any work around here."

"They won't do that. They adore you."

"Not as much as they adore you, I'm sure." Mary sighed again and drifted closer inside, her cleaning cloth pinched between two fingers.

"Oh, come now, Mary, you know how much the Bellmores love you." Kate waved her hand dismissively as if to clear the conversation from the air. "But enough of that. It has been a while since we've talked, hasn't it? We've both been so busy as of late. Tell me, how fares your family?"

"Well, since my father is the blacksmith in my village, he has had no time to rest—especially since it is summertime. Couples like Mr. and Mrs. Bellmore hail from London to relax in my village, and they hoist their jewelry onto him to fix. He makes no complaints, though. Summertime is the best time for making money."

"And your mother?"

"She is enjoying every bit of her days making pies and gossiping with anyone with a loose enough tongue." Mary rolled her eyes. "I swear, that may be the only reason she makes pies in the first place. Handing them out makes it much easier for her to lure others into conversation."

"She sounds like someone I know," Kate commented with a cheeky grin.

Mary slapped her lightly with her cloth. "I am not as bad as my mother, I assure you. If I was, I would have told you straight away that Phillip, the footman, has growing feelings for Hannah, our scullery maid, and wants to reveal them to her soon. He even said that he …" Mary trailed off, folding her lips into her mouth when she caught Kate's raised eyebrow. "Very well. Perhaps the apple does not fall far from the tree then."

That made Kate laugh. She moved away from the window, slipping into the chair before her vanity table. With Mrs. King, she hadn't even gotten a mirror. "And your sister?" she asked as she began to undo the chignon she had twisted her hair into earlier.

"She is set on marrying the—Oh, Kate, please let me do your hair."

Surprised, Kate looked at her. Mary advanced quickly, running her fingers through Kate's dark brown hair without warning. The loose tresses spilled over Mary's hand, brushing Kate's shoulders. "I've always thought that you had lovely hair and wished that I could style it. Oh, please let me."

"Of course, you may," Kate told her with a smile. Mary grinned victoriously and continued running her fingers through her hair, rubbing Kate's scalp now and again.

"As I was saying, my dear sister, Gillie, wants nothing more than to marry the vicar's son, though I cannot tell if it is because she truly loves him or because she believes he will secure her future."

"Is she getting very far in her advances?" Kate asked.

"Not as far as she'd like. They have formed a simple friendship, but the vicar's son is not pressed to marry. He is young, I believe. No more than four-and-twenty. I believe that he'll remain a bachelor until he is forced to take a wife."

"I wish your sister all the best in her endeavours, then."

"As do I, though I wish she would stop throwing herself at him. It is nice to be pursued. But enough about me. It hasn't been long since you've begun working for Mr. and Mrs. Bellmore, has it? How do you like it?"

It had only been two months. They had interviewed her in spring at their home in London and had instantly taken to her. And her to them. She had revealed her noble lineage to them during that interview without a second thought and was happy to know that she'd left her secret in safe hands.

"This is the first glimpse of peace of mind I've had since my mother died," Kate responded. It felt nice having Mary's hands in her hair. It felt even nice being this relaxed, with a friend to confide in and employers she adored.

"She died when you were a child, didn't she?"

"Yes." In the mirror, Kate caught Mary's somber expression and laughed. "You needn't be sad. My life may not have been very comfortable, but I'm here now, and that's what matters. I feel wanted and appreciated. But I know it won't last forever. The Bellmores are elders, after all, and I am nothing but an old maid."

"A beautiful young woman," Mary corrected firmly. "Even when you are thirty, you will have your beauty and shall have many men willing to marry you."

"I doubt that," Kate said with a laugh. But being an old maid didn't bother her. She'd never entertained the idea of marriage, even though she knew she was not hard to look at. With dark brown—nearly black—hair that fell well past her shoulders, a heart-shaped face, and eyes a cornflower blue, Kate knew she could find a husband if she truly wished it. She'd been called a beauty since she was a young child, though she didn't always pay her appearance much mind.

But becoming a wife was not something meant for her. In fact, Kate didn't think there was very much substance to her life altogether, but she didn't reveal those morbid thoughts to Mary.

"And there we go." Mary stepped back, hands on her hips, a satisfied smile on her face.

"My ..." Kate trailed off in awe. In such a short amount of time, Mary had done wonders. Kate's hair had been pinned up, the natural wave of her tresses brought to life. Mary had left a few tendrils out to frame her face, and for the first time in a long time, Kate felt like a true beauty.

"You see, with a face like yours and the wit and charm you possess, you shan't become an old maid. It is simply impossible. You just haven't met the right man yet. But that will change soon!"

"What do you mean?" Kate asked, turning to look at her.

Mary's brown eyes were glittering with excitement. "The London Season will be drawing to a close, and soon, there will be many visitors to the countryside. There, we will find our chance!"

"We?" Kate echoed with an arched brow, amusement playing around her lips.

Mary flushed. "Well, I want to be married too, you know. Who knows who we will meet?"

"That's true. And you are quite capable of attracting any man you please."

"Do you truly think so?" Mary leaned down to primp herself in the mirror, making Kate laugh.

"I do. No one will be able to resist your charm."

Mary smiled broadly. "Thank you for those kind words, Kate. And thank you for letting me do your hair. I should be going now, though. As much as I like to jest about Mr. and Mrs. Bellmore letting me go, I do not actually want it to happen. What shall you do?"

"Go for a walk."

"Oh, well, in that case, you should take the trail behind the house. It leads into a small forest, and there is a lovely pond hidden within. I'm sure you will love it."

"I shall, thank you."

Mary smiled and left the room. Kate waved at her friend as she slipped out of the room, leaving her alone once more. She turned back to the mirror to admire her reflection, her cheeks pink with excitement. She did not like to dream, to think about the kind of future many other women wanted for themselves. Kate only wanted to be happy and was content to seek that happiness without a man by her side.

But Mary's words lingered with her. And seeing herself now, Kate only wanted to shed the drab blue dress she wore and put on something prettier.

She hurried to her wardrobe to find something but all that was available were old dresses, seasons out of fashion. It was much better than what she was currently wearing, though, so she pulled out a sunflower yellow walking dress she'd had since she was five-and-ten, knowing it would still fit. Thankfully, she had a matching summer bonnet to wear as well. She slipped into the dress and carefully placed the bonnet around Mary's hard work.

The dress, while out of fashion, clung to her slim frame perfectly. Kate remembered how excited she'd been when she'd first received it, just a few months before she was meant to come out to society. But then her father had died, their dire financial state had been revealed, and Kate had learned the painful truth that she would not be able to debut.

The bitterness of that time had long since disappeared, and Kate was happy to know that she still admired the dress as much as she had when she'd first seen it. Slipping on her walking shoes, she left her room.

She heeded Mary's suggestion, taking the old trail behind the Dower gardens and headed towards the line of trees in the distance. The grass grew taller as she got closer, but the trail was still clear enough for her to see. Soon enough, with the wind at her back, Kate made it to the small cops of trees, a tiny pond nearby. She watched a bullfrog hop away from her and wondered if this was the pond Mary was talking about.

*No, she said it was hidden within the forest.*

But Kate was at a loss. Right at the entrance of the forest, there were three distinct paths heading in different directions. Which should she take?

Worrying her lip between her teeth, she decided there was no use turning back to ask Mary for clearer directions. She delved down the path in the center and prayed she would not find herself lost.

## Chapter Two

At the rate he was going, he was bound to wear a hole into the wooden floor soon. The thought didn't stop him. It spurred Emerson on, and he perched his chin in his hand, rubbing the smooth skin as he mulled over the letter he'd just read.

Sitting a short distance away from him, his two faithful dogs watched him go back and forth in the study. They panted heavily, a clear indication that they longed to go out and stretch their legs. But the large dogs remained quiet, watching their master.

Emerson paused for a moment to look at them. "What should I do?" he asked the older of the two dogs, who seemed to stare back at him with wise eyes. Her name was Lily, while her younger, more energetic brother's name was Liam.

He received no response, and Emerson suddenly felt foolish for expecting one. He began pacing once more, staring now at the letter on his desk.

The broken seal had once shown the Wellbourne crest. Emerson had felt excitement when he'd seen it, knowing who the letter was from. Its contents, though, now filled him with dread.

With a groan of annoyance, he marched over to the side table sitting a short distance away and poured himself a glass of brandy. He downed the glass in one fell swoop and grimaced at the harsh burn consuming his midsection. Before he could reach for another, there was a knock on the door.

"Come," he ordered brusquely.

Sparkes entered bearing a plate. Only a single sandwich laid on top, which he brought over to the desk. "Your lunch, Your Grace."

"I don't want it."

"You did not have breakfast, Your Grace. And it is only a small sandwich. You must eat."

"I said I do not want it!" Emerson hissed. Turning his back to the older man, he poured himself another glass. This time, he took a sip rather than throwing it down his throat.

Sparkes was quiet for a while. Emerson had expected him to insist. Sparkes did not like to see his master drinking, after all, especially when he had no food in his stomach. But instead, the other man asked, "Is there something bothering you, Your Grace?"

Emerson turned to face him, a grim look on his face. He pointed to the letter on the table, a silent gesture for him to read.

Sparkes rested the plate with the sandwich on the desk, picked up the letter, and read quickly. Then he lifted those wise eyes to Emerson. "Your friend will be visiting you."

"Yes," Emerson grumbled.

"I do not understand why this is a problem."

Emerson fought back his annoyance. "You know Bob as well as I do," he said. "It will not be a simple visit."

In fact, it may be the very thing that drove Emerson over the edge. Bob Cherry had been Emerson's closest friend since their school days at Westminster. And right now, Bob was Emerson's only friend. They hadn't seen each other in eight years as Bob had gone to France to work for his father. But now, the Earl of Wellbourne was dead, and Bob Cherry would be returning to England to assume the new title.

Emerson should have been happy to see his friend again. They exchanged letters often, and with Bob, Emerson could truly be himself. But Bob had been gone for so long. He did not know about the fire two years ago. He did not know that Emerson was now the Duke of Edendale. And he certainly did not know that, in the past two years, Emerson had become a recluse who did not dare show his face in society. Nor did he want to.

What would he say when he saw Emerson's horrible disfigurement? The scars he bore could not all be covered by his clothing. The worst of them all was on the left side of his face, twisting his flesh horribly. Emerson could not bear to look at himself. So how could his friend, who had remembered him as the sociable bachelor who had once enjoyed life and the company of others?

If Bob were to see him like this, there was no doubt in Emerson's mind that he would try to bring him back into society. The thought alone scared Emerson to death.

He grimly sipped his brandy as Sparkes watched him patiently. He knew the butler had something to say and was waiting, already annoyed, for him to just come out and tell him.

"I think it would be a good thing, Your Grace," Sparkes said after a brief silence. "It has been a while since you have been out among society. Perhaps with his visit, you two could go back to London and see a few old friends—"

"Nonsense! That may be the stupidest thing I've ever heard you say."

Sparkes was not outwardly perturbed by the rude comment. He only clasped his hands behind his back and raised his chin. "It is what I believe is best for you, Your Grace. Mr. Cherry—pardon me, Lord Wellbourne—has always been a good influence on you."

Emerson's annoyance rose tenfold. He downed the rest of his brandy with a grimace and stalked over to his butler. "You are of no help," he grumbled menacingly before he reached out and picked up the sandwich. Before Sparkes could assume that he would at least take a bite, Emerson shoved the sandwich into the pocket of the old pair of trousers he wore. Sparkes' eyes lit with muted disappointment, but the expression didn't last very long. The butler did let out a small sigh, though.

The defiant act did nothing to make Emerson feel better. If anything, he was even more annoyed—though it was directed at himself. Not caring to explore that feeling, he snapped his fingers at Lily and Liam, and the two massive dogs bounded to their feet instantly.

"I'm going for a walk," he announced, turning his back to his butler. "Don't wait around for me."

"Please eat, Your Grace," Sparkes tried once more.

Emerson ignored him. It was clear—with that crumbling sandwich stuffed in his pocket—that he would not be eating lunch today. With the way he was feeling, he doubted that he would have any dinner either. It wouldn't be the first time.

Before he left the room, he fetched his walking stick, which was propped against a bookshelf, and followed the dogs out the door. Excited as they were at the prospect of a walk, they hurried down the hallway, the sound of their steps being swallowed by the thick carpet. Emerson followed morosely. Right now, his dogs were the only company he could stomach. As they passed through the foyer, he spotted the housekeeper dusting in the corner, and she made a quick, respectful curtsy to him before she hurried away. Emerson didn't spare her any mind.

Outside, the sun hung high, its brilliant rays warming the earth below. It was an objectively lovely day, and Emerson hated it. A part of him wished the sky had been as dull and grey as his mood and that the sweet peas lining the path to the forest hung their heads instead of opening their petals for the world to see. He wished thunder would boom in the distance and that the promise of rain would chase away every woodland critter he saw as he trudged closer to the forest, his dogs leading the way.

Emerson was tired of the constant sunny days of Edendale and couldn't wait for winter. At that time, he could truly lock himself away, reminiscing on the winter two years ago and hating himself all over again.

But for now, the dogs wanted to go for a walk, and he needed to clear his head. What should he do about Bob?

Already a good distance from the house, he slowed, pulling the sandwich from his trousers. Emerson's stomach grumbled at the sight, but his appetite was well and truly gone. So, he broke off a piece and tossed it to Lily, who caught it elegantly between her jaws. Liam pranced around Emerson's body, waiting for his.

Absently, Emerson tossed the younger dog his piece as he thought about what he should do. Without a doubt, Bob was already on his way to England. There would be no use sending him a letter telling him not to come to Edendale. When he arrived at the door, though, could Emerson send him away? Claim that he had been afflicted by a terrible and contagious illness? Tell him that he was simply in no mood for company? No matter what he thought about, Emerson knew that the hardheaded Bob would barge in anyhow.

His mood grew fouler at the thought. When the sandwich was finished, the dogs rushed ahead, going in different directions. Liam chased a massive purple butterfly while Lily sniffed around. Emerson stabbed the ground with his walking stick, wanting to take his anger out on something.

At that moment, the sound of laughter reached his ears—children's laughter. Emerson paused, looking around. They'd made it a good distance from the house, already close to the entrance of the forest. Closer to the road, however, he spotted two blond heads bobbing above the tall grass, chasing each other around. He recognized the son and daughter of the smithy, who had a tendency to trespass on his property.

"You two!" Emerson bellowed, frightening even his dogs. "Get away right now!"

The children drew to a quick halt, but Emerson was already advancing. The moment they laid eyes on him, they burst into tears. Emerson stopped in his tracks.

"Monster!" the little boy cried.

"Don't hurt us!" the girl shouted.

They ran away from him, leaving him staring after them.

*Good riddance*, Emerson thought. He turned back in the direction of the forest, his dogs now somberly following.

*They think I am a monster. A beast. It's just as well. No one will dare trespass again when word gets around.*

Emerson tried to console himself with that thought, but his anger and frustration began to give way to something else nearly as debilitating. He didn't want that feeling to linger.

But there was no denying that, with the scars he bore, he was no better than a beast indeed. And when Bob came, he would see that for himself.

## Chapter Three

*I am well and truly lost.*

The good news was that she'd found the beautiful pond Mary had spoken about. Despite being tucked away in the center of the forest, a few rays of sunlight slipped through the foliage and shone brilliantly on the blue water. She spotted a lizard dipping into a moss-covered log, a frog hopping after its mate, and many ducks dipping their heads under the cool water to keep the heat off their backs. Kate sank onto a massive boulder with a conveniently flat surface and sighed happily at her peaceful surroundings.

The bad news was that she had no idea how she'd made it here, so she did not know how to return to Dower House.

But she didn't want to think about that right now. She was only sad that she hadn't thought to bring a small picnic with her and made a mental note to do just that the next time she decided to visit this pond. If she could find it again, that was.

*At the very least, I know I am not very far from home.* She hadn't walked for long before she came upon the pond after all. It may take a little longer than it could have, but she would eventually find her way back, so she wasn't too worried.

For now, she was content to sit and watch the ducks. The moment she relaxed, though, she heard rustling coming from the other side of the pond. Kate frowned at the sound, and a second later, two large dogs came bounding through the undergrowth. Kate shot to her feet just in time for the dogs to rush excitedly through the pond and launch themselves at her.

"Oh, goodness!" she exclaimed with a laugh. The smaller of the two dogs was shaggier—a boy, Kate saw—and his paws were far muddier. But he seemed to be ecstatic to see her, while the other—who Kate assumed was a girl, though she would have to take a closer look—seemed content to wait her turn.

"Where did you two come from?" Kate asked, scratching behind the shaggy dog's ears. With much effort, she managed to lean down and rub the other's head as well, and the dogs panted happily.

They were soiling her dress. If the mud stains dried by the time she returned home, it would take some effort to remove them from the fabric. Kate didn't care. She loved animals—dogs, especially—and shared in the dogs' excitement. She was as happy to see them as they seemed to be happy to see her.

Caught up in the animals before her, Kate did not notice that they had been followed until it was too late. A hand shot out past the trees on the other end of the pond, and a moment later, a thin, glowering man stepped through.

Kate's heart skipped a beat. She forgot about petting the dogs and they, clearly content with what they had received, ran off to explore around the pond instead, scaring the ducks. Kate hardly noticed, her hand lifting to her rapidly beating heart.

*He's so handsome*, she thought, drinking him in. He wore nothing but a thin white shirt and a pair of old trousers, matched with muddy riding boots. In his hand, he grasped a thin walking cane that closely resembled the one her father once had. His dark hair was long enough to cover both sides of his face and touched the top of his shoulders. He did not look at her, which gave Kate the chance to take in the fact that he was rather thin, yet tall and commanding enough to make her legs grow weak.

She put a hand on the tree next to her to steady herself.

"Come!" the man shouted, and Kate jolted out of her trance. The dogs looked up at his command, but rather than go to his side, they returned to Kate for more pets.

Kate smiled. "It seems they are not yet ready to leave," she said to the stranger.

The man stopped dead in his tracks, his eyes narrowing. Kate lifted her brows at that. Had he not seen her before?

For a moment, she thought her response would go unanswered, but then he asked, "Who are you?"

"I'm afraid I do not originally reside here," she responded with a friendly smile, though she did not answer the question. "Do you, sir? Perhaps you could assist me."

"You are trespassing on my property."

"Oh, am I?" Perhaps, had he said those words a little gentler, Kate would have heeded the quiet command to leave. She only grew annoyed. "Well, I am a bit occupied right now, if you cannot tell."

She made a show of petting the shaggier dog, and he leaned against her skirts companionably.

"Liam, Lily, come!" the man hissed. The dogs ignored him, staying by Kate's side.

"Liam, is it?" Kate said to the dog leaning against her. "What a lovely name for such a lovely boy."

"Do not pet them like that."

"Why not?" Kate asked without looking back at the handsome stranger. "They seem to like it. And judging by your reaction to it, it seems they do not receive it often."

"Who are you to tell me what my dogs receive?"

"I am only a passerby, I assure you," she said simply. She looked at him and saw the anger on his face, which only spurred her own.

She did not like to feel enraged, so she quietly calmed herself down. She'd done nothing after all.

Then, he did something unusual. He moved his hair from his face and twisted his head to the side, revealing the harsh scar covering the left side. Kate blinked in surprise. She recognized the scar as one made from fire. Her uncle had carried such a scar himself, received from his participation in the war, and she knew it was important not to show any outward reaction to such a sight. Even so, Kate couldn't help but think how endearing the scar made this man before her. He had been handsome before, but now … now, he was completely enthralling.

Questions filled her mind, rushing to her tongue. But she knew better than to voice them, so she took another approach.

"My apologies for trespassing, sir," she said. "But I am afraid this is an area I do not know well, and I am a bit lost."

"That is not my problem."

"Perhaps. But if you wish for me to trespass no longer, perhaps giving me some help would not be so inane."

His dark eyes glitter with anger. Kate couldn't help but wonder what she could have done to upset this man so. Simply because his dogs had taken a liking to her?

"Go away, woman," he hissed. "I have no more time for the likes of you. Liam, Lily, come!"

This time, the dogs seem to hear the seriousness in his command and come bounding over. Kate bristled at his rudeness, but she said nothing as she watched her new furry companions leave her side. Lily went calmly, but Liam went rushing over and scared a duck that had been hiding under the reeds. The duck flew into the sky with a loud quack and startled the handsome stranger, making him jump. The moment he did, he lost his footing.

Kate watched the scene unfold before her in horror. He could not regain his balance in time, and, with a grunt, he went crashing into the pond. Kate gasped, droplets of water wetting her cheeks. Her first instinct was to rush over and help him. But when he tried to get up, dripping wet from the roots of his hair, her urge to help dissolved into inescapable humor.

Laughter bubbled up her throat, and Kate could do nothing to hold it back. She giggled behind her hand at the sight of him, her stomach cramping as she tried not to let out the full force of her mirth. All that did was make her eyes water.

"Oh, goodness, let me help you!" Kate stifled the laughter as much as she could and rushed into the pond. The bottom of her skirt grew soaked with water as she grabbed ahold of his arm. Up close, he looked even more ridiculous, and she began laughing again.

The man glowered at her. "Leave me be!" he shouted at her, brushing off her hand. It forced Kate to step back, and she could only watch as he clambered out of the pond himself, his long black hair plastered to his face. This time, he made sure to keep the scar away from her view, eyes filled with fury.

Kate felt a pull of pity that had her humor dissipating. She was tempted to question him about the scar, but she bit down on her tongue instead. After a moment, she managed to ask, "Are you all right?"

"It is none of your business," he grumbled.

"Of course," she responded, expecting no different. "And I would love to leave you be, but I do not know the way back to Dower House."

The man looked at her, curiosity flickering in his eyes for a moment. Without a word, he pointed to the right of her, at the path she had certainly not come from.

"Thank you," she said to him, a little surprised that he'd helped her at all. "And I shan't repeat the error of trespassing again, I promise."

Of course, she received no reply to that, and Kate was surprised at the disappointment she felt. Lifting her skirts in her hand, she waded out of the water, now very much aware of how sodden her slippers were. It would be an uncomfortable walk home, but perhaps the sun would dry it a bit by the time she returned to the house. She made her way to the path the man had pointed to and glanced back at him.

He was watching her, his dogs by her side. Kate's heart thudded in her chest, and it took some effort for her to continue, remembering that she was not wanted there. She wanted so badly to ask about the scars, but proper decorum dictated that she pretend she had not seen it at all.

"Goodbye, Lily and Liam," she said softly, waving at the two dogs who watched her with steady eyes. Then she risked another look at the endearing, awful man and felt another pull she was hard-pressed to ignore. With more effort than she cared to admit, she turned and continued down the path.

It wasn't until she was a good distance away did his words come rushing back to her.

What did he mean by *his* property?

## Chapter Four

"Your Grace, I just do not understand. What could have caused this?"

Emerson glanced up at Francis' face in the tall mirror. For the past thirty minutes, as his valet waited for the maids to finish preparing Emerson's bath, Francis had been watching Emerson with a confused expression. Emerson knew he'd planned on asking why he had returned to Angelfield House dripping wet but was waiting for the right moment.

Now, as the layers of wet clothes were stripped from his body, Emerson did not know how to answer him. The truth, after all, filled him with shame.

"There was a trespasser on my land," Emerson explained gruffly. "And when I caught them, they ran off. I took chase and happened to fall into the pond."

"A trespasser?" Francis' confused look deepened. The wet shirt landed in a heap next to Emerson's muddy boots. "That cannot be. Everyone knows that they cannot and must not trespass on your land."

"Everyone but the smithy's children, it seems."

"Yes, but they were not the ones, were they?" The valet's blond brows knitted together. He was a rather handsome fellow, just a few years older than Emerson's eight-and-twenty years. "Did you get a good look at the man?"

*I most certainly did*, Emerson thought grimly. As a matter of fact, he could not get that mysterious woman's face out of his head.

She was a natural beauty, though she wore an old dress and a tattered bonnet. Like a princess right out of a fairytale, she'd looked so out of place yet at peace with her surroundings, a few tendrils of her dark brown hair shifting in the wind. Her blue eyes were as bright as the sky above, watching him with curiosity, kindness, and amusement. And her slim figure and lovely smile made the shame bearing down on Emerson consume him even more.

He felt a little guilty for lying to Francis, but how could he tell him about how rudely he'd treated the stranger in the forest? Yes, she had been trespassing, but it was as clear as day that she was not familiar with the area. He could have shown her a bit more kindness and grace, and yet he had bared his fangs at her and tried to chase her away by showing her his scars.

And she hadn't even blinked at it.

Emerson was used to others running from the sight of it. Though he loathed to admit it, it was partly the reason why he secluded himself upon his property. He was a monster, through and through, and his physical appearance could chase away the most compassionate of hearts. Yet, the beautiful woman hadn't reacted in the slightest.

*Perhaps she didn't see it*, he thought to himself. But how was that possible? Even when she'd come closer to help him out of the pond, it should have been obvious. Why hadn't she reacted to it?

Embarrassment washed over him, and it took all he had not to hang his head.

"Well, Your Grace?" Francis pressed. All of his soaked clothes now lay in a neat pile, and Francis moved towards the steaming bath. "Did you?"

"Don't question me," Emerson snapped. "I didn't get a good look at him, no."

If Francis was put out by Emerson's rudeness, he didn't show it. He was used to it. "Then it must not be one of the locals. Surely, this person knew no better. It would have been nice if you'd seen them so that we could find him later."

"Find him later to do what?"

"Tell him the errors of his ways, of course."

Emerson didn't respond right away. He sank into the heated bath and let out a sigh of contentment. He did not find pleasure in much lately, but a hot bath was an exception.

"Considering the fact that he ran, I think he is quite aware that he was doing something he shouldn't have," Emerson said. He didn't like the fact that he had to lie, but he didn't want Francis to know how rude he'd been to the woman. Though he wouldn't dare to show it, Francis would disapprove. And Emerson didn't like when his valet disapproved of him.

"I suppose so," Francis said, clearly still mulling it over. He opened his mouth to say something else but was interrupted by a knock on the door.

"May I, Your Grace?" came Sparkes' voice on the other end.

Emerson closed his eyes, resting his head on the back of the bath, and waved his hand at Francis to open the door. He listened as Sparkes entered.

"Your brandy, Your Grace," Sparkes announced.

"Give me a glass and leave the decanter by my bed," Emerson ordered. "And then you two, leave me be."

"Will you be having dinner, Your Grace?" the butler asked.

Emerson took a moment to respond. In truth, he was ravished and felt a little regretful for having wasted the sandwich. He didn't dare to show it. "I shall."

"Very well, Your Grace."

Emerson received his glass and then listened as the two men left him alone. In the silence of his bedchambers, Emerson opened his eyes, staring blankly at the ceiling. Unbidden, the woman's face popped into his mind once more.

*Who is she?*

It did not make any sense to him. A woman—especially a woman who possessed her beauty—did not look at a monster such as him and not run for the hills. He'd seen it many times before. Young maidens who had strayed too close to his house without realizing it had grabbed their skirts and ran the moment they spotted him. A combination of his terrible manners, his angry eyes, and that horrid scar on his face was all it took for them to fear him.

But there had been no fear in her eyes. If he was being honest with himself, he thought he might have seen a moment of intrigue instead.

Emerson sipped his brandy, her laugh echoing in his head. Though she'd tried to, she hadn't been able to hold it back. Which made him all the more certain that she was not a local, as no woman who knew of him would dare laugh at him that way. He was the duke, after all. And from the look of it, she was just a common woman.

Yet, she had watched his graceless fall and could barely contain her giggles. Who was this woman to neither fear him nor hesitate to laugh at him?

While his shame at his behavior earlier lingered, his curiosity grew as well. Emerson finished his brandy without realizing it, his need to know who she was mounting by the second. He couldn't ask Sparkes or Francis, though. They would grow curious as to why he cared and would think it was more than it actually was. And Emerson was convinced that it was nothing. He only wanted to know who she was, that was all. He only wanted to pay her a visit and give her a firm warning never to trespass again. Then he would have his peace of mind.

The dogs would love to see her as well, he realized. They'd never disobeyed him before, and yet, upon meeting this stranger, they'd stuck to her side as if she was their mistress. Traitorous beasts, they were.

He sighed, sinking further into the water and letting the empty glass dangle between his fingertips. He wondered if she'd made it out of the forest and back to Dower House ….

Suddenly, Emerson sat up, water sloshing over the side. That's right! She'd wanted direction back to Dower House, hadn't she? If that was where she was staying, then it wouldn't be too difficult to find her, would it?

A plan rapidly formed in his mind, and for the first time in a long time, Emerson felt a shadow of a smile.

## Chapter Five

The sun was hanging low in the sky by the time Kate found her way back to Dower House. Luckily, the afternoon had been hot enough to dry her somewhat, and as she made her way up the steps leading to the back door of the house, she was feeling only mildly uncomfortable.

She headed for her bedchamber, intending to change into something warmer. On her way there, she ran into Mary, who was carrying a tray of dirty dishes from the drawing room.

"Oh, heavens! What happened to you?" the maid exclaimed dramatically.

Kate nearly sighed. "Honestly, I am not entirely sure what happened. It feels oddly like a dream."

"Does it?" Mary's eyes glittered with curiosity. "You will have to tell me all about it when you have the time later. For now, though, you should change. There are visitors."

"Visitors?" Kate glanced behind Mary at the drawing room she'd just left. If she listened closely, she could hear the sound of laughter. "Who is it?"

"Parson Dewhurst and his eldest daughter, Miss Eve, have come to pay the Bellmores a visit. They wish for you to join them, of course."

Kate frowned. She didn't recognize the names. "Very well, I shall change quickly then. Have they been here very long?"

"Not very," Mary said with a shrug. "Perhaps one hour?"

"That *is* long!"

"But they will be here for a while longer, so don't worry. Oh, I wish I could do your hair once more, but Mrs. Bellmore has requested another serving of tea."

"Don't worry." Kate touched Mary's ruined work with a bit of regret. She'd truly looked pretty before her walk and had hoped it would last. Sadly, much of her hair had fallen from the hold, and the ends were tinged with water. "I can do it myself, thank you."

Mary sighed but brightened up once more as she said, "Don't forget to tell me what's gotten you so disheveled."

Kate laughed, shaking her head as the maid drifted away in the direction of the kitchen. Try as she might, Mary could not stop herself from gossiping. Kate was happy she had a bit of time before Mary would come demanding to know what had happened. She still hadn't sorted through it entirely herself.

She headed upstairs to her bedchamber and quickly pulled out a proper, yet dull, brown dress. Once the dress was one, she sat before her vanity table and began to take down her hair.

*Who was that man?*

That question had plagued her every step of the way back to the house, and Kate was no closer to figuring it out. She was still shocked at his rudeness but was even more surprised at the fact that her heart would skip a beat every time she pictured his scarred face. Though he'd been unkempt, his hair clearly not styled in a while, and his arms far too thin for a man his age, his endearing handsomeness had shown through. He may not have been very kind, but there was no denying that he was interesting.

Kate remembered how he'd fallen into the water and paused for a moment to let out a small chuckle. It hadn't been nice, she knew, to laugh at him like that, but she hadn't been able to hold herself back. Had she offended him further by doing that?

She might have, but it was unlikely she would ever see him again.

That thought brought on a wave of disappointment, which she quickly shoved aside. There was no need to be disappointed. He'd been mannerless and harsh to her. Why should she want to see him again?

Shaking her head at the very idea, Kate quickly twisted her hair into a chignon and rose to leave the room. She hurried down to the drawing room, knocking gently before she entered.

"Oh, Kate!" Mr. Bellmore greeted amicably. "There you are! Come, sit right here. We've been waiting for you to return."

Kate drew closer and sat on the sofa on the other side of Mr. Bellmore. Mrs. Bellmore occupied an armchair next to him, and across from the couple was an older man—perhaps near his fiftieth year—and a woman closer to Kate's age. The man and woman looked very much alike, with sandy brown hair and bright, expressive green eyes.

Mrs. Bellmore spoke next, clinking her cup of tea against her saucer. "Kate, allow me to introduce you to Parson Dewhurst and his daughter, Eve."

"It is a pleasure to meet you both," Kate greeted respectfully. "My name is Kate Cooper, a companion to Mr. and Mrs. Bellmore."

"We've heard much about you, Kate," Mr. Dewhurst said with a twinkle in his eye. Unlike the others, he was gorging on a lemon cake rather than a cup of tea.

"Have you?"

"Yes," Eve responded with a grin. "Mr. and Mrs. Bellmore have spent the past twenty minutes telling us all about the wonderful young lady they'd hired before they'd left London."

"All good things, I hope?"

"Oh, you know how much we adore you, my dear," Mrs. Bellmore interjected. "We were growing worried when you did not return home in time. Did something keep you?"

Kate expected the question and still did not know how she should respond. "Yes, something like that."

"Oh? What's the matter? You seem concerned about something."

Mr. Bellmore straightened. "Are you hurt?"

Kate quickly shook her head. "No, nothing of the sort. Though I cannot say that my pride is not bruised a little."

The other four exchanged confused glances. "I'm afraid you will have to give us a little more detail, Miss Cooper," Mr. Dewhurst urged.

"Well ... I went for a walk through the forest in search of a small pond. I grew lost after a while, but I managed to find it in time. I was enjoying the ambient surroundings when two dogs came charging toward me. They were very friendly," Kate said quickly at the look of alarm on Mrs. Bellmore's face, "and I was very taken with them. But I soon realised that their owner was nearby and was not fond of me petting them."

"Wait a moment," Eve interrupted with a raise of her hand. "Two dogs, you say?"

Kate nodded, frowning. She watched as Eve glanced at her father, and the two exchanged knowing looks.

Eve turned back to Kate with a concerned expression. "Please tell me you did not come upon the duke and his dogs?"

"The duke?" Kate echoed bemusedly.

"The Duke of Edendale. His house is bordered by the forest, and much of the forest itself belongs to him. He is known to prowl around his land with his dogs in tow. Everyone in the village knows those two massive animals."

A duke? Kate thought back at the disheveled man and could hardly believe it. He looked nothing like a duke, save perhaps for the expensive-looking walking cane he'd had in his possession. But the parson and his daughter were looking at her with such a serious expression that she knew they told no lies.

"Well, I suppose that may be why he shouted at me and told me that I was trespassing," Kate said to them.

"Oh, heavens, it is never a good thing to get on His Grace's bad side," Eve said. "He is known for his horrible temper, and everyone knows never to walk on his land. He hates trespassers more than anything. Why, one time, I heard that he'd even set his dogs loose on a man who'd wandered too far, though I do not know how much truth is in that tale."

Kate couldn't imagine the excited Liam and the calm Lily ever attacking anyone. She leaned closer, interested. "Do you know the duke well, then?"

"I know of him," Eve explained. "Though I have never had the misfortune of meeting him myself, thank goodness."

"Then do you know of the scar he bears?"

"Scar?" Mrs. Bellmore asked. She looked as invested in what was being said as her husband was. "He bears scars?"

"Yes," Kate responded. "He has a terrible burn scar on the left side of his face. I saw it plainly when he scolded me for petting his dogs and trespassing on his land. And I couldn't help but wonder how he'd gotten it."

Silence descended within the room. The Bellmores and Kate stared at Mr. Dewhurst and his daughter, waiting for the explanation. It was clear that they knew the answer but were uncomfortable with telling the story.

Mr. Dewhurst spoke first. "There was a terrible fire two years ago. The original Angelfield House was burnt down, and the Dowager Duchess and Duke of Edendale perished from the smoke. The current duke had been returning from London when the fire started and had rushed into the burning building to save his brother and mother. However, it was not meant to be. As I've heard, a burning beam fell down on His Grace while he was attempting to drag his brother out, and he was knocked unconscious. When he came to, he was outside in the snow. The flames had been put out by the servants, and the former duke and dowager duchess were dead."

"The current duke had been taken to Foster's Inn to have his wounds treated," Eve continued, her tone somber. Kate couldn't tell if there was truly a shimmer of tears in her eyes or if she was imagining it. "Mr. Renner, the village physician and personal physician of the duke's family, had been tending to the wound when my father arrived. I remember accompanying him to help tend to the others who had been hurt in the flames. I had passed by the duke's room as my father had been praying over him and ...." She trailed off, swallowing.

Her father picked up after taking a sip of his tea. "The duke was still in a state of shock. So much so that I do not think he felt any pain that night. His face was sweltering and red, and blood had soaked through his clothes. He'd been cut and bruised all over, but the worst of it all had been the scar on his cheek. My heart had broken for him that night, and I do not think the duke had ever been the same again."

"That's horrible," Mrs. Bellmore murmured. Kate noticed that the older woman was on the verge of tears and quickly fetched a handkerchief for her to dab her eyes. Mr. Bellmore laid a hand atop his wife's to console her.

Kate felt the same horror and sadness at the tale. Now, all she could think of was how he'd tried to hide his scar when he was getting out of the pond. She couldn't imagine what he must feel, to have that constant reminder of such a horrible day.

"He hasn't left his property since the new Angelfield House was built," Eve continued. "Some say it is for the best. That night changed him, of that I am certain."

"I agree with you, daughter," Mr. Dewhurst said. "He hates children and anyone who trespasses on his property. I am surprised your encounter with him was not worse, Miss Cooper."

"I think it may be because he'd fallen into the pond," Kate said without thinking.

Eve let out a surprised giggle, her cheeks coloring as she held her hand to her mouth. "He fell?"

Kate nodded. It was too late to take it back now, though she no longer found it as funny. "I tried to help him, but he chased me away."

"If he is as bad as they say, then that comes as no surprise," Mr. Bellmore said with a decisive nod.

Mrs. Bellmore agreed with her husband and said something in response, but Kate stopped listening. Now, the scar was all she could think about, pity welling within her. It was a badge of honor, a reminder of his love for his family. He'd done all he could to save them and had failed in the end. To her, it only showed his compassion.

But to him, it was surely a brand of failure. Now, he lived all alone with the constant reminder of what he'd lost. How could anyone fear such a man? How could they not think of him as simply a man in pain?

She thought of his black eyes and wondered if he would ever know peace again.

"It would certainly not do to anger him again, Miss Cooper," Eve said, breaking Kate out of her reverie. "I do not think you will be so lucky next time."

That was the last thing Kate wanted to happen. "I would like to be better acquainted with my surroundings then. Could you help me by showing me all the safe paths that would avoid his land?"

"Certainly," Eve said with a bright smile. "I could do so after church this Sunday. Will you all be attending?"

"Yes, it has been a while since we've attended church, hasn't it, Thomas?" Mrs. Bellmore said to her husband.

"It would be nice to go this Sunday," Mr. Bellmore agreed.

Mr. Dewhurt grinned and clapped loudly, rising. "Then it is settled. We shall see each other once more this Sunday for service."

"We could go for a walk after church," Eve said to Kate as she rose along with her father. "I could show you the paths then."

"That would be lovely." Respectfully, Kate stood, sensing that they were ready to take their leave. She felt a pinch of excitement at the thought of Sunday, already seeing a friend in Eve. She hasn't had many friends before.

Kate gestured for them to follow her, and she led them to the door. Goodbyes were exchanged, and soon enough, the Dewhursts were gone. Kate returned to the drawing room and heeded the request of Mr. Bellmore to fetch them a pack of playing cards. She didn't miss the look of competitive fierceness in Mrs. Bellmore's eyes and knew that they would be occupied for some time. They wouldn't need her.

Once the game had begun, Kate announced her intention to go to the library. She slipped away from the competing couple and found solace amongst the tall bookshelves and the smell of old books. She milled around the room, and once she found the map she had been looking for, she went to the desk and sat, spreading it wide.

Her intention was to do a bit of studying on her own, to learn what areas were off-limit, but Kate could not concentrate. Not when a pair of angry black eyes kept filling her mind and distracting her.

She sighed, staring out the window instead. Night had fallen, and a gentle breeze wafted in past the curtains. In the distance, she saw the spires of Angelfield House poking into the sky and thought of the lonely man within. The house must feel so big for him.

Her heart went out to him. His rudeness earlier felt inconsequential now, and all Kate could think about was that there was certainly pain hidden deep within. The same man who had dived into a raging fire to save his family must have been locked away behind walls of shame, anger, and regret for having failed them. Now that she looked back at their encounter, she did not see a rude man but a man who used his pain to lash out.

*It would have been better if we'd met under different circumstances*, she thought with a sigh.

But he was a duke and one intent on staying away from everyone. They would never meet again.

The pang of regret she felt at that knowledge was a little harder to ignore this time.

## Chapter Six

"You seem to know what I should do."

Emerson stared into the deep brown eyes of his faithful dog, Lily, and could have sworn that when she cocked her head to the side, she was giving him the affirmative. He sighed, shaking his head. Liam had rushed off to do his business, so Emerson had paused along the path for the younger dog to finish and catch up.

Lily looked patiently up at him, as if waiting for him to unburden himself onto her.

Emerson stooped to scratch her behind her ears. "Don't look at me like that, you wise dog. Though sometimes, I wish you could speak. I have a feeling you would have a lot of great advice for me."

Lily barked in response, and at that moment, Liam came rushing up, sniffing at the ground. The two dogs continued their walk down the seemingly endless path, and Emerson followed behind them, his mind drifting back to the issues that had been plaguing him for a few days now.

Bob Cherry and the mysterious woman he'd met at the pond.

Bob was the most pressing of his problems, he was afraid, since Emerson was certain that his friend would be arriving at any moment. And he still hadn't thought of what to do or say to him when he did. Emerson was only certain of what thing—that he did *not* want to return to society. He wanted to remain the recluse he'd turned into ever since that horrible day. Emerson wasn't very keen on upsetting his daily routine of waking up, growling at everyone who came near him, and only being able to stomach the company of his dogs. And sometimes caring to eat, when the hunger turned into pain that he could no longer ignore.

The London Season was still underway, he knew, but once summer was over, it would be drawing to a close. Bob would be eager to take advantage of the time they have left and would undoubtedly try to drag Emerson everywhere with him. Balls, parties, hunting ….

The very thought made Emerson shudder.

"But I cannot just turn my friend away," Emerson mused aloud. Lily looked back at him for a second but did not stop her happy prancing down the path. "I have not seen him in eight years, and while it was nice to exchange letters, it would be even nicer for us to speak in person, won't it?"

Emerson wasn't so sure. He had such little patience for the company of others that he didn't know how he would act once Bob arrived.

Still, he continued to voice his thoughts out loud, not caring that he may seem a bit mad if someone were to hear him. "He will not approve of my lifestyle. He'll try to change me. He won't understand what I'm going through. No one understands."

The somber realization soured his mood even more. Emerson couldn't let him come to Angelfield House. The bad consequences would certainly outweigh the good.

"Should I feign sickness? Should I lie to him and say that I had to go to Scotland for urgent business and that I shall see him once I return?" He shook his head at that, brows furrowed. "No, he will wait for me. Worse, he may just see right through the lie."

Nothing he thought of was a good enough excuse to prevent Bob from coming here. Emerson sighed so heavily that it felt as if it shook the world around him.

He couldn't let Bob see him like this. As much as he wanted to remain hidden away from everyone, Emerson could admit to himself that he felt a twinge of shame that he had allowed himself to become like this.

Without warning, the sound of laughter filled his mind, a sharp memory that had been following him since that day at the pond. Emerson slowed his pace as he thought back on the smile that had played around the mysterious woman's lips, the mirth dancing in her beautiful blue eyes. No matter how hard he tried, he could not summon the anger he should have felt at her laughing at him. No ... all he felt was intrigue, and all thoughts of Bob drifted away.

She was all he could think of now. He did not take note of the path the dogs headed down, only following them aimlessly. For the past few days, he'd lain awake at night, thinking about her. Wondering who she was, where she'd come from, and if she was thinking about him as well.

That last thought made his cheeks grow hot with embarrassment, a little ashamed to admit that he hoped that she was. He wished he had at least learned her name.

But if that were the case, what did she think of him? Surely, much like everyone, she would only remember a scarred and horrible man with a crass tongue.

Yet a part of him didn't think she did. The way she looked at him that day ... he didn't feel any fear from her. No pity, no disgust. She'd only seemed intrigued, though the expression had lit her eyes for just a moment. It was enough to keep her present in his memory for the days that ensued after.

That, and the fact that she was the most beautiful woman he'd ever laid eyes on.

He didn't want to meet her again. Or at least, that was what he kept telling himself. But as he thought of her now, Emerson now knew how much he lied to himself. He wanted to see the mysterious woman again. To apologize? To ask her the questions he'd been asking himself? He honestly didn't know, and he didn't want to think about it.

And his only clue as to where to find her was Dower House.

Emerson paused, looking in the direction where he knew the house stood, though all he could see right now were trees. Dower House had once been a part of the estate, but he'd sold the property to the Evans family a while ago. Was that mysterious woman their niece? Had she come to visit them in the countryside? For the first time in a while, Emerson felt a pang of regret that he'd failed to keep up with the lives of the people around him. It would have been so easy to simply pay them a visit had he not sequestered himself to his land.

He shook the regret away, deciding there was nothing he could do about it now. He should stop thinking about her. He'd made it clear that she was never to trespass again, and if she meant to heed his warning as she'd promised, then it was very unlikely that he would see that angelic face again. Emerson tried to commit himself to that truth, but it only made him disappointed.

"Come, Lily, Liam." He whistled at the dogs, and they instantly turned around and trotted up to him. Without stopping to think, Emerson changed courses.

He took the same few paths each time he was out on a walk. The path he headed down now was not one of them. It was a spur-of-the-moment decision, and he would not allow himself to think about what he was doing. With every step he took, he drew closer to the village until the thick trees began to grow sparse and he stepped out into a wide and open field. A beaten road lay just a short distance away, and, thankfully, there was no one going by. The last thing he wanted right now was to be spotted.

Despite the risk, Emerson kept going. His heart began beating faster as he drew closer to the village but settled a bit when he was able to delve back into the forest. This bit of land was not a part of his property, he knew, so there was always the chance that someone may come upon him. But he kept going, feigning nonchalance, eyes peeled for the very slim chance that he may spot her.

Suddenly, he drew to a halt. *What am I doing? Am I really risking being seen by others just for the nearly nonexistent chance I may see that mysterious woman again? I must be out of my mind.*

Annoyed with himself, Emerson turned, intending to head back to the house. There he could lock himself away in his study and hopefully distract himself with a good book and a glass of brandy.

But then the sound of bells rang through the air. The church bells. Emerson halted.

*That's right. It's Sunday.* That must be why there was no one around. Everyone was attending Sunday church service.

Slowly, he looked over his shoulder, spotting the church's spires poking into the sky. It wasn't very far from where he was now, and, if he was careful, he might be able to avoid interacting with anyone as he got closer.

Surely, she would be in attendance? Everyone attended Sunday service. As a matter of fact, before his life had fallen into shambles, Emerson himself had gone a few times. If she was truly a visitor here, wouldn't she go as well?

The very thought was enough to make him swivel on his heels. He only wanted to see, he told himself. Perhaps he could follow her a bit, if she truly was there. It wasn't a very gentlemanly thing to do, but he was no longer a gentleman. He was a monster.

Consoling himself with that thought, Emerson set off in the direction of the church.

## Chapter Seven

With the church service now over, Kate was feeling a little overwhelmed. Even though she'd been in Edendale for a while now, she hadn't had the chance to go out and meet many of the locals. With her days spent catering to the Bellmores and then cherishing the precious alone time she was afforded, Kate hadn't truly realized just how many people were in the village.

And they all wanted to talk to her.

She had been approached first by the blacksmith, his wife, and his two children. The children played around their parents' legs as the older couple introduced themselves excitedly. Kate tried to engage them in conversation as much as she could, but she was quickly interrupted by the baker and his wife, who had approached with a thinly veiled plan to match her with their son. One by one, the rest of the congregation crowded around her, and Kate, though she appreciated their kindness, wanted nothing more than to escape.

As if she sensed her panic, Eve appeared in the midst of them. "If you would all excuse us, Kate is needed," she said to them all and firmly grasped Kate's wrist, leading her away. She didn't provide any more of an explanation.

Kate let out a breath of relief once she was away from the throng. "I don't know what happened there," she admitted.

"Don't worry about it," Eve said with a dismissive wave of her hand. "The villagers here always get overexcited when there are visitors, and there is something about a good church service that makes their camaraderie grow. They mean no harm, I assure you."

Kate had assumed as much. Eve led her out the back entrance of the church and down the steps. "Where are Mr. and Mrs. Bellmore?" she asked, looking around for them. There were so many people that she'd lost them in the confusion.

Eve pointed off to the side. The elderly couple was talking with Mr. and Mrs. Dewhurst. "They had been ambushed as well," Eve said with a chuckle. "But Father and Mother saved them."

"I must find a way to show my gratitude to your family, then." Kate laughed. She followed Eve over to her parents and the Bellmores, whose eyes lit up when they saw Kate.

"Kate!" Mrs. Bellmore greeted her with a broad smile. "I was wondering where you'd disappeared."

"A few of the locals wished to speak with me," Kate told her.

"Which really means that they had hoisted themselves upon her," Eve explained, "and she is far too kind to tell them to leave her be."

"That sounds right," Mrs. Dewhurst said with a smile. She was a homely-looking woman with blond hair already shot with grey. Kate had sat next to her during the service and was already growing to like her.

"Kate, my dear," Mr. Bellmore spoke up. "The parson and his wife have invited us to have a cold luncheon with them at the parsonage. Isn't that nice of them?"

"That sounds lovely." Kate, as respectful as she'd been raised, turned to the parson and his wife with a grateful smile. "Thank you for your kind invitation."

"It is nothing, my dear," Mrs. Dewhurst said with a wave of her hand. "We are happy to have you all."

"That won't be until a few hours, won't it?" Eve asked. She turned to Mr. Bellmore. "Will you be going there now?"

"Yes, that is the plan," he confirmed.

"Then," Eve looked at Kate, a sparkle of excitement in her eyes, "we could go for our walk until it is time for lunch. We should be able to return in time. There is a teahouse by the river, and I'm sure you will enjoy it."

Kate hadn't forgotten about the walk. As a matter of fact, it was the only thing she had been looking forward to since the service ended. She felt a fierce kinship with Eve and eagerly wanted to explore her growing friendship with her. Before she answered, though, she looked at the Bellmores for permission. She didn't doubt that the elderly couple would happily send her on her way, but she also didn't think it proper to leave them without asking them first.

"Oh, don't look at us like that," Mrs. Bellmore grumbled. "You know we have no qualms with you enjoying your walk with Miss Eve. Just be back before lunch is served. I'm sure Mr. and Mrs. Dewhurst will not mind either."

"Not at all," the parson assured.

Kate smiled happily at Mrs. Bellmore. "I shan't be long, I promise."

With that, she turned and followed Eve as they left the church and made their way onto the road. The primrose-colored bonnet she wore protected her face from the bright overhead sun, and a gentle breeze against her back kept most of the heat away. Kate had donned one of her loveliest dresses for today—though it was still woefully out of fashion—and felt quite pretty as she made her way down the road. It hugged her slim figure and matched her bonnet perfectly. The slippers she wore were only donned on special occasions, and she hoped Eve would not notice how expensive they looked.

"I'm certain you will love the teahouse," Eve expressed excitedly. Her sandy brown hair was braided over one shoulder, a few stray wisps flying about in the wind. She looked rather lovely herself, wearing a deep blue that resembled an evening sky. "They serve the loveliest of cakes, and the sound of the lapping water from the river nearby is quite relaxing. Whenever we get the chance to, Mother and I make frequent visits."

"I don't doubt that I will love it," Kate agreed. "Perhaps we could make it a ritual of ours to go to the teahouse after church every Sunday."

"Oh, that would be wonderful! But you will not be here for long, will you?"

"Sadly, no. Once summer is over, I'm sure Mr. and Mrs. Bellmore will wish to return to their London home, and I must go with them. But until then, we can enjoy the time we have together. I quite enjoyed the service after all, and I'm sure they did too. They will certainly want to return next time."

"Yes, many have said the same once they've heard my father preach," Eve said, her voice filled with pride. "I do not think there is a single person in the village who does not come to church on Sunday if they can help it. Well, except the duke, of course."

Kate's heart skipped a beat at the mention of the reclusive duke. She didn't dare to admit that she'd been hoping to see him at church and had felt a sharp stab of disappointment when she saw that he was not in attendance.

What else should she have expected from a man who hated the company of others? A full church was the last place he would be. Kate felt a little silly at the hope she'd harbored.

"Has he attended church before?" she asked casually, hoping Eve would not think she was a little too interested in him.

Eve answered easily. "I have seen him sitting amongst the congregation in the past, but that was before his father died. At that time, His Grace was far more likely to spend time hunting than in the church."

"I suppose he does neither now."

"Yes, I would bet on it. Father has tried on many occasions to get him to come to church since the fire, but he hasn't even gotten far enough to see the duke himself. His butler would always take the message at the door and send him away."

"Do you think that message reached him?"

"I don't think it would have mattered if it did."

Kate thought about it and shook her head. "I don't doubt that. If he speaks to his servants the way he spoke to me that day, no one would risk engaging him if they did not have to. You should have heard what he said to me."

"Oh, pray tell," Eve said excitedly, coming closer to slip her arm through Kate's.

"He said that he has no more time to waste on the likes of me. With the manner in which he chased me away, it was like he was shooing a pesky rat. I certainly could not have said those things in front of Mr. and Mrs. Bellmore."

"Oh, goodness, then you should hear what he says to Father! Once, Father had the misfortune of spotting him during one of his walks and invited him to church directly. The duke looked him in the eye and said he would much rather be afflicted with consumption!"

Kate gasped in horror. "How horrible!"

But Eve only laughed. "Father did not take the offense to heart, though. You really cannot when speaking with the duke. He is rude to everyone, the positive beast that he is. It is truly hard to believe that he had once been a very handsome man and an eligible bachelor."

"Once been?"

"Yes, he was quite good-looking. His scars have spoiled him, I'm afraid."

Kate frowned at that, remembering the dark eyes smoldering with something she could not name, hidden deep under the surface-leveled rage. The scars certainly did *not* spoil him. "I'll have to disagree," she admitted. "They are a shame, of course, but I do think they add to his attractiveness."

Eve looked surprised at that. "In what way?"

How could she put it? "They show his noble heart," Kate said after a moment. She thought of the way he'd hidden the scar when he'd climbed out of the pond—they showed his hidden pain as well. But she didn't say that.

Eve was still frowning, clearly not understanding. "You are an unusual woman, Miss Kate Cooper," she said.

Kate laughed at that. "It is what I truly believe, though. His Grace has not lost his physical charm at all. Though I cannot say much for his terrible personality. It is his behaviour that makes him seem like a monster, not the way that he looks."

"That is very kind of you to say, Kate, but I doubt he will ever be accepted into society with the way he looks now. I do not know much about the nobility and their ways of doing things, but I do know that they are not very accepting."

Kate had to agree. She hadn't gotten her chance to debut, but that didn't mean she was not well-versed on the *ton*. At best, they would be polite to him. At worst, they would scorn him as an outcast altogether.

Here though, it seemed as if the duke was scorning himself. He was the one rejecting the outside world, not the other way around.

They heard a sharp snap of a branch and halted. They'd gone quite some distance from the church, so they were alone on the road, the teahouse still a ways ahead.

"Did you hear that?" Kate asked, looking in the direction of the forest on the other side of the road.

"Yes, but it may just be a badger," Eve said without a care. She was already tugging Kate along to continue.

But Kate sensed something else, the uneasy feeling of being watched. She searched the line of trees even as Eve continued talking about the duke and his scars, but she did not spot anyone.

*I am just being silly. There is no one there.*

Convincing herself of that, she looked away, happy to continue their pleasant walk to the teahouse by the river.

## Chapter Eight

Emerson couldn't believe what he was doing—crouching down in the bushes across from the church, holding on to the scruff of his dogs' necks so that they didn't rush out to meet the dark-haired beauty he'd gone in search of.

That usual wave of shame washed over him, but he didn't move. For the past ten minutes, he'd sat here, waiting for her to emerge from the building. He'd thought about leaving, of giving up his search, and berated himself in silence for having gone this far. But before he could, she'd stepped out, looking as refreshingly lovely as the day he first saw her.

Now, Emerson knew he stood no more chance at leaving. She wore a dress even prettier than the one he'd first seen her in, a lovely pink bonnet sitting atop her dark hair. Most of the tresses had been wrapped into a chignon at the nape of her neck, but she had left a few strands out to frame her face. The smile that lifted her lips was enough to send Emerson's heart racing, and he slowly put a hand to his chest, trying to calm it.

Thankfully, Lily and Liam must have caught on to what he was doing and stayed quiet, only their soft pants audible. Emerson felt his ankles creak from the weight of his body, but he didn't move, watching instead as the dark-haired woman was dragged down the steps by whom Emerson believed was the parson's daughter. His memory of everyone was a bit hazy, and she'd certainly grown since the last time he saw her.

The two women approached the parson and his wife, who stood with another elderly couple. They spoke for a while, and then the parson's daughter and the mysterious woman walked away, heading down the road. Emerson rose and dipped back into the forest, following.

*I'm crazy*, he thought, keeping his eyes on them. The more they walked, the closer he came to them, until he could hear the sounds of their voices. *I am completely and utterly mad.*

But he continued, his curiosity desperate to be sated.

"... well, except the duke, of course."

Emerson frowned. He hadn't expected to be the topic of discussion, though he shouldn't be surprised. It was always fun to talk about the monster that hid himself away in his lonely home.

"Has he attended church before?"

Her voice was lovely, music to Emerson's ears. Clearly, the dogs heard her, too, because they grew excited. Emerson grabbed ahold of Liam before he could run out into the road and pulled him deeper into the forest. Here he could not hear the response to her question.

He put a finger to his lips. "Hush!" he whispered to them both. "For all that is good and pure, do *not* give me away."

Liam made a low bark that sounded eerily like a grumble.

Emerson thinned his lips. He looked back to see that the two women were steadily leaving him behind. Longing to hear what was being said about him, he looked back at the dogs.

"I shall give you treats and take you on walks every day," he promised. They only blinked at him, and Emerson wasn't convinced that they would heed his commands. Sometimes, he loved his dogs' personalities, which was why he'd never gotten them professionally trained. But at a time like this, it was only frustrating.

"You shall receive all the pets you want, and I will even take you to the pond so that you can play with the ducks. Is that enough?"

In response to that, Lily lowered into a sitting position, panting amicably. When her brother didn't do the same, she put a heavy paw on his back and forced him down.

"God, you are too smart for your own good," Emerson mumbled. But he took that as a sign that he could resume his discreet following.

He walked briskly to catch up with the women.

"Yes, he was quite good-looking," he heard the parson's daughter say. "His scars have spoiled him, I'm afraid."

His heart sank. They were talking about his physical appearance. He should have assumed that would happen, but Emerson didn't want to listen to this. He didn't want to hear them say how disgusting he was, how a face like his should never be shown in public.

He thought of the way the mysterious woman had looked at him even when he'd shown her his scar and hoped that, for once, he was wrong. He stared intently at her face, watching those delicate brows furrow as she thought. Emerson braced himself for the emotional and mental torture he was about to endure.

"I'll have to disagree," she said. "They are a shame, of course, but I do think they add to his attractiveness."

Emerson's brows shot into this hairline. She thought he was attractive? That could not be! No one could look at him and think he had any physical appeal. Perhaps he was wrong. Perhaps the conversation had moved on to someone else while he was talking to the dogs.

But he kept up the pace, the dogs trotting dutifully next to him, eager to hear more.

The parson's daughter looked at her with surprise. "In what way?"

This time, her furrowed brow smoothed out, and she lifted her eyes to the sky in thought. For a moment, a pink tongue darted out to lick her lips. "They show his noble heart," she said after a long moment.

Emerson couldn't believe what he was hearing. Noble ... heart? Whatever heart he had left was now tucked away behind a wall of anger and regret. After their meeting, she should think of him to be a crass and mannerless man. She should think he was a horrid creature! What noble heart did a man like him possess?

Something warm filled him, spreading through his body like a salve. Emerson clenched his fist tightly, a strange emotion bearing down on him. It had been so long since he'd felt anything other than fury and shame that he couldn't tell what it was. All he knew was that as he looked at her face, he saw the sincerity that lay there. It was not a cruel joke. She meant every word.

Clearly, the parson's daughter thought the same thing, looking at her with a mixture of confusion and horror. "You are an unusual woman, Miss Kate Cooper," she said.

*Ah, so that is her name.*

Miss Kate Cooper let out a musical laugh. "It is what I truly believe, though. His Grace has not lost his physical charm at all.

Though I cannot say much for his terrible personality. It is his behaviour that makes him seem like a monster, not the way that he looks."

Each word she spoke felt like a blow to Emerson's chest. He didn't know what to think, didn't know how she could possibly believe such things. He was certainly a monster, true and true. Only a monster would follow a woman like this and eavesdrop on their conversation!

With a start, he realized what the foreign emotion was—longing.

For what exactly, Emerson wasn't quite sure. All he knew, as he studied Miss Cooper's angelic smile, was that he wanted to see her again.

"That is very kind of you to say, Kate," the parson's daughter said as she shook her head, "but I doubt he will ever be accepted into society with the way he looks now. I do not know much about the nobility and their ways of doing things, but I do know that they are not very accepting."

That much was true, and those words were like a bucket of cold water, washing away his warm feelings. He couldn't be accepted—not only by society but by anyone. Even his own friend Bob would not be able to look at him like the man he'd once known anymore, even if he could see past the horrible scar.

*She is far too kind to know the error in her words*, he thought as he watched Miss Cooper. Her face was expressive. Whether it be confusion, disagreement, or if she was simply thinking about something, it could all be seen as clear as day. Emerson felt as if he could watch it forever, but then he accidentally stepped on a branch, and the women halted.

"Did you hear that?" Miss Cooper asked, looking in his direction. Emerson held himself still. She searched the area, but from the bewilderment on her face, it was clear she couldn't see him.

"Yes, but it may just be a badger," the parson's daughter said without sparing a glance and tugged her along.

For a moment, Emerson felt like their eyes had met. When she looked away and continued behind her friend, though, he felt foolish for even having the thought.

His heart was still racing, his body flushed with excitement. He could not leave now, he knew. Though he'd satisfied his curiosity—and had learned her name!—Emerson wanted to see more of her.

Knowing how wrong it was, he kept following them. Their conversation moved on from him directly to the parson's daughter telling Miss Cooper all the routes she could take to avoid trespassing on his land. Emerson suddenly felt bad, watching Miss Cooper as she earnestly listened and asked questions for clarification. She'd been serious, he saw, about not trespassing again.

By the time they were done with that, they had arrived at the river. Sitting just a short distance away from it was a small, homely building with a sign that marked it as Johnson's Teahouse. The two women went inside, and Emerson was forced to crouch again, waiting for them to emerge. Lily and Liam grew bored and wandered around behind him, sniffing for heavens know what.

After a long while, they both emerged and sat at the table near the entrance. A plump lady, whom he assumed was the owner or the owner's wife, followed behind them, bearing a tray. She set their table with their cups, saucers, teapot, and a few small sandwiches, then left them to enjoy.

"We should not fill out stomachs, Eve," Miss Cooper warned, even as she lifted a sandwich to her lips. "Or else we won't be able to have lunch."

"Mother won't like that," the parson's daughter—Miss Eve—agreed. She, too, ignored her tea and instantly picked up and sandwich, taking a small bite. "She adores having others over for meals and won't be satisfied if you and the Bellmores do not leave with full stomachs."

"Mrs. Bellmore will love her then. She is very much the same."

"I can tell they have similar personalities," Eve said with a giggle. "I shall miss you and them both when you return to London."

Emerson raised his brows at that. *She hails from London, then? And who are the Bellmores?*

Miss Cooper only smiled in response, finally lifting her tea to her lips.

"I have never been to London, you know," Miss Eve continued. "Please tell me all you can about it. I've always wanted to go, but Father thinks that the butcher's son will ask for my hand soon and does not want me to ruin his chance."

Miss Cooper looked interested at that, but she answered Miss Eve's question. She told her about Hyde Park, about the communities she'd lived in, about the general hustle and bustle of the city. Her every word was vague, revealing nearly nothing about herself, which made Emerson all the more curious. Miss Eve, however, didn't seem to notice. She continued asking questions about London, and Miss Cooper indulged her without saying a single personal thing about herself.

By the time they were finished with tea, nearly an hour had passed. They headed back inside for a while, and then when they emerged again, they were walking arm in arm, continuing down the road. Emerson got to his feet and followed.

The conversation they engaged in was nothing of particular interest to him. It centered around Miss Eve and her odd relationship with the butcher's son. She did not like him, but she had no other prospects, she said. Her father adores the family and thinks it would be a good match. She did not know how to tell him that she wants to marry someone she could fall in love with instead. Emerson listened with half an ear, admiring Miss Cooper instead. She was invested in Miss Eve's story, appearing concerned and even horrified at all the right moments. Once, she even shook her head in disapproval, and Emerson nearly smiled at how motherly she seemed.

They kept talking as they headed deeper into the village and finally came upon the patronage. Emerson remembered the home, as he and his brother had been invited to dine with the parson and his family once. Some improvements had been made to the house, which now appeared a bit larger than before. The women headed straight inside, leaving him alone once more.

Emerson felt something nudge his side. He looked down to see Lily staring up at him. "Are you ready to go?" he asked her. She began to pant, not breaking eye contact.

He was starting to get hungry, in truth. The only thing he'd had for breakfast was a glass of brandy and a good brooding session before he'd left the house. It would do well for both him and the dogs to return. He'd gotten what he'd wanted anyhow.

But something held him there. His curiosity was not yet sated. He wanted to know more.

So he waited. And waited. The sun drifted slowly across the sky, and the midday heat began to lift. Just when he thought he could wait no longer, Miss Cooper exited the patronage alongside the elderly couple he had seen at the church. They were too far away to be heard, but he assumed they were saying their goodbyes. Then the three of them set off down the path that would take them to Dower House. Emerson trailed behind.

They arrived within five minutes and disappeared inside. This time, Emerson doubted he would be seeing her again.

*They must be the Bellmores*, he thought as he finally turned and walked away. The dogs followed eagerly. *But what are they doing at Dower House? Did the Evans rent it to them for the summer? She did say that she would have to return to London.*

Hope bloomed in Emerson's chest. If she was truly staying the summer, that meant it would be a few more weeks at least before she was due to leave. There was still a chance of seeing her again.

Not that he would, he told himself. There was no need to. His curiosity had been satisfied, and he knew she did not harbor any hard feelings over their encounter. That should be enough.

*It should be*, he thought grimly. But Emerson was beginning to think she had lit a flame in his heart that would not be able to put out.

## Chapter Nine

"Oh, goodness, these old bones do not work the same as they used to."

Kate looked worriedly at Mr. Bellmore, watching as he rested his body against the door jamb leading into the drawing room of Dower House. There was a light sheen of sweat on his brow, and his breathing was very slightly labored.

"Which is it?" asked Mrs. Bellmore, her slightly anxious voice betraying the worry that her face would not reveal. "Your hips? Your back?"

"My legs," he answered. He knocked a closed fist against his thigh as if that would awaken the old bones he complained about.

Kate drew closer, already undoing the laces of her bonnet. "Perhaps you should return to your chambers for rest, Mr. Bellmore. It is almost near your nap time anyhow."

"And admit defeat?" he sighed.

Mrs. Bellmore raised a brow at him. "Admit defeat about what, you old man?" she asked, not unkindly. Because Kate knew them so well, she could hear the affection in Mrs. Bellmore's voice. And because Mr. Bellmore knew his wife the best, he grinned. The elderly lady caught the broad smile and rolled her eyes. "Come now, I know you are tired. Let us settle down for a nap so that we do not worry Kate further."

"Oh, no, you needn't think about me, Mrs. Bellmore," Kate said to her, but the older woman just waved a dismissive hand. She took her husband's arm, and together, they changed directions and made their way toward the staircase.

Kate watched them go for a few seconds before she called out, "I shall have tea prepared for when you awake."

The couple did not answer. She heard their voices murmuring to each other, and she wondered if they had heard her at all. Kate smiled warmly at them as she watched them retreat, and then, once they were gone, she pulled her bonnet from her head with a sigh.

"Oh, I could have sworn I heard Mr. and Mrs. Bellmore's voices," came someone from behind.

Kate turned to see the homely cook, Mrs. Henry, standing behind her, wringing her hands in her apron. Her face was covered with sweat, and she wiped tiredly at her brow as she looked up at the staircase. "Have they gone for a nap?"

"They have. Is something the matter?" Kate asked.

"I had only wished to remind them that I shall be leaving shortly, since I have asked for the rest of the afternoon off."

"Ah, yes, you're right. I'm sure they remembered. And if not, I shall make sure to remind them once they awake."

"Thank you, Kate." Mrs. Henry gave her a warm smile. "I have prepared a cold supper for them, so they may have it at any time. Yours is ready whenever you wish to have it as well."

"I'm grateful for your kindness, Mrs. Henry," Kate responded with a thankful smile. "I hope you enjoy your afternoon off. What do you intend to do with the time, if you don't mind me asking?"

"I shall be doing nothing at all. I am looking forward to it already." Mrs. Henry let out a happy sigh, and Kate giggled. She, like a few others, had already been employed to the house when the Bellmores and Kate arrived. She lived in the village and so would return to her own abode when the day was over, returning early in the morning to prepare for breakfast.

Kate waved goodbye to the cook and stood there to watch her leave before she turned and began making her way to her bedchamber. The heavy meal she'd partaken in at the patronage still sat heavily in her stomach and brought a sweeping exhaustion throughout her body. She debated the idea of heading in for a nap as well, even as she began to remove the pins that held her chignon together. In her chambers, she sank onto the chair before her looking glass, letting the pins fall onto the vanity table.

The luncheon with the parson and his family had been splendid. Kate greatly enjoyed their company and was already looking forward to spending more time with Eve. She was already considering the girl a dear friend, something Kate had not had much of. And as she thought back on the luncheon, her mind wandered to the walk to the teahouse and the conversation they'd shared.

The reclusive duke ... Kate didn't think she could possibly get him out of her head. Every time she had a moment to herself, his scarred face would appear before her mind's eyes and would bring equally staggering waves of confusion and warmth. But warmth for a man who had spoken so rudely to her? Surely not.

Kate sighed once more as her dark locks tumbled over her shoulders.

"What has gotten you so down?" Mary asked as she breathed into the room, bearing a tray of teacups, small lemon cakes, and a teapot.

Kate watched her approach with a broad smile. Mary brought everything over to the quaint table and chairs on the opposite side of Kate's room. Kate had considered moving the chairs and table closer to the window so that she could sit there and gaze out whenever she had breakfast or dinner alone, but for now, it sat in the other corner.

"I've brought tea," Mary announced.

"I can see that," Kate observed. "Whatever for?"

"Well, I had prepared it in anticipation of your return with Mr. and Mrs. Bellmore, but I heard from the cook that the couple had decided to go down for a nap instead. I didn't want it to go to waste."

"How smart of you." Kate made her way over while Mary got started with pouring out the steaming water.

"Also, I wanted to talk to someone. I was afraid that if I didn't, I would burst from anger."

"Oh?"

Mary's eyes flashed with fury. She leaned back and nibbled on a piece of cake before she said, "I was out in the village not too long ago, picking up a few things for Mrs. Henry, and I came across the blacksmith and his family coming back from work. I overheard them talking, and would you believe that the two children were crying? They told the blacksmith that the duke had chased them away from his land and that they couldn't even sleep at night because he's terrified them so!"

"Truly?" Kate whispered, her heart thundering. Hearing those words filled her with sharp disappointment, though she couldn't understand why.

"I stopped them to ask about it, and, well, they said it as plain as day. The duke had nearly set his dogs on them! To children, no less! How can such a man, who lords over this territory, be so cruel to his people?"

"Perhaps it is not as they say. You know how children tend to exaggerate with their wild imaginations."

"They could not have imagined their fear." Mary shook her head, eyes still hot with anger. "I would love to see this duke for myself. I've heard what they say about him, you know. How terribly scarred he is. It is only fitting that he has a personality to match, I suppose."

Kate knew Mary was right. After her own encounter with the duke, how could she doubt this story? He was most certainly the type of man to scare off little children without an ounce of remorse, and the thought brought on a wave of anger. She imagined those sweet faces who'd wanted to play with her at the church, cheeks streaked with tears as they recounted what had happened with the duke. It was one thing to be crass with a woman near his age. It was another thing entirely to nearly set his dogs loose on unsuspecting children.

The more Kate thought about it, the more that anger dissolved into disappointment and pity. The duke's dark eyes and shoved the pity aside.

"That is really sad to hear," Kate sighed, sipping her tea. "Though I am not surprised. My own encounter with him was not very pleasing."

"You've met the Duke of Edendale?" Mary gasped.

Kate blinked. "Ah, yes, I hadn't gotten the chance to tell you, did I? It was the same day I returned from my walk quite disheveled."

Mary leaned closer, eyes glittering with curiosity. "Tell me all about it."

And so Kate did, beginning from when she had lost her way going through the forest and ending the way the duke had reluctantly shown her the way back home. Mary stayed quiet throughout it all, not for lack of expression. Her brows shot into the air, her mouth fell open, and now and again, a gasp left her lips.

"How horrible!" Mary exclaimed once Kate was finished. "He truly is terrible!"

"I cannot deny it," Kate said, surprised at how reluctant she felt to say that aloud. "He has most certainly proven himself to be the beast everyone calls him. A part of me wishes I could meet him again, just to tell him exactly what I think of him."

"I would want to be there with you when you do."

Laughter spilled from Kate's lips. Mary's nosiness was borderline admirable. "It will never happen. His Grace never leaves his property, so I've heard."

"That is another thing! Don't you think it is rather rude of him not to have called upon Mr. and Mrs. Bellmore? He is right next door, after all. It would have only been proper to give his greetings."

Kate contemplated telling Mary why the duke would not leave his home and thought against it. She did not think it was right to spread that sad tale to anyone who would hear it. At least, not without reason.

"I suppose," she agreed halfheartedly. "Though I think it is more likely that we will not be seeing His Grace at all during our time here. And we should take care to avoid him and his property as best as we can."

"I shan't make that mistake, I assure you." Mary sighed. "It almost feels like my fault that you came in contact with him in the first place. I was the one who sent you to that pond, after all."

"You did not know, and neither did I. Now that we do, we won't make that mistake again."

"Hmm," Mary hummed. She brushed the crumbs from her fingers. "That is true. But maybe one more time, just in case he falls into the water again. I would love to see that."

Kate, despite herself, let out a giggle. They laughed about it for a while longer before the conversation, thankfully, moved on to other things. Mary talked endlessly about her time in the village market and about the handsome man she'd bought the chicken eggs from while Kate sat, listened, and spurred her on with a few comments. But her mind was elsewhere, thinking about the duke and those shadowed eyes.

Her thoughts remained on him long after Mary was gone, and she lay in bed, staring blankly at the ceiling. She'd changed into a simple white wool dress, the soft fabric resting delicately against her body. Idly, Kate ran her hand up and down the covers of the bed as she recalled the once-eligible duke. At least, according to Eve, though Kate was not inclined to agree.

On the contrary, he was one of the most handsome men she'd ever laid eyes on. The most handsome of them all, perhaps, had his personality been a little more tolerable. There was simply no doubt that he was not someone Kate should be acquainted with, or even think about, but there was something about his sad, black eyes that troubled her.

*Is it the scars or those eyes that scare women away?* Either way, he was most certainly still eligible.

With a sigh, she let her eyes drift shut. What would he look like without the scars? She tried to picture it and found that she couldn't. But she could imagine him smiling, that horrid countenance shed with a warm personality in his place. Was it possible? Could the monstrous man become human once more?

## Chapter Ten

There was a carriage in his driveway. Emerson drew to a sudden halt, fury washing over him at the sight. Who would dare come here without sending so much as a word? It was parked to the side as well, the horses gone. Whoever it was had been taken inside. Sparkes would have to answer for this.

Emerson drew nearer, Lily and Liam leading the way. As he came close to the front door, he heard Sparke's voice and then finally spotted him in front of the carriage, ordering the footmen hidden on the other side to take the trunks inside.

The trunks? Emerson's fury increased tenfold. He charged up to the aging man, and Sparkes, to his credit, turned to face him with a good measure of calmness.

"Your Grace," he greeted. "You've returned—"

"What is the meaning of this?" Emerson demanded to know, his voice already hoarse from his shout.

"The Earl of Wellbourne has arrived, Your Grace," Sparkes answered, "and is in the library awaiting your return. He has decided to make himself at home, I'm afraid."

"And you just stood by and let him?"

"There was not much I could do against Lord Wellbourne." Sparkes tone was matter-of-fact. He glanced at the footmen who idled nearby with the trunks in hand, clearly not entirely sure whether they should continue their task. "It seems he has come to stay for a while."

Emerson sucked in an angry breath, pinching the bridge of his nose. He shouldn't be surprised, in reality. He knew Bob nearly as well as he knew himself. And Sparkes was right. The new earl was not the sort of man who would take no for an answer. Shouting at Sparkes would serve no purpose.

His butler regarded him, clearly expecting more of an outrage. Emerson bit back his curse and turned his back to him, stalking up the steps to the front door. Behind him, he heard the footmen get back into action, no doubt at Sparke's quiet command.

Lily and Liam were taken away to be washed after their walk, and Emerson stormed his way to his bedchamber. There, Francis was already waiting for him, Emerson's clothes laid out on the bed.

"I have prepared a bath for you—"

"Save it," Emerson hissed. "I do not want to hear what you have prepared, or what I shall wear, or anything else you deign to say out your mouth."

Just like Sparkes, Francis did not seem to be as perturbed by Emerson's answer. "As I suspect that you would not like to wait too long to be dressed, I have prepared only a basin so that you can clean up."

Emerson marched over to said basin and stood still as Francis proceeded to undress him. His mind was running too fast for his liking, waves of emotions consuming him. There was mostly his anger, familiar and safe. But there was also fear hidden deep within now that his friend was here. It would not be easy, he knew. Bob might not even recognize the person who stood before him.

The thought sent a shudder through Emerson, and Francis stilled just as he'd touched Emerson's back with a wet cloth. "Too cold, Your Grace?"

"It's fine," he mumbled.

Francis resumed his task. "I assume you are not pleased that Lord Wellbourne is here?"

"Of course, I am not pleased! I do not like when my personal space is invaded. I can barely tolerate *you* in my room, so how will I tolerate my overbearing friend, whom I've only communicated with through letters for the past eight years, wandering around my home?"

Francis was quiet for a while, and Emerson felt a stab of guilt at his words. There was no need to be so mean, he knew. But sometimes, he just could not help himself.

"If you wish, Your Grace," his valet said finally. "We could come up with an excuse so that he will leave earlier."

"That won't work. Nothing will deter him."

Again, Francis fell quiet, and it lasted until Emerson was washed and dressed. When they were done, he stood back and said, "I hope it goes well."

Emerson didn't answer him. He couldn't. His mind ran at full speed, his heart pounding as each second went by. With every breath he took, he came closer to facing one of his biggest fears. His past.

As he made his way to his study where Bob was, Emerson could not stop thinking about all the things that could go wrong. Perhaps if he was lucky, Bob would be instantly horrified at the sight of him and take his leave. If he was not, his friend would stick by his side and try to pull him out of the trench Emerson was content to lay in. Either way, it would be a strike at Emerson's already fragile ego, and he didn't want to have to deal with it.

But deal with it he must and spared himself no more time before pushing into the room. There, Bob stood with broad shoulders and a wide stance by the window, a glass of brandy in his hand. He turned upon Emerson's noisy entrance, a smile pulling his wide. "Emerson, at long last! I have been waiting forever—"

He broke off suddenly, the smile slipping away as quickly as it came. "Goodness me."

Shame took such strong hold of Emerson that he could not manage to stand still. Desperate to hide his face, he marched over to the sideboard in the corner of the room, needing a stiff brandy brewing in his stomach. He hoped his hair would hide his scars, but Emerson had a strong feeling that the long, unruly hair was nearly as horrible as sight as the scars were.

"Emerson …." Bob sounded closer. Emerson glanced over his shoulder to see his friend approaching, a deep frown on his face. "What the hell happened to you?"

He didn't know where to start, so he only said, "A fire."

"I can see that!" Bob was as naturally loud as I remembered him. "But when? And how? And how come you never told me anything about it?"

Too many questions he had expected. Too many questions he still didn't know how to answer. Emerson gave himself more time by pouring his glass as slowly as he could and then taking a long sip. Once the warmth of the brand began spreading throughout his veins, he mustered up the courage to face his friend fully. Bob's expression didn't change, the frown as deep as it could possibly go.

"It happened two years ago. I had gone to London for a hunting trip, and when I returned home, the fire was already raging. Mother and my brother were trapped inside, caught unaware by the flames in their sleep. I rushed in to save them. I ... didn't."

"Damn." The curse rolled off Bob's tongue with ease, something Emerson had always admired about him. He ran a hand over his face and then came to stand directly before Emerson, clapping a heavy hand on his shoulder. "I'm sorry to hear about what happened. I must admit, on my way here, I had heard rumors ... but seeing you myself allows me to see how terrible that fire must have been."

"I would understand if you cannot stand the sight of me—"

"Cannot stand the sight of you? Come now! You must wear them as a badge of honour! I have seen far worse than these. What really concerns me is how thin you have become. And your skin ... it is as if you've spent all your days sick and in bed."

"I have been going out quite often," Emerson murmured, his surprise nearly quieting him altogether. He couldn't believe his ears. Bob did not think the sight of him was abhorrent? Did he not want to run away now, to seek the company of anyone else but the monster who stood before him? A badge of honor? The words felt as foreign to him as Miss Cooper's had been.

"You could have easily fooled me," Bob said strongly. He looked Emerson up and down and shook his head. "Have you been wasting away since the fire? When was the last time you had a full meal? Do you engage with society anymore?"

"I don't need any of that," Emerson protested. He didn't like the interrogation and walked away from him, dreading the questions that were to come.

"You don't like having good eating habits, Emerson? You are not happy with entertaining an active social life? My God, when was the last time you had a haircut?"

"None of that does me any good."

"Neither does keeping yourself shut away from everyone like this." Emerson looked sharply at him, and Bob only crossed his arms. "It would not take a genius to see what you are doing to yourself."

"Bob, do not start this."

"You are the one who's started this, Emerson." Bob let out a long sigh. With long legs, he walked over to Emerson's desk and fished out one of the long cigars sitting on top. Emerson watched, a little amazed at Bob's gall. "What has gotten into you, Emerson? Why aren't there a gaggle of children running around these halls and your beautiful wife to greet me?"

"Because I hate it all." The words rolled off his tongue with ease. Emerson didn't want to tell him, but there was no escaping it. Bob would not be satisfied until he learned the truth, and Emerson could not bear to hold on to it any longer. Or at least, the truth he was willing to admit. "I resent the ton. It is as simple as that. I can no longer stomach the thought of being a part of society, and so I have shut myself away here. I do not intend on getting married, siring children, or passing on the dukedom. I do not care to do anything but live out the rest of my days in this manor with my two dogs."

"Heavens, it is worse than I thought." Bob took a long drag of his cigar. "What utter nonsense."

"Excuse me?"

"That doesn't sound like the Emerson I know," Bob declared. "The one who could stay up until all manners of hours and was always ready and waiting as soon as an invitation was sent out, no matter what it was. Ball, hunting, a trip across the world. You would be there. I find it hard to believe that that man has suddenly decided he hates it."

"Time changes people."

"Not time alone. Never time alone." Emerson frowned at that, but Bob was already moving on, waving a dismissive hand. "It is a good thing I'm here then. I shall help you get back into the swing of things."

"I don't want to—"

"Nonsense. We shall take it slow first. There's no need for us to go to London, as I'm sure there are more than enough events happening in the countryside for us to attend. I shall find out and let you know."

"Bob, there is no reason for you to do this. I am content as it is."

"But are you happy?"

The question went unanswered. Even Emerson couldn't bring himself to lie. So, he let out a quiet sigh and tried to force a smile onto his face. He couldn't bring himself to, and so he simply made his way over to the desk, picking up a cigar himself. With a grin, Bob lit it for him.

"It's good to see you, Bob," Emerson said to his friend, only because he simply couldn't smile. He'd clearly forgotten how to, and the last thing he wanted was for Bob to think he was unwelcomed. Even if, deep down, Emerson would much rather Bob stay elsewhere.

"It's good to see you too, old friend!" Bob bellowed with another heavy clap on Emerson's back. "Even if you are much thinner and more unkempt than I last saw you."

Emerson shook his head and asked Bob how he fared in the time they'd been apart. He hoped Bob would go on about every small detail that happened in the past eight years apart—things he had not told him in his letters—and was not disappointed. He provided Bob with a good amount of brandy and cigars as his friend droned on about his life abroad and all the things he wished to do now that he was Earl.

Meanwhile, Emerson's mind would not stay still. His heart was racing, his fingers tapping nervously on his sleeve as he thought about what Bob had said. The very thought of being forced to attend an event threatened to break him out in cold sweat. Emerson couldn't bring himself to do that. He knew it was hard saying no to his strong-willed friend, but he would simply have to when the time came. There was absolutely no way he would do such a thing.

But what if he could not say no? What if Bob got his way, and Emerson found himself surrounded by the people he'd shunned for the past two years? What if ... what if he came face to face with Miss Cooper again?

At this point, Emerson could not hear a thing Bob was saying, his mind firmly focused on the idea of seeing Miss Cooper again. It made the idea of going to an event a little less terrifying, but his nerves grew as a result. He wanted to see her again, but how could he after he'd been so rude to her? She may not abhor the sight of him, but she does not fancy his personality in the slightest. She'd made that very clear during her conversation with Miss Eve. How could he bring himself to face her when he could not summon the strength to apologize? Would he even try to if given the chance?

He tried to picture her lovely blue eyes coming to life under the night's stars. He tried to imagine her dancing, laughing with her friend, and enjoying herself. And every time he pictured approaching her, the daydream would end with horror and embarrassment as that smile would inevitably drop, and she would become cold and distant. Emerson could not face that possibility.

Which meant that, no matter what, he would resist Bob's attempts … even if it meant he lost his only friend in the process. It would be the least he deserved after all the wrongs he'd committed in his life.

## Chapter Eleven

"Oh, Miss Kate! It is a pleasure to finally meet you! My dear sister sang your praises in every letter she writes me, so much so that I have come to see you as a daughter of my own!"

Kate laughed in surprise at Lady Caroline Wharton, the Dowager Viscountess Reed's excitement. The heavyset lady bustled into Dower Manor with her arms spread wide, already enveloping Kate in a tight hug before she could say anything in return. She smelled citrusy, the warm scent wrapping around Kate and instantly making her relaxed in the lady's company. She hugged her back, enjoying the warmth of her hold.

"I can say the same, My Lady," Kate said respectfully once they pulled away from each other. "Mrs. Bellmore talks about you so often, though she is usually complaining that you do not visit her as much as you used to."

"Which is why I'm here so that my sister will complain to me rather than talk your ear off." Lady Reed gave Kate a broad, rosy-cheeked smile, and she patted Kate's face before she looked over her shoulder, searching for her sister. "Now, where is she? I bet she is grumbling under her breath about how loud I am being already."

"She and Mr. Bellmore are waiting for you in the drawing room," Kate said to her.

Lady Reed nodded, looking pleased, but she didn't move further into the house. Instead, she stepped away from the door just in time for a tall gentleman to come sauntering forward. Pride shone in her dark brown eyes as she gestured to the man. "Kate, my dear, allow me to introduce you to my son, Lord Archie Wharton, Viscount Reed."

Kate was well acquainted with Lady Reed's story. Mrs. Bellmore had told her all about it, how her younger sister had caught the eye of the previous Viscount Reed and had married him within a few months of meeting each other. To the surprise of nearly everyone around them, Lady Reed had grown to love her elderly spouse as much as he had loved her, and they spent five years in blissful marriage before he died of old age. He hadn't left the earth without leaving her a hefty inheritance and a son. That son had assumed the title of Viscount the moment he came of age.

Lord Reed was a pleasant-looking man, bearing the same brown eyes and sandy-colored hair as his mother. He looked quite simple for a lord in a plain pair of trousers, black boots, and a matching brown waistcoat atop his thin white shirt. With sun-kissed cheeks lifting at his smile, Lord Reed ducked into the house and instantly captured Kate's hand before she could sink into her curtsy. "Miss Cooper, I have heard much about you," he professed. "It is a pleasure."

Kate blinked in surprise when he pressed a soft kiss on the back of her hand. She knew it was a standard greeting for many men being introduced to women, but she wasn't entirely comfortable with it. As soon as it was appropriate, she slipped her hand away from him.

"It's a pleasure meeting you as well, Lord Reed," she said kindly. "I'm sure Mrs. Bellmore would be happy to see you."

"Yes, it has been a while since I've seen my aunt. She will go on and on about how much I've grown, I'm sure."

"Then we should not keep her waiting. Please, follow me." Now that the introductions were over, Kate turned and began leading the way to the drawing room. Just as Lady Reed predicted, Mrs. Bellmore was complaining to her husband about how often he cheats during whist, while Mr. Bellmore maintained amused ignorance. Their bickering was cut short upon their entrance.

"Caroline!"

"Hester!"

The two sisters met in the center of the room with a tight hug. Kate took a seat on the sofa close to where the Bellmores sat, and she was a little surprised to see Lord Reed take the seat next to her.

"When last have I seen you?" Mrs. Bellmore asked as soon as they pulled away. Lady Reed sat next to her sister with a wide smile.

"It has only been a few months, Hester, don't be dramatic now."

"A few months?" Mrs. Bellmore frowned. "Has it truly been that long?"

"Long, she says," Mr. Bellmore chuckled. "Well, considering the fact that you two were nearly inseparable once upon a time, I suppose that would be a long time for you."

"And I have missed my sister dearly in that time, Major," Lady Reed said with a sigh. "It is truly good to see you both. And I have met your lovely Miss Kate Cooper as well. She is as beautiful as you said, Hester."

"Isn't she?" All eyes fell on Kate, and it took all her strength not to hang her head in embarrassment. She couldn't keep the blush from creeping across her face. "It is so lovely having her here with us."

"I would love to get to know you a little better, Miss Cooper," Lady Reed said, shifting to face Kate fully. "Don't you, Archie?"

"Certainly, Mother." Lord Reed responded with quick ease. "I am certain Lady Cooper is as intriguing as she appears."

"You flatter me, my lord," Kate responded humbly.

"If I do, then I hope you will indulge me with your answers. Where did you grow up, Miss Cooper?"

"London," Kate said, calm. It was not her first time being questioned, however innocently, and so she knew how to give answers that would satisfy her interrogator without telling them anything she didn't want them to know.

"Ah, I see!" Lady Reed's eyes glittered with excitement. "Then you and my son have a lot in common. He's spent all this life in London, as well. He rarely ever leaves the city."

"Why is that, my lord?" Kate asked, only slightly curious.

"I have everything I need in London. My stewards take care of my properties outside of London, so there is no need for me to leave. Though, I am very pleased to be in the countryside now, visiting family and making new friends."

Kate looked away at that last comment. Thankfully, there was a knock on the door, and Mary entered bearing trays of tea. A comfortable silence fell over them all as the tea was laid down for everyone to enjoy, and Mary slipped out once more.

At that point, Lady Reed spoke again. "I wonder if there is anything else you two have in common?"

Before Kate could answer, Mr. Bellmore said, "Kate likes to read. And she enjoys going on long walks."

"Do you enjoy reading as well, Lord Reed?" Kate asked.

The viscount was already shaking his head. "I have never read a book in my entire life," he said with a confidence that alarmed Kate. "I do not even read newspapers, other than the horse racing section. I do enjoy hunting, fishing, and shooting, however."

"Perhaps you would enjoy going for a horse ride as well?" Lady Reed glanced hopefully at her son. "Archie is a lovely rider."

"Mother, please," the viscount said, but he did not sound flustered. As a matter of fact, he sounded eager, as if he knew exactly what his mother would say next and was looking forward to it.

"Don't be modest now," Lady Reed said with a wave of her hand. "You are quite good. Isn't he, Hester?"

"I do recall my nephew having a love for horses, yes. A part of me wondered if you would participate in the races."

"I have thought about it," Lord Reed expressed. "But I am not sure I will have the time. What do you think, Miss Cooper?"

*What do I think about what?* Kate blinked at him, a little bemused. They were talking about horses as if it was quite an impressive feat, but Kate did not care about such things. She caught the keen interest in Lady Reed's eyes and felt her heart sink. Suddenly, she knew what was happening here.

Clearly, Lady Reed is hoping to pair her son with Kate. The thought soured Kate's mood a bit. There was no denying Lord Reed's pleasant face, but that was as far as she could compliment him. He seemed like a decent man as well, but Kate felt no attraction towards him. Certainly nothing close to what she felt when she was near the duke ….

The thought caught her off guard. *Attraction? For the duke? Surely not!*

Shoving the thought aside, she answered exactly how they expected her to. "It would be a lovely sight to see, my lord."

"Surely, it would be." Lord Reed grinned at her agreement, and Lady Reed took that as her chance to continue talking about all her son's prowess. Kate listened with half an ear, her mind trailing elsewhere.

Toward the duke. How could she think, even for a moment, that she was attracted to him? He was certainly attractive, yes. Perhaps that was where her confusion lay. His Grace was a very handsome man, and it was very likely that she was confusing her emotions. It was one thing to acknowledge his handsomeness and another thing entirely to fall victim to it. It simply did not make sense for Kate to think she was attracted to a man who had treated her in such a loathsome manner.

Without thinking, she glanced up at Lord Reed, who was nodding to something Mr. Bellmore was saying. He didn't notice her at first, so she was free to compare him to the duke without even realizing what she was doing. He was clean-shaven, his hair cut Brutus-style, and his skin had a healthy glow. And, more than that, he bore no scars. Yet, he lacked something that the duke possessed. Lord Reed appeared more boy than man, while the duke was nothing but pure, unadulterated masculine energy.

Lord Reed looked over at her, and Kate quickly averted her eyes, blushing at being caught. She hoped she had not given him any ideas.

"Miss Cooper, I am hoping to stretch my legs," Lord Reed said. "Would you accompany me on a walk?"

Kate's heart sank. That was the last thing she wanted. She had nothing in common with the viscount; he'd never even read a book before! How could she spend time alone with him on a walk? Would she be forced to listen to his tales about horse racing the entire time?

Before she was forced to respond, Lady Reed said, "Oh, Archie, remember we do not intend on staying long. I am tired after the long ride, after all, and wish to return to our countryside manor soon."

"Ah, yes, Mother. I had forgotten." Lord Reed seemed disappointed. Kate was breathlessly relieved.

Mrs. Bellmore sat up straighter. "That is some distance away, is it not? When shall I see you again?"

"Fear not, dear sister. I've already thought ahead. A ball will be held at the Farringdon Estate in a few days, and I would love it if you all could accompany us."

"I would love to!" Mrs. Bellmore exclaimed even as her husband shook his head.

"I'm afraid I may not be up to attending, considering how unwell I have been feeling lately," he said sadly. "But I implore you all to enjoy yourselves in my absence."

"We shall," Mrs. Bellmore responded with no remorse, and Mr. Bellmore only smiled warmly at her. The elderly lady looked expectantly at Kate. "Kate, you will come with us, yes?"

Kate hesitated for a second. She could see right through Lady Reed's plan, could read behind the excitement in the viscountess' eyes. There was no doubt that she would use the ball to try and pair Kate with her son. Without a doubt, Kate would be forced to spend all evening fending off Lord Reed's advances. The thought nearly made her sigh.

But she'd never been to a ball before. And she truly enjoyed dancing, though it had been a while since she'd done it, so she wasn't entirely sure if she remembered how to. Kate didn't want to give up the chance to attend just to avoid the viscount.

"Yes," she responded. "I would love to."

Lady Reed clapped her hands happily. "Lovely! We shall have a grand time, I assure you."

Kate didn't doubt it. For a moment, a wishful thought crossed her mind. What if the duke was in attendance?

As quickly as she dismissed that possibility, another thought occurred, more daunting than the first. With a closet full of old dresses, what would she wear?

\*\*\*

It had been a few weeks since Lord and Lady Reed visited Dower House and left with their invitation to the Farringdon ball in their wake. Kate had been thinking about what she would wear since then and had mentioned it to Eve in passing. The parson's daughter had promptly suggested that they search the village for ribbons or lace to refresh any old dress she had, since purchasing a new one was simply out of the question.

They walked arm in arm, talking once more about Eve's unfortunate romantic situation, and entered the fabric shop. There, they split ways and began to search for anything they could use to renew Kate's dresses, but after a while of looking, nothing seemed suitable.

Kate returned to Eve's side with a sigh. "I'm afraid our quest will end in failure, Eve."

Eve mimicked her sigh, twisting her lips to the side in thought. "Perhaps you could borrow one of my dresses," she suggested.

"That's very nice of you, Eve, but you are far taller than me. Your dresses won't fit."

"If anything, it may only look like you are wearing one that belongs to a doll," Eve tried to joke.

Kate laughed along, but she couldn't shed her disappointment. It was one thing donning those old dresses for a walk in the forest or for Sunday service but another thing entirely when she was attending a ball. Nothing she had was currently fashionable. No matter how pretty she may be, she would look very drab in such clothing.

"We'll find a solution," Eve said, breaking into her thoughts. At Kate's slightly confused expression, Eve grinned. "You aren't very good at hiding your thoughts, you know. I can tell you're still worried about what you'll wear. But we'll figure something out, I'm sure. In the meantime, let's return home so that we may make it home in time for lunch."

Kate nodded and linked her arm with Eve's once more. They left the shop together, and as soon as they stepped through the exit, Kate's shoulder bumped into someone else's.

"Oh, pardon me, my ladies," came a silky voice of a dapper gentleman. He bowed with a hand over his chest, lifting his head to fix them both with a charming smile. "Though perhaps I should say thank you, as you've both so wonderfully graced me with your beauty."

Kate smiled at his smooth words. "You flatter us, sir."

"Please, the name is Lord Bob Cherry."

"Lord?" Eve questioned.

"I am the Earl of Wellbourne, but my title matters not right now. I'm afraid after living abroad for so many years, I still find it difficult adjusting to being back in England—and with an earldom, no less. May I ask what you two lovely ladies are up to?"

"We were on our way home," Kate explained.

"Ah, so I've just missed you then."

"I wouldn't say so, since you seemed to be heading somewhere yourself."

"But I would not hesitate to drop my plans to spend the evening in your company."

Eve giggled. "That is quite bold of you to say, my lord, seeing that you do not know us. We could be horrendous company."

"Oh, don't say such blasphemy," Lord Wellbourne stated with an exaggerated shake of his head. "Our God up above would never be so cruel to pair such beauty with horrible personalities. May I ask your names?"

"I am Eve Dewhurst, the parson's daughter," Eve responded eagerly.

"And my name is Miss Kate Cooper," Kate told him after.

Lord Wellbourne nodded his head at the introductions, a smile playing around his lips. "It is a pleasure to be acquainted with you both, ladies. So, shall I put it to the test?"

Eve tilted her head to the side with a frown. "Put what to the test?"

"Whether our Lord and Savior have truly forsaken me?"

Kate could not keep the smile off her face. Lord Wellbourne was quite charming and friendly, in an easy manner that somehow did not seem flirtatious. She was already relaxing in his company, and she could tell Eve was enjoying it as well. "How so?"

"Join me for tea tomorrow. And if the weather is still fine, perhaps we may have a picnic by the lake. I am staying at Angelfield House."

Angelfield House? Kate exchanged a look with Eve, but she doubted her friend's heart thudded at the mention of the forbidden abode. It brought to mind the brooding man hidden within, and Kate felt her toes curl in her shoes. She couldn't imagine the reclusive duke having someone stay with him, especially someone with such a vibrant personality as Lord Wellbourne.

"Doesn't the duke refuse all visitors?" Eve asked with a deep frown.

Lord Wellbourne only gave them a hefty shrug. "You needn't worry about that. I need only know if you are willing to visit."

"We would love to." The acceptance rolled off Kate's tongue without a moment of hesitation, surprising even herself. She couldn't understand it. She knew she should stay far away from the duke and his monstrous personality, but all Kate wanted to do was to get closer to him. She blamed it on her unbridled curiosity, but that idea didn't sound very right. What did, she hadn't a clue.

"Lovely!" Lord Wellbourne's face lit up at her acceptance, and he clapped his hands happily. A moment later, he fished a pocket watch from his pocket and frowned before saying, "I'm afraid I cannot spare any more time right now, but I shan't forget our engagement. I look forward to spending time with both of you ladies tomorrow. As for now, I bid you adieu."

He swept into an extravagant bow which brought another giggle out of Eve. Together, they watched as the earl sauntered away, his head held high and a pep in his step. Absently, Kate heard Eve make a comment about the earl's vivacious personality, but Kate couldn't focus on it. Only two words echoed in her head.

Angelfield House … Angelfield House … Angelfield House ….

Where the duke resided.

It didn't make any sense. After all the things she'd heard, after what she'd learned herself after meeting him herself, Kate could fathom the thought of the duke entertaining anyone from the village in his home. Perhaps Lord Wellbourne was a relative of his, whom he had no choice but to house in his manor. Perhaps the earl was unconcerned about the withdrawn personality of the handsome duke. Kate couldn't understand it, nor could she comprehend the odd tingly feeling she was getting in the pits of her stomach.

"Tea with a handsome earl and the duke?" Eve's excited voice floated back in, snapping Kate out of her thoughts. "What do you think will happen?"

"I don't know …."

Eve kept chattering about the invitation, then slowly pulled the conversation towards the upcoming ball. Kate only listened with half an ear and felt a twinge of relief when Eve said her goodbyes once they were upon the patronage, leaving Kate to her thoughts once more.

What if the duke had her thrown off his property for trespassing? She had made a promise, hadn't she? Clearly, he did not want her anywhere near him. Did he want anyone near him at all? How had the Earl of Wellbourne gotten close?

She thought about it all the way to Dower House, her curiosity transforming into deep trepidation. She would honor her acceptance, of course. And she could not deny to herself that she wanted to see the beastly duke once more, though she wasn't entirely certain why. All she knew was that there was a strange excitement brewing within her.

# Chapter Twelve

"You accursed man!"

Bob tilted his head back and bellowed a laugh, the sound echoing around the large parlor. Emerson maintained his scowl, resting his elbow atop his cue as he stared at the ivory balls before him. Bob had suggested they play billiards after lunchtime, and Emerson had given in, even though he had not looked at the thing since the house was rebuilt. And his lack of practice was clearly showing because Bob was soundly beating him.

"What's wrong, Emerson?" Bob asked, watching him with a taunting grin. "Perhaps you would like some time to get yourself together."

"Be quiet," Emerson pushed through gritted teeth, his eyes focused on the table. "I am concentrating."

"Take all the time you need, though I doubt it will be enough to salvage a win."

Emerson groaned a little, his brows deepening into a frown. Bob was right. He'd well and truly lost, even though the game was not over. Emerson considered just ending it here, but he realized with a start that, though he was losing, he was not so engrossed in his self-hating thoughts as he usually was during this time of the day. He wasn't at peace, but at least he was distracted from the thoughts that plagued him.

"While you're trying to figure out your next move," Bob went on, putting his cue down to head over to the sideboard, "there is something I must tell you. We will be expecting guests."

Emerson froze. A surge of anger took ahold of him, and he tapered it as quickly as it came, looking up at his friend. Bob was calmly pouring himself a glass of whiskey. "What do you mean?"

"Just as I've said it. Tomorrow, for tea, I have invited two lovely women from the village. They have gratefully accepted, though that came as a surprise. I was certain they would have turned me down the moment they heard I was staying at Angelfield House. I thought your reputation preceded you, but perhaps not."

"Who?" The game forgotten, Emerson put down his cue and faced Bob, crossing his arms. "Who did you invite here?"

"Miss Eve and Miss Kate. Perhaps you know Miss Eve? She says she is the daughter of the parson."

Emerson felt the ground give way beneath him. Trying to hold his composure, he made his way over to the closest armchair and sank into its comforting folds letting out a breath. So many thoughts ran through his head at once, but only one stood out to him.

Miss Kate had agreed to come *here*.

Panic took hold of him. The thought of Miss Kate—of anyone, really—coming to his abode felt like a sick and cruel joke. He'd spent so much time away from the company of others, so how could he entertain two lovely women? He couldn't even imagine it. No, it couldn't happen.

"They were quite charming," Bob went on, oblivious to Emerson's inner crisis. "It was rather disappointing that I had to leave, due to my appointment with the tailor, because I would have loved to spend a little more time with them. I'm already looking forward to seeing them tomorrow. I suggested a picnic as well, you know. By the lake. We should have cold chicken available, as well as wine, cakes—"

"Cancel it."

"Pardon me?"

Emerson glowered at him, but Bob met his heated look with a calm one of his own. "Cancel it. I am in no mood to entertain anyone."

"I would assume so, since you have not kept the company of anyone but your dogs and your servants in two years. But you will relax as time passes, I'm sure. They have quite amiable personalities. It will do you some good."

His panic deepened. There would be no convincing Bob, Emerson knew. He'd already made up his mind, and Emerson would simply have to sit back and allow it. What could he do to stop this? Feign illness? No, Bob would only say that a bit of fresh air would do him a world of good and force him out. Fall off his horse and break his neck? He humored the thought for a desperate moment but decided it was far too much of a risk. With a sinking heart, Emerson realized there was nothing he could do to stop this.

But he could not come face to face with them. Especially not Miss Kate.

"I cannot remember the last time I have been in the company of women," Emerson said in a low, deceivingly calm voice. "I don't know how to talk to them. They giggle, and they laugh at everything you say, but we would share no interests. Reading, history, geography, nature ... I won't be able to talk about any of it. And even if I do, I shall bore them to death."

"You must take care not to judge them before you get to know them," Bob said wisely. "They may very well enjoy all the topics you've just named. Commoner women are much different from noble ladies, you know."

Since his attempt didn't work, Emerson switched tactics. "They shall react with fear when they see me and the scars I bear. What woman wouldn't? I am a monster in the eyes of others, even before I've even opened my mouth. And what will I wear? I have nothing fashionable in my wardrobe as I have not gotten new clothes in years, and I am in desperate need of a haircut. I am in no position to see others, as you can clearly see."

Bob laughed at that, downing the rest of his whiskey. The sound made Emerson long for a glass of his own. "There are plenty of women who would gladly marry a duke, whether they be scarred or not."

"Marriage? Who said anything about that?"

Bob ignored him. "And, as for everything else you've mentioned, it can easily be fixed. New clothes and a haircut? Why, I can have that taken care of within the hour."

Emerson faltered, grappling for something else to say. He was given a little bit more time when there was a knock on the door, and Sparkes' voice sounded on the other end, "Your Grace, my lord, dinner has been served."

"Sparkes, you are just the man I was hoping to see!" Emerson leaped out of his chair and bounded for the door, throwing it open to reveal a slightly confused Sparkes. He ushered the elderly man in. "Come, tell me about the state of our larder. I doubt there is much that can facilitate a picnic, is there?"

Emerson caught Sparkes' confusion, making sure his back was turned to Bob when he gave him a pleading look.

"As a matter of fact, Your Grace, the larder is always well-stocked. We could have a dinner party tonight if you wished it."

Emerson hung his head in disappointment as Bob huffed a loud laugh.

"What about a picnic by the lake, Sparkes?" Bob asked him. "Do you think that could be facilitated?"

"Quite so, my lord."

"Traitor," Emerson mumbled under his breath, and the bemused butler looked even more befuddled.

"We shall be having a picnic tomorrow, then," Bob announced to the butler. "With Miss Kate Cooper and Miss Eve Dewhurst. Everything must be perfect! It has been a while since my dear friend has entertained anyone."

"A picnic, my lord?" Sparkes shot Emerson a surprised look, but Emerson didn't bother to say anything. Admitting defeat, he sloped back to his chair with a silent sigh.

"Yes, and Emerson does not believe he has suitable clothes to wear."

"I'm certain Francis will be able to find something proper, my lord. Something even suitable for a ball."

"Excellent! Come then. There are arrangements that need to be made regarding the picnic itself. I shall leave the outfit and the duke's appearance to your discretionary instructions."

Sparkes nodded in understanding and allowed Bob to drape his arm around his shoulders and lead him out of the room. Once he was alone, Emerson allowed himself one deep, soul-shattering groan.

Picnic with Miss Kate? It still didn't make any sense to him. Why would she even agree to such a thing?

*They show his noble heart.*

Miss Kate's words echoed in his mind, softening the anger. Was that the reason she decided to accept the invitation? Was she interested in seeing him again, even though she had made it quite clear that she thought his personality atrocious? The thought made the anger and horror melt away just a little, leaving a forbidden bit of excitement.

But he couldn't allow himself to be excited. Be excited about what? Being humiliated the moment they laid eyes on him up close and saw the horrors that were his scars? Sinking into the shadows of Bob's overwhelming personality? Emerson should not feel any excitement. Right now, he should be spending every waking second praying that something would happen to save him from this arrangement.

Despite knowing that, his heart skipped a beat at the thought of seeing Miss Kate again. It was unusual, this feeling. How could she have this effect on him when he hardly knew her?

Would she be at the ball? He'd received an invitation to the Farringdon ball and was already planning on ignoring it, though the kinder thing would be to reject it if he did not intend on going. But now, the thought that Miss Kate might be in attendance had him entertaining the idea once more. Was he willing to go, despite his revulsion of crowds and the attention of others? He was bound to be the topic of discussion the moment he set foot inside that ballroom. Was he willing to risk that at the slightest chance of seeing Miss Kate again?

Goodness, there was no telling anymore. Only a short while ago, he'd been content to spend every remaining second of his life locked away in this house, with only dogs to keep him company. But now that he'd met Miss Kate, it felt as if he was questioning every decision he'd ever made. And he was wanting to change ….

# Chapter Thirteen

Angelfield House was a sprawling manor of white brick. The columns that bordered the wide front porch were a similar white, with a balcony standing atop it. Massive mahogany doors stood as the front entrance, and the long, open driveway that sat before it was bordered by a thick line of purple orchids. As Kate and Eve made their way towards the massive building, stones crunched under their feet, both silent in awe of the magnificent structure.

"Is this how the previous Angelfield House looked?" Kate whispered to her friend, as if she couldn't dare to speak any longer before such greatness.

"I don't know," Eve whispered back. "I cannot remember. But I don't think so."

They approached the porch, lifting their skirts to make the trip up the steps. Kate made sure to wear one of her best dresses, one of the mint green walking dresses she had been gifted in her previous life as a lady, when she had expected to do much walking through Hyde Park with potential suitors. Thankfully, the dress still fit quite well, and she paired it with a white bonnet and matching white slippers.

Eve looked quite lovely herself, wearing a sky-blue dress and leather shoes. Rather than wear a bonnet, she had opted to braid her hair over one shoulder, letting her cheeks grow red from the sun. They had met with each other near the patronage and had made the trip to Angelfield House together, with Kate's trepidation growing with each step. The closer she came to the house, the more wrong it felt. And the more her excitement grew.

Right now, her heart beat rapidly in her chest as she stood before the door and considered using the ornate door knocker that was on both doors. Before she could do anything, though, the front doors opened wide, revealing a tall, aged man.

"Miss Kate, Miss Eve." He swept into a deep bow fit for a queen. "We have been expecting you."

"Ah, Mr. Sparkes!" Eve exclaimed. "How lovely it is to see you again!"

"It has been some time, Miss Eve, indeed. I have not seen you since you were a young child. I am surprised you remember me."

"As am I," Eve said with a laugh. Then she gestured to Kate. "Please, allow me to introduce you to Miss Kate Cooper. She is staying with the Bellmores, who are renting Dower House."

"Miss Kate, I have heard much about you." Mr. Sparkes turned to Kate fully and bowed once more. "An honour. Please, come inside."

Kate gave him a grateful smile and swept past him into the cavernous foyer of the house. Along the sides sat end tables bearing luxurious vases, with paintings lining the walls. A large burgundy rug extended from the front doors all the way to the large staircase spread out before them. Kate hardly had any time to admire everything in detail when Lord Wellbourne came bounding around the corner of the staircase, coming from a hallway she could not see.

"My lovely ladies!" he boomed, his voice ricocheting off the walls. "You have arrived! Welcome."

"My lord," both Kate and Eve greeted, curtsying respectfully.

"Oh, come now, there is no need for the formalities. You should both call me Bob. Welcome, welcome." He came close enough that Kate thought he would pull them into a hug. She wouldn't have been surprised if he made an attempt, but he only came to stand next to Mr. Sparkes. "You two look beautiful."

"Thank you," Eve responded with a blush.

Bob gave them a regretful look. "I'm afraid our host is a little indisposed at the moment," he said. Kate didn't miss the look he and Mr. Sparkes exchanged. "But I assure you, he will be joining us shortly."

"Ah, of course," Kate said, a little breathlessly. She hadn't realized just how much she had been looking for the appearance of His Grace until just now. Blushing, she tried to reign in her eagerness. But she couldn't help but wonder if they were truly expecting him to arrive at all, given his personality.

"It is a lovely day outside, ladies, so I would like to suggest we take this party to the lake for a picnic," Bob suggested. "What do you say?"

"A wonderful idea," Eve said excitedly. "It has been so long since I've had a picnic by the lake."

"Ah, our minds are in sync, Miss Eve. Then shall we make our way there?"

"Yes, let us!"

Eve excitedly traipsed out of the house as Bob accepted a large basket from a housekeeper who came by. Kate expected them to head down the driveway, but Bob turned towards a path off the side instead. They followed dutifully, though Kate felt a bit naughty for walking on the duke's land. She had to remind herself that she was here at the invitation of the earl and not because she was trespassing.

Conversation flowed between the two of them as they went through the duke's overgrown garden and delved into the forest. Kate didn't think they were anywhere near the pond where she'd met the duke because, only a few minutes later, they were moving past the trees out onto a wide plain. Soon enough, Kate could hear the quacking of the ducks occupying the lake.

"Shall we stop here?" Bob asked once they were near the lake's bank. The stretch of deep blue water under a lovely, cloudless sky was absolutely breathtaking. Kate was already nodding before she knew it.

"Right here is perfect," she declared.

With that said, the earl had the large, soft blanket spread and the food laid out. Kate gasped at the sheer amount of it. There were cakes, sandwiches, cold meat, and even wine! Eve looked quite eager to dig in, and when the earl commented on her obvious excitement, she blushed to the roots of her hair.

They talked about everything and nothing. Kate indulged in nearly everything she saw, not caring about how it may look to Bob. He seemed happy to see them enjoying themselves and began asking them about themselves. Kate allowed Eve to do most of the talking at that time and only responded to say that she was a companion of the Bellmores and had lived all her life in London. The topic soon moved on to other things, like upcoming events in the village, past events that Eve was more than willing to describe in acute detail, and Bob's time while abroad.

The entire time, Kate was looking out for His Grace.

It might have been an hour before she spotted a figure in the distance. Her belly was full, a smile on her face, and she was quite happy with the current company—but she could not shed that pinch of disappointment. Until now.

She knew it was the duke the moment he appeared. He was still quite some distance away, and, since Eve and Bob sat with their backs turned to him, they didn't notice him until he drew close. But Kate couldn't take her eyes off him. As he drew nearer, his scars came into view, harshly contorting his face. His magnetizing handsomeness had her heart racing in her chest, and she forgot that she was meant to be conversing with the others, unable to take her eyes off him.

His dogs were in tow. Kate didn't notice until Liam barked and bounded towards her, Lily on his heels. Kate stood instinctively to receive their excited hugs.

"Oh, you two are still so lovely!" she exclaimed, scratching the dogs behind their ears. She used them to distract her from the tall, thin, handsome man who was now standing at the edge of the blanket.

"Good evening." His deep voice washed over her, bringing goosebumps to her skin. Kate finally looked back at him and felt a sharp tug of surprise at the apologetic look on his face. He scratched the back of his head awkwardly.

"That's just fine," Bob said heartily, standing to clap his friend on the shoulder. "I'm just happy you made it. But did you have to bring the dogs?"

"I'm happy that he did." Eve, despite her opinions on the duke, smiled kindly at him and reached out to pet Lily. "They certainly bring some excitement to the picnic."

"Are you saying that I'm not exciting enough, Miss Eve?"

"Certainly not!" she said with a cheeky grin. "Or perhaps I am."

Bob and Eve laughed at that, but His Grace did not even crack a smile. Kate couldn't help running her gaze down the length of him. The last time she saw him, he wore an old, plain shirt and old boots. But now, he was in a white shirt, dark waistcoat, white gloves adorning his hands, and a black, heavy coat overtop. His black breeches were tucked into black boots, looking no less than a proper duke. Kate licked her lips, her throat suddenly dry.

She sank back onto the blanket, happy that the exuberant Liam decided to sit down as well. To her surprise, the duke sat next to her, Liam between them. Lily stayed by Eve, content to accept the gentle pats she was receiving from her.

"Miss Eve?" came Bob once more. "Would you like to go for a walk by the edge of the lake?"

Eve was already getting to her feet, a bright smile on her face. "I would love to." She looked at Kate. "Will you be all right?"

Kate nodded, though she wasn't entirely sure. The very thought of being left alone with the duke was both terrifying and exhilarating. He'd only just arrived, and now she was to be alone with him?

At her nod, Bob and Miss Eve went off together closer to the lake's edge. To her surprise, Lily and Liam bounded after them. Perhaps they thought they were going on an adventure, Kate thought.

The silence that fell over them was deafening. Kate took a sip of her second unfinished glass of wine, trying to think of what to say.

"I must apologise, Miss Kate." The duke's voice caught her by surprise. She looked over at him, noticing how he kept his head tilted away from her, hiding his scars. "For my behaviour when we first met."

"I have already forgotten about it," she said. "But I suppose now I can forgive you. Apology accepted, Your Grace. And what of the smithy's children?"

She caught a flash of surprise in the duke's eyes, and she was taken aback by how endearing it was. For that moment, he was not so much intimidating as he was misunderstood. "Pardon?" he murmured.

She didn't know why she brought that up, but it was too late to take the words back. "The blacksmith's children," she explained. "I have heard how rude you were to them when they wandered upon your land as well. You made them cry. I think it would be nice for you to apologize to them as well."

Kate might have been mistaken, but she could have sworn she saw a hint of red color his cheeks. Even so, his deep dark eyes bore into her, penetrating deep with an intense emotion she could not name. "I did not know you would be aware of that …" he said after a long moment of silence.

"I think everyone in the village is aware of it," Kate responded.

"I see. I shall make sure to send my apologies soon."

She nodded in satisfaction, feeling a wave of awkwardness come over her from the stilted conversation. This was not what she'd imagined it to be when she saw the duke again. Then, she hadn't imagined much at all. Even now, he was nothing but an enigma that she could not figure out.

Silence sank around them like a heavy fog. Kate watched as Eve and Bob meandered along the bank of the lake, their laughter drifting towards them. The dogs sniffed ahead, searching for something to entertain them, and the world sat and was peaceful. It would have been quite calming had it not been for the uneasiness settling in the pit of Kate's stomach.

She tried her hardest not to look at the duke and failed. His face was stoic, his body tense and rigid, as if he was expecting to be attacked at any moment. Even so, he made sure to angle his face away from her, his long hair shifting into his face with every brush of the wind.

"Miss Kate," the duke said suddenly, clearing his throat. Kate's heart leaped. "Tell me a little more about yourself."

She thought about it before she answered, sorting through and discarding her usual responses to such a question. For the duke, she wanted to be as open as she possibly could without revealing too much of her past.

"I am the companion of Major Bellmore and his wife, who are currently renting the Dower House for the summer," she began, her voice soft. "We've been in the village for a few months now and are set to return to London once the Season is over."

"It is not unusual for an elderly couple to seek solace in the countryside during such a busy time in London," he remarked.

"That is true, and I'm pleased that I could join them."

"And how are you liking the village so far?"

"I will certainly miss it when I am gone. It has a very quaint charm I've come to greatly admire, though I admit I am not yet used to the area as yet. That is why I became lost that day."

The mention of their first meeting made him shrink away from her. Kate instantly regretted her words, but before she could offer a word of comfort, he said, "I acted quite untowardly to you."

"It is water under the bridge, Your Grace."

"Please," he said quietly. "Call me Emerson."

Kate's heart threatened to beat right out of her chest. She could not take her eyes off him and did not miss the deep loneliness she saw hidden within his guarded gaze. It was all she could do to keep from reaching a hand out to him.

"In that case, Emerson," she began again, needing to fill the quiet before it bore down on them for too long. "May I ask you a question then?"

Emerson tilted his head slightly towards her, eyebrows raised in question. "Yes?"

"You strike me as the sort of man who likes to spend hours on end locked away in a library. Am I correct in my assumption?"

He nodded slowly. "Very much so. Though I suppose I have not read anything new lately."

"What is the last publication you read?"

He lifted his eyes to the blue sky above them in thought. "*Travels of England and Wales* by James Brome."

"Oh." Without realizing it, she pushed her bottom lip out in thought. "I have not had the opportunity to read that one. Could you tell me more about it?"

"Are you certain?" Emerson asked, clearly surprised.

She nodded. "Why not? I've always had an interest in books, and my love for reading is greater than no other. Perhaps I could pick up that piece once I am in the local bookstore within the week. Do you think they will have it?"

Emerson shook her head. "I doubt it. But allow me to tell you what I can without giving too much away."

And then he launched into a full-blown explanation of the publication. He spoke breathlessly, with such eager fervor, and his words ran into the other. It felt as if he had not spoken this much in a long while. Kate listened, enraptured by the rise and fall of his tone, by how rapidly he would go off on several tangents while trying to explain one point. She didn't realize she was smiling until a giggle escaped her lips.

Emerson stopped suddenly. Whatever life had washed over him disappeared in a second. "What is it?" he asked. "Have I bored you?"

"Not in the slightest, Your Grace," she said hurriedly. "On the contrary, I am quite enamored by your interest in the topic."

"Interest in what topic?" came Bob's voice as he and Eve came upon them once more.

Emerson turned his face away as the two of them hunkered down onto the blanket. Kate couldn't tell if he was hiding a blush, but the very thought was enough to make her smile even wider, her heart as light as a feather. "On the topic of travel," she explained. "His Grace was just telling me about a book he's read."

"A book?" Bob wrinkled his nose as he shook his head. "Would it not be better to seek such information by travelling yourself?"'

"Indeed, my lord," Eve agreed with a nod. "I have always hoped that one day, I would be able to do just that. I think reading about it would only make me quite anxious."

"I suppose only true lovers of books would understand us, don't you think, Your Grace?" Kate asked. She looked at Emerson as she posed the question, but he only gave her a curt nod, his head still slightly hung. The sight was rather intriguing. At first glance, she would have thought he was shunning them, not wanting to endure this picnic any longer. But after their conversation—after she listened to him ramble on about the work of James Brome—Kate could see the shyness that bolstered his actions.

Despite his lack of response, a lively discussion ensued, and talk of travel drifted once more to a tale from Bob about a time he had visited India. Kate tried to listen, but her mind was far more focused on the quiet man next to her. What was he thinking now?

He appeared to be listening, but he made no contribution to the conversation, so she could not truly tell. Was he enjoying himself?

Hoping to settle her constantly wandering thoughts, she reached for a still-chilled bottle of champagne. At the same time, Emerson did the same, and their fingers met before they could do anything to stop it.

"Oh, pardon me," he said quickly, pulling his hand back. But the damage was done. Her heart was racing in her chest, her body flushed with heat. Kate was happy that Bob and Eve were too busy talking to notice how red her face had undoubtedly become, and she quickly tried to pour herself a glass of champagne as a distraction. She sipped the cool liquid, her eyes darting toward the duke.

He was watching her. Kate nearly choked on her drink, and it was all she could do to keep her composure. His expression was guarded, so she could not tell what he was thinking. But even when their eyes met, something passed between them, and he didn't look away, watching her steadily.

"Isn't that right, Kate?" came Eve's voice, pulling Kate back to the present.

"Y-yes, right," Kate responded quickly, not entirely sure what she was agreeing to. Eve noticed how flustered she was and frowned but said nothing. And the conversation went on and on until the sun began to drift towards the horizon and the afternoon warmth faded.

"It is getting quite late," Eve announced suddenly. "I'm afraid I won't be able to stay any longer, as I have choir practice to attend."

"Then we shan't keep you," Bob stated, and he instantly got to his feet and offered a hand to Eve for her to stand. Kate began to shift herself, moving her skirts about so that she could get to her feet, but then a gloved hand appeared before her face.

She looked up to see Emerson hovering over her, his arm extended. Kate's mouth went dry even as she accepted the hand and allowed him to help her up. As soon as that was done, he cleared his throat and stepped back awkwardly.

They said their goodbyes quickly as the things were packed up. Within a few minutes, Bob and Emerson were heading back towards the forest after both Eve and Kate had refused Bob's offer to let them escort them to the church. Kate stared after the duke, disappointment washing over her the further he got away. It felt as if it was all over too soon. She wished she could have spent a little bit more time with him.

Pushing that feeling aside, she fell in step with Eve, walking in the opposite direction of the men. After a while, she couldn't hold it back any longer.

"The duke is rather interesting, don't you think?" she asked, feigning nonchalance.

"Interesting?" Eve echoed, then nodded. "Yes, I suppose so. I thought him to be rather monstrous, but he did not seem so scary. I wished he had spoken a little more, though."

"I think he is shy. It has been a while since he's been around others, after all." Kate couldn't hold back her sigh. "Even so, I cannot believe he is the same man I met at the pond. He'd been so crass at that time, cursing and shouting at me. Yet today, he was rather gentle and even a little friendly."

"I cannot understand it either," Eve said.

Kate left it at that, but her mind was running at full speed. She wouldn't let her friend know how intrigued she was by Emerson and his sudden change of behavior. Nor could she explain this strange, tingly feeling she had after their time together, not even to herself.

"Well," Eve said after a while. "We will see him again soon, so maybe then we'll know what he's truly like."

"What do you mean?"

"Lord Wellbourne told me that both he and the duke intends to attend the Farringdon ball next week, so we shall all meet there again. It will be rather fun, I'm certain. I can't wait!"

And now, neither could Kate.

She'd been eager to attend her first ball before, but the thought of the duke being in attendance filled her with desperate excitement. It was all she could to keep herself from talking about him, voicing to Eve the questions she'd wanted to ask the duke. She wanted to know more about him. Would she get her chance at the ball? Would he truly be in attendance?

A part of her was skeptical, but she was excited. It could not come any sooner.

## Chapter Fourteen

"My, that was quick."

Emerson frowned a little at Francis' chipper tone as his valet drifted through the door. He instantly made his way over to Emerson and began assisting him with his boots. Emerson tried ignoring the glee in Francis' eyes, but it was hard since he could feel a murmur of it light his heart. He took a moment to respond.

"I suppose it was," Emerson murmured as he gazed out the window, seeing nothing but the lovely blue of Miss Kate's eyes.

"Yes, well, it is the first time I've seen you pay such keen attention to your style of dress in such a long time, so I suppose I cannot blame you for arriving late. Did you enjoy yourself, however?"

Emerson managed a shrug, hoping Francis couldn't see through his façade. "It was all right," he said simply.

"All right?" Francis paused to look at Emerson as if he was staring at a ghost. "Goodness, that is better than I expected."

Emerson couldn't help frowning at the overexcited valet. He said nothing for a while, mulling over the best words to use in this situation. Explain how anxious he had been the moment he laid eyes on Miss Kate and how he had to resist the urge to turn back? Or should he lay bare the odd feelings brewing in his chest, filling him with equal parts excitement and dread?

If he could sort through his feelings in full, perhaps he would have chosen to explain it all to Francis. Certainly, his valet would understand, would be open to listening and giving him advice wherever he could. But the thought made Emerson grimace.

Francis, however, was staring expectantly at him, pulling Emerson's boots off his feet as he awaited a response.

"I don't understand what you mean," Emerson finally stated.

"You have not been in a social setting in two years! And you decided to attend a picnic with two lovely ladies. Certainly, Lord Wellbourne coming to visit was a great decision."

"Don't push it, Francis," Emerson muttered, with none of the venom that would usually make the valet stand down.

Francis helped Emerson out of his heavy coat. "But am I wrong, Your Grace? If it were not for Lord Wellbourne, you would not have even considered the thought?"

"He does have a rather persistent attitude, I will admit. But …."

"But?" Francis pressed, eyes twinkling with interest.

The words left his lips without thought. "He was not the reason I decided to go."

"Oh? Was it the lovely Miss Eve, the parson's daughter? Or perhaps Miss Kate, who hails from London?"

"How do you know who was there?" Emerson asked, taken aback.

But his valet only shrugged. "I only had to piece the bits together, Your Grace. I know Miss Eve would be there, and, well, word has spread about the beautiful Miss Kate. They have been inseparable as of late, so it was not unreasonable to assume."

"How astute of you. And what a marvelous way of saying that you have been gossiping."

"Gossip is such an ugly word, Your Grace. I reject it."

"Reject it all you'd like. It is exactly what you did. Unless you would like to admit that you followed me there instead?"

"Certainly not, Your Grace!" But Francis' grin was as broad as ever, undeterred by Emerson's words. And, to his surprise, for some reason, Emerson did not feel the usual bite of annoyance that would usually follow Francis' pestering. Rather, he felt more inclined to respond to him, the words rushing to the tip of this tongue without a moment's hesitation.

"I must say, though, Your Grace, that you looked quite dapper today," Francis made sure to point out. "Though I may speak in jest, I truly hope that you enjoyed the outing."

"I did …" Emerson trailed off, not knowing how to continue. He opened and closed his mouth a few times, trying to figure out how best to explain the awkward situation between him and Miss Kate, how she had smiled and laughed at him, and it had somehow felt as if the dark cloud which hung over his head had dispersed for a small moment.

"And I have had the pleasure of meeting the Bellmores myself, I'll have you know," Francis forged on. "They are a remarkable couple. Major Bellmore served in the army, and now they spend the rest of their days in retirement, with Miss Kate as their companion."

"The army, you say?" Emerson murmured, though he was really hoping Francis would volunteer more information

Before he had the chance to, however, the door banged open, and Bob came sauntering in, his arms thrown wide and a broad grin on his face. "What a lovely day to be alive!" he bellowed, so loud that the rafters shook just a little. "A marvelous day, I must say. A truly wonderful occasion."

"You're being too noisy," Emerson complained even as he watched the earl stagger over to the window and lean heavily against the sill. It was clear that he was inebriated, an amazing feat considering the fact that they had not been back to the house for very long yet.

"Were you this in your cups by the lake?" Emerson had to ask, frowning.

Bob just waved a heavy hand. "Of course not," he slurred. "I would never deign to disgrace myself in front of those lovely ladies. But I must say I truly enjoyed myself. Didn't you, Emerson?"

Emerson sank onto the bed, finishing now with dressing for bed. Sensing that it might not be the best time to say anything, Francis drifted away to stand by the door while Emerson stared at his flushed face friend, wondering how best to respond.

"It was as horrible as I thought it would be," he said after a long while.

"I'll take that as a resounding 'Yes, Bob! I am so happy you decided to drag me along!'. And to that, I say, you're welcome, Emerson." Bob's grin was so wide it caused new crinkles around his eyes. He tried crossing his arms, but they fell to his side as if he hadn't the strength to hold them upright for much longer than a second. "It is always a good time when you spend it with fine fillies. Especially the young Miss Kate. She was particularly beautiful, I must say."

The white-hot jealousy that surged in Emerson threatened to choke him. He curled his hands into fists, biting down hard to keep from launching to his feet. The force of his emotions took him by surprise, and it was all he could do to force it back down.

For what reason should he be jealous? It was certainly true that Miss Kate was a marvelous lady, beautiful both inside and out. Anyone with eyes could see that, and he couldn't get upset at everyone who decided to point it out, could he?

A resounding *yes* echoed in his mind, and Emerson briefly closed his eyes to force the thought away, letting out a long breath.

"Perhaps it would be best to have a bit of coffee, my lord," came Francis to the rescue. He strode by quickly, reaching for the earl's elbow while throwing an anxious glance Emerson's way. It was clear he knew how upset Emerson was getting and was trying to diffuse the situation.

"Coffee?" Bob questioned with a deep frown. "Why would I do such a thing? That will only make me sober."

"And perhaps that is not a bad thing, my lord." Expertly, Francis steered Bob towards the door.

"Why don't you come and drink with me, Emerson?" Bob called over his shoulder as he was led away.

Emerson waved a hand. "I would rather go to bed."

"What a bummer you are. But it is fine. We shall have plenty to drink when we attend the Farringdon ball in a few nights' time."

*The Farringdon ...* Emerson shot to his feet. "What?"

Bob planted a hand on the door jamb just before he was about to leave, giving Emerson a broad smile. "I informed Miss Eve that we will be in attendance. Surely you do not mind?" Emerson opened his mouth to respond, but Bob was already walking out, shouting over his shoulder, "It doesn't matter if you do because you are going, and that is the end of that!"

And then the door was closed. For a few seconds, Emerson contemplated going after him, nipping this in the bud before Bob convinced himself further that he would attend the ball.

But then, a brief image of Miss Kate flashed in his mind, clad in a lovely muslin ballgown, her hair pinned to the top of her head, flowers in her hair ….

The most beautiful woman in attendance.

And that image led to more imaginations—of Emerson holding his hand out to her and Miss Kate taking it with a smile, of him leading her out to dance, pulling her close, drifting through a waltz.

He hadn't danced in years, but the thought of doing that with her had the fight going out of him, and Emerson sank back onto the bed. With a sigh, he fell back, seeing nothing before him but Miss Kate's face.

First a picnic, now a ball? People would talk. They would wonder what has brought the monstrous duke out of his lair, and Emerson would be the center of attention once more. Gawking, whispering, laughing at his scars.

But she wouldn't laugh. Emerson wondered if she even saw them. With the way she looked at him today, it was as if they didn't even matter, as if the scars he hated so much were as normal to her as lips or eyes or a nose.

Was that enough to pull him further out of his shell? Bob might have succeeded in having him attend the picnic, but he could easily turn down going to the ball if he wanted to, if he was determined enough. The only thing he could focus on right now, however, was seeing Miss Kate again.

*No.* Emerson shook his head, closing his eyes. He couldn't do it. He'd shut himself away from society for so long that he couldn't possibly try to integrate himself once more. A picnic with only two kind ladies was one thing. An entire ball …? He wouldn't be able to handle it.

Or was Bob, Sparkes, and Francis right all along? Had he made the wrong choice by shutting himself away like this, despite his scars?

It doesn't matter. He didn't have proper clothes for a ball anyhow. It wouldn't hurt to miss it. He'd missed so many over the past two years, so another would hardly matter. Yes, he could stay home with the dogs and ignore these unusual feelings he harbored for Miss Kate.

But no matter how much he tried to convince himself of that, only one thought persisted. *She will be there.*

# Chapter Fifteen

"Oh, dear God."

Mary rushed up to Kate, her face stricken with worry. She grasped Kate's shoulder as she quickly took in every inch of her, searching for what might be wrong. "What is it?" she asked a little breathlessly.

Kate blinked, coming back to herself. With a forced smile, she tried to console Mary by saying, "Oh, it is nothing. I don't know what came over me."

Mary stepped back with a frown but said nothing. Kate could tell that she hadn't convinced her completely.

And there would be no hope of that, seeing that the dread sinking within her body at that very moment was too much to hide. Mary had come up to tell her that Lord and Lady Reed had come to visit again ... which was the last thing Kate wanted to hear.

The thought of having to entertain the viscount again, knowing that both the Bellmores and the dowager viscountess would try to match them, made Kate's shoulders sag in defeat. There was nothing she could do about it, sadly. For the next few hours, she would have to smile with Lord Reed as he so blatantly tried to flirt with her. Kate didn't know what to say to get out of it.

"I'll be downstairs in a few minutes," Kate said to Mary, hoping her smile was a little more convincing this time.

Mary narrowed her eyes, but she nodded, backing away towards the door. "I'll let Mr. and Mrs. Bellmore know."

And then she was gone, leaving Kate to her thoughts. Alone, she sat at her vanity table and let out a sigh. It had already been a few days since the picnic by the lake, and, right now, that was all Kate wanted. To go back to the lake to spend time with Eve, Bob, and the duke. She had been getting ready to go for a walk before Mary came. Now, she would have to pretend she didn't want to be anywhere else but there.

With another sigh, Kate replaced a few of the pins she had taken out of her chignon, stood, and smoothed the skirt of the grey-blue dress she wore. Taking another breath of confidence, Kate made her way down to the drawing room, where she knew the others were.

Mrs. Bellmore was in the middle of a fit of laughter when Kate walked in. The moment the elderly woman spotted her, she waved her over, tears glimmering in her eyes. "Oh, Kate, you missed it!" she wheezed. "Lady Reed was just telling us the most hilarious tale."

"I wouldn't mind saying it again for your benefit, Miss Kate," Lady Reed responded, sipping her tea with a smile. She sat next to her sister, with Lord Reed in the armchair opposite of them and Mr. Bellmore sitting in the chair by the hearth.

Kate took a moment to look around the room, her heart sinking when she realized she would have no choice but to sit closer to Lord Reed. Forcing the smile to stay on her face, Kate sat on the chaise lounge next to the viscount, resisting the urge to perch on the very edge. It would be too obvious she was trying to be apart from him, she feared.

"I would love to hear it, if you don't mind," Kate said politely.

"I am happy to recount every detail for you, dear Miss Kate," Lord Reed spoke up. He even leaned a little over the armrest closer to her, and Kate forced herself to look at him.

"Certainly, my lo—" Thankfully, there was a knock on the door before she could finish her sentence. Mary slipped in a second later.

"Dinner is served," she stated, her head bowed slightly.

"Shall we make our way over then?" Kate was the first to stand, already heading over to Mr. Bellmore to assist him with his cane. Mrs. Bellmore waited until her husband was on his feet before she slipped her arm through her sister's, and the two of them made their way out of the room. Kate had hoped that Lord Reed would go on ahead, but he lingered, gesturing for Kate to take the lead when she looked expectantly at him.

The short walk to the dining room was filled with chatter from Mrs. Bellmore and Lady Reed, talking about stories from their past and people who were now long gone. They didn't cut the conversation short until they were about to settle at the dining table.

"Kate, why don't you sit next to Lord Reed? I'm sure he would love the company."

Kate's heart sank at Mrs. Bellmore's words, and she tried her hardest not to reveal how disappointed she was at the suggestion.

"Wouldn't that be nice, Miss Kate?" Lord Reed spoke up, suddenly far closer than Kate had anticipated he would be. "That way, I could talk to you rather than listen to my mother jabber on about her past."

"Jabber?" Mr. Bellmore echoed, chuckling. With Kate's quiet help, he sank heavily down into the chair at the head of the table. "The youth these days, I tell you."

"He has had to listen to me talk about all manners of things on the way here," Lady Reed stated with a smile. "I certainly wouldn't mind him seeking company elsewhere. I'll borrow his ear another time."

It seemed as if the decision was already made for her. Kate knew she had no choice. Once everyone was seated, with Lady Reed sitting next to her sister, Kate stiffly made her way over to the chair next to Lord Reed. He didn't bother to stand as he pulled the chair out for her.

"Thank you," she murmured.

"You are most welcomed, my dear."

Kate cringed away from him at the endearment. The next few hours might just be the longest she'd ever had to endure. And she didn't know why exactly the thought of being near him disturbed her so. He wasn't too unagreeable and had a pleasant appearance. He seemed to dote on his mother and was in a very favorable position in status, though Kate could not care less about that. They did not have much in common, yes, but was that enough to dread the very thought of sitting so close to him?

She only had to catch the look Mrs. Bellmore gave her sister to know why this bothered her so. They'd placed her here for a reason. Once again, the two sisters were up to no good, trying to match her with the viscount. And Mr. Bellmore would go along with their plans, of course, leaving Kate with no choice but to entertain him while he was here. That alone made Kate wish she was dining in the solace of her room.

"Did you enjoy your day, Miss Kate?" Lord Reed asked, his voice low enough to keep from involving others. As the first course was served, Kate noticed that the Bellmores and Lord Reed were talking about a ball they had once attended together and the events that had taken place during that time. They seemed very content with pretending Kate and the viscount were not at the table.

"I did," she responded after a while. "I had tea with Mr. and Mrs. Bellmore, helped the gardener with some work, and then went to my room to read before you and Lady Reed arrived. A very relaxing day, I'd say. What about you, my lord?"

"Oh, 'my lord' sounds far too stuffy for us, don't you think? Please, call me Archie." She maintained a polite smile while the word *no* resonated in her head. He continued, "I spent the day hunting in the nearby forest. There is much game there, I've learned, so I shall be frequenting it."

"Do you mean the forest near Angelfield House?" Kate probed.

Lord Reed shook his head, the sand-colored tips of his hair moving as well. "Further than that. I like to ride out to get to my hunting spots, so it is well outside the village. There is nothing better than feeling the wind run through your hair while atop a horse, I'm afraid."

"Except perhaps having a successful hunting excursion."

"Yes, certainly!" He seemed excited at that. "And let me tell you, the pheasants would not make it easy for me. My hunting dogs and I had to work for it."

And then he proceeded to detail every bit of his hunting trip. Kate tried her best to listen, to even make comments now and again out of sheer politeness, but the conversation was quickly wearing down on her.

"Of course, my lord. It sounds lovely," she responded for the tenth time, much to the viscount's oblivion. The food tasted bland on her tongue, every nerve in her body itching for her to leave. As the first course was taken away, Kate longed for the night to be over.

"Doesn't it?" Lord Reed was excited and, without a second of warning, went straight into how often he'd won one horse race after another. Kate had tried contributing, but she found she could think of nothing else but a novel she'd read where the main character had a slight fondness for horses.

They had nothing in common, but it was clear that Lord Reed did not care. He went on and on, and at some point, Kate decided not to say anything at all. The viscount did not seem to notice, or if he did, he didn't care. He was content to talk, clearly expecting her to listen.

She did, but her mind was elsewhere. While she nodded along and tried her best not to be rude, Kate was thinking about the duke who had gone on about his book of travels. The similarities between them were many, and yet they were so vastly different that Kate felt wrong for comparing the duke to this self-absorbed man.

With the duke—with Emerson—she felt she could talk about her interests. In that short span of time together at the picnic, she'd seen a side of him she never thought possible, a side she wanted to explore. She'd thought about those few minutes with him nearly every second since they'd left the lakeside, and her excitement for the ball grew more and more. But Lord Reed would also be in attendance ….

The thought made her shudder, and Lord Reed stopped what he was saying, looking at her with slight alarm. "Are you cold, Miss? Would you like for me to fetch you a shawl?"

Kate shook her head, surprised by the attentiveness. "No, my lord, I am fine. Thank you."

"The way you've shuddered reminds me of the time I spent the night in a forest in Bath. It was a terrifying and exhilarating outing, I assure you. We had gone …."

Kate stopped listening. She couldn't handle it anymore. She went through the motions of eating her meals and counted the seconds until this was over. Deep down, she wished she was anywhere but here. Perhaps lingering on the edge of the duke's property, wondering if she should risk trespassing for a chance to see him again.

The thought made her smile a little. How quickly she'd changed ….

"Does it amuse you, Miss Kate?" Lady Reed spoke up suddenly. The plates that had once held the pudding served for dessert were being cleared away, but Kate knew the night was far from over.

"Does what, my lady?"

"My son's tale regarding his night in France. He tells it all the time, and I never tire of hearing it."

Kate hadn't even realized that he had moved on to talking about his travels to France. "Oh, ah, yes. It is quite interesting."

"Shall we take this to the drawing room then?" Lord Reed offered, rising from his seat. "I could continue the story there if you'd like."

"I, oh—" Surprise rushed through her when the viscount attempted to pull her chair out for her. "Thank you. I … would like to, yes. Shall we?"

Kate knew she had no choice. They would retire to the drawing room anyway to have a few glasses of wine and relax before it was time for bed. A guilty part of herself hoped that the elderly couple would feel too tired to stay up for much longer and the evening would end all the quicker.

Thankfully, Lord Reed and Mr. Bellmore decided to lead the way this time, leaving Kate and Mrs. Bellmore walking from behind. The elderly woman sidled up to Kate's side just as they made it to the door leading to the drawing room. She waited for the men to walk in first before whispering, "He is quite handsome, isn't he?"

Kate quelled her annoyance. "He is rather pleasant, I suppose."

"And quite charming too. I think you two would make a lovely match."

"I see."

"And I can tell that he really likes you. What do you think about him?"

"Perhaps we could discuss this another time, Mrs. Bellmore." Kate patted the older woman on the hand, steering her towards the chairs by the hearth where her husband sat. She knew this conversation was not over, though, and her dread increased tenfold.

This time, Kate went to sit alone on one of the plush couches, not too close to anyone else.

"Miss Kate, I hear you are the daughter of the late Earl of Cookham," Lady Reed stated the moment her bum began to warm the seat. "It is truly sad, as I heard what happened to him. But it is good to see that you have found your way in life."

"How ...." Kate was too stunned to finish. She looked from Lady Reed to the sheepish expressions of the Bellmores' and resisted the urge to sigh.

"Oh, they did not want to tell me, but I wheedle it out of them," Lady Reed said quickly. "My sister and I tell each other everything. You understand, I'm sure."

*I do not*, Kate wanted to say. *I have no sisters. No family. No one but the Bellmores, who could not keep my secret.*

She tucked her bitter thoughts aside and only nodded.

Lady Reed seemed pleased with that response. "Did you get the chance to debut?"

"I did not, no."

"How sad." And she seemed truly upset at that thought. "Then what about your training? I heard rumours that the earl was impoverished before his death, but surely he had enough funds to prepare you for the Season, did he?"

"Caroline!" Mrs. Bellmore gasped.

"What is it? What did I say?"

"It's fine, Mrs. Bellmore," Kate managed to say, even though it was most certainly *not* fine. She took another moment before she said, "I am quite adept at watercolours and the pianoforte."

"Oh, the pianoforte?" Lord Reed clapped his hands in excitement. "Excellent! I do love the sound of such an elegant instrument. Why don't you play for us?"

"Oh, well, it has been a while and ...."

"Nonsense," Mr. Bellmore spoke up, clearly oblivious to Kate's growing discomfort. "You play for us all the time. I'm sure you won't suddenly forget where the keys are." Lord Reed laughed along with him.

Kate couldn't see any way out of it. Slowly, with all eyes on her, she made her way to the small pianoforte sitting in the corner of the drawing room. Her back now turned to the others, she could scowl as much as she wanted to without feeling any guilt, praying for the night to be over. Maybe there would be a miracle, and her playing would lull them all into a deep sleep. *That would be lovely.*

She nursed the idea as she opened the book of music perched in front of the pianoforte. Before she had a chance to begin, though, someone sank onto the stool next to her.

"Let me help you," said the viscount. Kate didn't say anything, only watching as he leafed through the pages and finally came to a stop. "I like this one. Go ahead."

The words that rushed to the tip of her tongue could not be said aloud, so she swallowed them, giving herself a moment to compose herself and quell her rage. The room was quiet, the Bellmores and Lady Reed waiting for her to begin. She could hear Lord Reed's wheeze with each breath he drew in, the heat of his body making her want to run from the room. He was far too close to her.

At long last, she began. Music filled the silence. For a few seconds, Kate wanted only to lose herself in the music and forget all the people around her, but when it came time to turn the page, Lord Reed did it for her.

She paused for a moment, and he gave her a smile. "I'll help you," he whispered, and a shudder went down her spine.

Still, she continued, hating every moment of it. Each time the viscount turned a page, he would press closer to her just a little bit more. She couldn't tell if he did it on purpose or if he was just unaware of how much of her personal space he was invading.

To help curb her annoyance and discomfort, Kate decided to lose herself in something she had not done since her father passed away. She began to sing. The lyrics flowed from her lips, her voice as angelic as it was those days she'd spent singing in the garden of her old home in London. She had once entertained the thought of singing at a dinner party, entertaining her hosts who may one day introduce her to the man she would marry. Now, those days were long past, but she found her love for the art had not gone away.

As the song poured forth, her fingers flying expertly over the keys, Kate could ignore the vexatious viscount sitting next to her. When it was finally over, Lady Reed clapped happily from behind. "Lovely! Just lovely. Why don't you play us another?"

"Actually, I would like to be excused for a bit," Kate said quickly, rising. "I need only get some fresh air, is all."

"Are you all right, dear?" Mr. Bellmore asked with genuine concern.

Kate nodded. "Yes, I'm just feeling a little … overheated. If you'll excuse me." She slipped out before anyone could stop her and made a beeline for the backdoor, escaping into the gardens bathed in silvery moonlight.

Now that she was alone, Kate felt like she could breathe again. She drew in a deep breath, letting it out through her nose as she made her way over to the stone bench covered in the creeping vines of the overgrown foliage. It faced the woods, nothing but deep, unmoving shadows at night. But the sight comforted her more than anything else, knowing what lay within.

"A beautiful night, don't you think?"

Kate gasped, shooting to her feet. Lord Reed stood behind her, his eyes glittering. "My lord! What are you doing?"

"What do you mean? I came to check if you were all right."

"I said that I was. Don't you know it is not proper for us to be seen alone like this?"

He took a step closer. "There isn't anyone around to see us, Miss Kate."

Kate took a large step back, holding out her hand to keep him from advancing. Rage filled her at the sight of him, at the situation she now found herself in. "Even so, it is still improper. Please, I would like to be left alone."

"Surely, you do not mean that?" He had the audacity to sound hurt by her demand. "I thought you enjoyed my company. Did you not? I could tell you more about the lake where I go fishing at home."

"I don't want to hear any more of your stories, my lord. Please, go back inside."

Lord Reed looked dejected at that. His shoulder slumped, but he backed away like a dog who had been kicked. For a moment, she felt a little bad for being so harsh, especially since she had been trying her best to remain polite the entire evening, but she did not take back her words.

"Very well. I shall let the others know that you are fine." With that, he turned and stiffly marched back into the house. Kate waited until the door was closed behind him before she sank onto the bench, letting out another sigh.

To think he would be attending Farringdon ball as well. Now, she didn't want to go. Not if it meant she would have to endure his annoying advances the entire time, with his mother and the Bellmores cheering him on from the sidelines. Kate didn't want to disappoint Mr. and Mrs. Bellmore, but how could she handle being around the viscount while he talked about hunting, horse racing, or fishing? It was clear he was not truly interested in her, and neither was she in him.

She would have to miss the ball, then. It was a pity. She had been looking forward to it for days now, her excitement growing stronger after the day at the lake. And now she would miss out on her first ball and potentially spending time with the duke. Curse that blasted viscount!

## Chapter Sixteen

He could not sleep. It was one of those nights when painful memories would resurface in the most horrible ways, stealing his fatigue and his peace of mind. Emerson sat up, his mind racing, those horrid images playing in his head. His body was washed in sweat, his heart racing, his nerves trembling as he tried to quell the memories and couldn't.

With a curse, he shoved the sheets aside and swung out of bed, pacing the room barefooted. He ran his hand through this hair, finding that no amount of movement was helping to forget. Desperate for an escape, he made for the balcony doors, needing fresh air.

The moon hung large and heavy in the night sky, surrounded by millions of stars twinkling at him from their spots in the sky. They seemed to laugh at him, watching how desperate he was for an escape. He gripped the balustrade so tightly that his hands began to lose feeling, squeezing his eyes shut to push the thoughts aside.

And then he heard it: a small bark.

Emerson opened his eyes, looking below. Shrouded within the shadows, Emerson could make out the wise brown eyes of the ever-faithful Lily. Liam was standing next to her, prancing around in excitement.

He pushed his hair out of his eyes, squinting down at them. They were often left outside, mostly because Liam had a tendency to race around the hallways bumping into everything in his way, and Lily would often give in to his excitement without stopping him. On those few nights when they were allowed to stay in Emerson's room, he didn't suffer from nightmares. Those excitable beasts would calm him in ways he could not understand.

Lily stared up at him as if she knew that he needed them. Emerson let out a sigh. "Should I come down?" he asked the dogs.

Liam's response was to prance even higher as if he sensed that an adventure was in his near future. Lily only let out another soft bark.

"Very well. I shan't leave you waiting for long."

Emerson re-entered his room but only stayed long enough to don his shoes and a robe before slipping out the front door. He didn't bother to take a candle with him, opting to traverse the dark hallways without any light. He'd done so many times before, his troubled mind and inability to sleep most nights often leading him to wander these halls like a haunting ghost. Within a few minutes, Emerson managed to make his way to the back entrance, leading out to the vegetable garden near where the dogs were kept. He unlocked the small gate that kept them—or rather, Liam—from digging up the gardener's hard work and carefully closed it behind him before making his way to where they were.

Liam ran up to meet him, jumping up on Emerson with dirt-covered paws. Emerson didn't mind. He sank to the ground, knees digging into the soft, dew-soaked earth, and wrapped his arms around the massive dog. When Lily trotted over, he enclosed her in the embrace, burying his face into their fur.

"I don't know what I would do without you two," he said to them, tremors of gratitude reverberating throughout his body. These dogs were the only things that kept him sane, the only beings that were capable of keeping him from completely sinking into self-loathing. With them around, Emerson felt as if there was still a life worth living—even if that life was spent locked away on his property hating everyone around him.

Already, he could feel those horrible memories fading into the back of his mind where they belonged. Emerson held on to them for as long as Liam would allow before the restless dog wiggled out of his hold and began to jump on him once more. That was his sign to stand.

"Shall we go for a late walk then?" he asked, looking up at the sky. It was cloudless, moonlight showering everything within its sight. It was enough light for a walk, he decided.

The dogs thought so as well and eagerly rushed up to the gate, waiting for Emerson to let them out. He did so and watched as Liam rushed on ahead, taking the path they usually took towards the forest, while Lily seemed content to stay by his side.

As he went through the overgrown clearing separating Angelfield House from the forest, Emerson's mind began to wander to the house that stood not too far away—and the dark-haired beauty within. Already, it had been a few days since the picnic, and Emerson had been itching to see her again, a sensation he did not know how to handle. Every time he thought of the Farringdon ball, he would entertain the thought of attending more and more. He wanted to see her, if only to speak with her one more time.

Would it be incredibly improper for him to pay a visit to Dower House right now?

Emerson shook his head, dismissing the thought as it came. It was too late at night, and he was not properly dressed. No, now was not the time. But perhaps tomorrow? Would he be able to do it?

Right now, his longing to see Miss Kate was enough to make him think hard about it, but Emerson doubted he would have the same strength in the morning. Even so, he found himself heading towards the house, the dogs sniffing around next to him.

Soon enough, Emerson ended up behind a thick hedge that bordered the Dower House's garden. He was close enough to see the candlelight shimmering within and could hear music pouring out from one of the open windows.

It was a lovely sound, a pianoforte, he believed. Was it Miss Kate playing?

In the next moment, an angelic voice drifted to his ears, mixing so perfectly with the pianoforte that Emerson was struck still. He didn't dare to move, his heart thumping in his chest at the sound. That was certainly Miss Kate. There was no doubt about it.

It was a lure, tempting him to go closer. He wanted to see her sing, to hear it more clearly. He wanted to be in the room with her while she was so clearly losing herself in the music, not hiding out behind her house like this. For a moment, Emerson seriously considered the thought, and the only thing that stopped him from giving in to it was the dogs nearby, who seemed content to busy themselves with finding sleeping squirrels in the trees around them.

Miss Kate stopped singing all too soon. Emerson didn't realize he had been holding his breath until silence pervaded the air and the world was still again. He stared at the house for a while, still very much in awe.

A minute later, the door opened, and Miss Kate herself walked out. Emerson ducked, even though the hedge was tall enough and far enough away to keep him hidden. After a moment, he peered over the top again. What was she doing out here?

He watched as she made her way to a stone bench and sank onto it, her shoulders sagging as if she'd let out a heavy sigh. She didn't move, the moonlight caressing the gentle curves of her ivory skin.

*Here is the beauty with the voice of an angel*, he thought.

A moment later, someone else came to join her. A man. Emerson narrowed his eyes, hearing the audible gasp Miss Kate let out when he approached.

Emerson recognized him instantly—the Viscount Reed, Lord Archie Wharton. They'd run in the same circles once upon a time, but Emerson had always made it a point of duty to stay away from the doltish viscount. He was a whippersnapper, a well-known idiot. What was he doing here with Miss Kate alone?

He clenched his jaw, jealousy coursing through him like hot lava. He couldn't hear what was being said, but judging by how heated Miss Kate looked and the pink tinge on her cheeks, there was clearly some amount of passion between them. Was this the sort of man she fancied? A fool who could not focus on anything but mindless sports? Emerson had once tried to have an intellectual conversation with that man and had been left with the desperate urge to get away from him as quickly as possible. Surely Miss Kate was not serious?

But there was no denying that she was. Emerson couldn't watch their interaction any longer. He turned his back, his jaw tight, and stiffly marched away, the dogs instantly at his heels. Fury began to mingle with the envy, aimed mostly at himself. For entertaining any thoughts of her, for thinking she might be different. The viscount was a handsome man with a title. Of course, she would be interested, even if she knew how foolish he was. Emerson himself was stupid for assuming she would ever look his way.

Why would she when there was a perfectly capable man by her side? Why would she even pay any attention to the monster with the scars? What had he been thinking?

At least, he knew one thing for certain. There was absolutely no way he would be attending the Farringdon ball now.

## Chapter Seventeen

"Will you tell me now?"

Kate resisted the urge to sigh. She stopped what she was doing, steam lifting elegantly from the teapot to caress her chin, and looked over her shoulder at Mary. The other woman was standing on the other end of the kitchen, helping Mrs. Henry wash and peel apples.

"Honestly, Mary, you are rather persistent, aren't you?" Kate said, barely able to keep the exasperation from her voice. "No matter how many times I tell you that there is nothing to say, you will not listen."

"Because I do not believe you. Do you believe her, Mrs. Henry?"

The cook, sitting a short distance away with her arms plunged in a large bucket of water, scrubbing away at the green and red apples, paused only for a moment to shake her head at Mary. "I do not."

"See!" Mary exclaimed. "It is not I alone who think you are hiding something. And it only makes me all the more curious to know what it is."

Kate said nothing, continuing to laden the serving tray with Mr. and Mrs. Bellmore's favorite teacups. The steaming green tea wafting from the teapot had been brewed a little too long ago, and Kate feared it would be cool by the time she made it back to the drawing room where the elderly couple waited.

Mary was, however, quite persistent. From the moment Kate entered the kitchen, the maid had hounded her every move, trying to wheedle out information that did not exist. Or at least, Kate wanted her to believe it did not, but she clearly wasn't doing a very good job of that.

Ever since a few days ago, when Lord and Lady Reed came to visit, Mary had had an inkling that there was something going on between her and the family. Whether it was good or bad, Mary didn't know, but she was determined to find out.

She'd thrown out many possibilities—a rift or family feud—but was clearly hoping that there was an intimate relationship between her and Lord Reed. Mary, like many others like her, romanticized the thought of a commoner marrying a lord.

"Won't you tell me?" Mary, abandoning her task, rushed up to Kate's side. "Why would you keep such a thing for me? From us?"

"Mary, there is absolutely nothing to say," Kate said once more after taking in a calming breath. "I was feeling tired that day and wanted to rest, that is all."

Mary hung her head dramatically. "Oh, how you have forsaken me, Kate."

Mrs. Henry chuckled. She, too, paused her task. "Would you leave her be, Mary? Miss Kate clearly does not wish to talk about it."

"There is nothing to talk about, Mrs. Henry," Kate persisted. But the cook only continued washing her apples. It was obvious that she wasn't convincing anyone.

Neither was she convincing herself. To her dismay, they were right. There was something going on, something Kate could not bring herself to face. It had been a few days since their visit, and the memory still brought back waves of shame and annoyance. How evidently the Bellmores and Lady Reed had tried to push them together, Lord Reed's blatant impropriety by following her into the gardens, the way in which she had to mind his ego as he droned on and on about things that did not interest her.

The Reeds were looking forward to her attending Farringdon ball, but the thought of entertaining the viscount once more only brought on nothing but dread. She hadn't yet told Mr. and Mrs. Bellmore that she would no longer be attending.

That was another conversation she was dreading.

Seeing her chance to escape, Kate quickly picked up the tray and left the kitchen, heading back to the drawing room as fast as her feet could take her.

"Kate!" Mr. Bellmore exclaimed the moment she returned. "Thank God you are back. My dear wife has been making my pains worse."

Mrs. Bellmore rolled her eyes. "Do not listen to him, Kate. He is only being overdramatic."

Just as his wife stated, Mr. Bellmore leaned back in his chair, putting his hand to his temples as if he'd just fainted. "You know how she can be, Kate. I complain about my aching joints, and she does not even pay me any mind."

"And is that any reason to act as if you have just been shot?"

"Yes." Suddenly full of vigor, Mr. Bellmore sat up and grabbed Mrs. Bellmore's hand, caressing the back of it with his thumb. "Because I need only a single touch from you to make all the pain go away."

Mrs. Bellmore tossed his hand aside, but Kate didn't miss the furious blush that erupted across her cheeks. Kate giggled as she poured them both a cup of tea for both of them.

"Now, now," she chided gently. "You two have been bickering all evening. It is a wonder you are not yet tired of each other."

"I am quite tired of him," Mrs. Bellmore stated. But when her husband reached back out to touch her arm, she did not move away. If anything, Kate could have sworn she leaned into the touch. As usual, she was all bark and no bite.

"So you say," Mr. Bellmore drawled. He sipped his tea gently. "But even when you do, I shan't give up on our love."

Kate laughed again. Mr. Bellmore loved to make a habit of teasing Mrs. Bellmore, knowing that she was not used to receiving such blatant affection. She waited until she had reclaimed her seat across from them to ask, "Mr. Bellmore, is your pain getting worse?"

"Better, I'd say," he responded. "I cannot tell if it is from my dear wife's adoration or if it is from your wonderful tea, my dear Kate. I am already feeling much better."

"I'm happy to hear that. Then I doubt you will mind us going for another round of card games?"

Mr. Bellmore chortled, and it ended in a wheezing cough. "I would love to, but I'm afraid of being beaten soundly by you two. Let me nurse my wounds first."

"Then would you like for me to read for you?"

"No, no," Mrs. Bellmore chimed in. "There is something we'd like to speak with you about, actually."

Kate's heart skipped a beat. Even Mr. Bellmore's countenance grew serious. "What is it?"

"Are you excited about the ball?"

Kate sipped her tea to avoid showing her expression. The truth was, she truly wanted to attend. Just the thought that she might see the duke again was enough to fill her with excitement. She fell asleep at night wondering what it would be like to see the duke smile, if it was even possible. How would it feel to have his arms wrapped around her, twirling her around the room in a scandalous waltz? She would entertain the idea until the irritating image of Lord Reed invaded her thoughts and ruined her good mood. When she thought of him, she could not stomach the thought of attending.

Nor did the idea get any more pleasing when she looked at the hopeful faces of Mr. and Mrs. Bellmore, knowing exactly why they were looking at her like that.

Not knowing how best to answer as yet, Kate sipped her tea once more and said, "I have never been to a ball before," hoping that would tide them over for now.

Mrs. Bellmore seemed satisfied with that response, nodding. "Yes, you've told me that once. So the moment Caroline told me about the Farringdon ball, I just knew you had to attend. You are a lady, after all. You should attend a ball at least once."

"Mrs. Bellmore …." Kate glanced uneasily at the door. Her secret might have been revealed to Lord and Lady Reed, but Kate didn't want anyone else to know about it. God knew what would happen if Mary got ahold of that information.

"Oh, don't worry about it," Mr. Bellmore cut in with a wave of his hand. "Mum's the word. No one knows but us, though I'm certain that will not make your ball any less exciting."

"It's not my ball—" Kate began, but they were no longer listening.

"I think so too!" the elderly woman exclaimed excitedly. "She is such a beauty that no one will care if she is a commoner or not. Noblemen and commoners alike will be begging to write their names on your dance card."

"Certainly! She could be dressed in the drabbest gown known to man and would still capture the attention of everyone in attendance."

Their dramatics chased away some of Kate's trepidation, and she managed a laugh. "I doubt that will be the case," she stated humbly, but both of them simply waved her off.

Before they could say anything in response, Kate heard the faint sound of a knock on the door. "I'll get it," she announced and quickly got to her feet. She escaped out of the room, letting out a breath now that she'd bought herself some time to think of how she would tell them that she did not intend on attending.

By the time she made it to the front door, she hadn't figured out what she was going to say. She opened the door, revealing a lanky-looking man wearing patchy clothing and clutching a pristine white box under his arm.

"Miss Kate Cooper?" he asked, his voice tilted by an accent.

"Yes, that's me." Kate glanced confusedly at the box as he held it out to her. "Is this for me?"

The man didn't deign to respond, simply waiting for her to accept the package. Uncertain, she took it from him, and the moment it was out of his hands, he tipped his hat to her and sauntered away. Kate watched him go for a moment, confused.

The box was heavy and unmarked. There might be a letter inside, but she did not want to open it. Perhaps it was for the Bellmores, but the delivery man was given her name since she was their elderly couple's companion. That made more sense, she supposed, and quickly tucked away the insane, fleeting thought that the duke might have sent her a gift.

*Goodness, I think I might have lost my mind.* It could not have been the duke. He hardly knew her and had spent less than thirty minutes in her presence. Surely the impact she had on him was far less significant than the one he had on her. So why would he send her anything?

Dismissing the slight pang of disappointment, Kate made her way back to the drawing room.

"Mrs. Bellmore, a delivery man—"

"Oh, good," Mrs. Bellmore cut in, her voice high and excited. "It has finally arrived. Go ahead, Kate. Open it."

Kate stared blankly at her. "Is it truly for me?"

"Who else would it be for?"

Not knowing how to react, she slowly made her way back to her seat and rested the box on her lap. She took in the expectant looks of Mr. and Mrs. Bellmore before she opened the box.

Kate gasped. "No ...."

"Let us see it!" Ms. Bellmore said excitedly.

Slowly, Kate pinched the thin fabric between her fingers and lifted it. It unfurled, revealing a beautiful gold-colored ball gown. The bodice was laced with a white ribbon, an overlay of silk covering the main part of the gown. Hemming the short sleeves were tiny embroidery, the likes of which could only be done by the most skillful of modistes. Sitting beneath the gown was a pair of long white gloves with matching embroidery at the hem.

It was the most beautiful gown Kate had ever seen, and it must have cost a fortune.

"It is your first ball," Mr. Bellmore said, breaking into Kate's shocked silence. "We wanted to make sure you felt like the most beautiful woman in attendance."

"This is ... this is too much!" But she could not take her eyes off it. Somehow, Kate knew that it would fit her perfectly, that she would certainly feel beautiful in a gown such as this.

"Ah!" Mrs. Bellmore rose from her seat with a speed that was a little alarming to Kate. She hurried over to the mantle above the hearth and picked up an ornate box Kate had not taken notice of at first. The moment she laid eyes on it, though, Kate knew what to expect.

Mrs. Bellmore brought it over to her. "Now that the dress has arrived, I can give you these." And then she opened the box to reveal a lovely pearl necklace and matching pearl earrings.

Kate did not know what to say. She had not owned such lovely things, even when she still held the title of an earl's daughter. She'd always known that the Bellmores had retired with a fortune, but to have them spend so much of it on her was more than she could handle. Yet, how could she turn down such kindness?

"Thank you," she breathed, remembering her manners. "I will treasure them dearly."

"As long as you enjoy yourself, my dear, that is all that manners. The more you dance, the better!"

Mrs. Bellmore laughed as she returned to her seat, but Kate could not share in her humor. Kate knew exactly what that meant. She knew that, deep down, the Bellmores were hoping she would find a suitor at the ball—even if it was not Lord Reed. Their eyes glittered with their hidden intent; they could not hide it any better if they tried.

Kate gently put away the dress, closed the box, and rested the ornate jewelry box on top. She didn't know how best to express her gratitude, torn between keeping the gifts and handing them back to them since she knew what they wanted deep down. Instead, she rose. "I shall put them in my room."

"Then I suppose it is time we take our nap, my dear, don't you think?" Mr. Bellmore asked, holding out a hand to Mrs. Bellmore.

"Yes, I am feeling a bit tired." The elderly woman rose and helped her husband stand, waving Kate off when she tried to assist. "We can make it on our own, Kate. Why don't you try on the dress and tell us if there are anything alterations that need to be done?"

"Thank you," Kate murmured again because she could not think of anything else to say in response.

Mrs. Bellmore just gave her a cheeky smile and, guiding the aching Mr. Bellmore, left the room. The moment they were gone, Kate looked back at her gifts.

She could not disappoint them. They had put so much into this that the thought of killing their hope bore heavily on Kate. Which meant ... which meant she had no choice but to attend.

A sliver of relief rushed through her at the thought. She would suffer at the hands of Lord Reed and his terrible company, certainly. But now, left with little choice, she would see the duke. That was worth it, at least.

# Chapter Eighteen

"Surely it is not as bad as you say. You've always managed to be rid of these ailments within a day or two. Why are they plaguing you so much now?"

Emerson considered ignoring Bob, but knowing full well that it would not get to him to leave, he responded by saying, "That was then. I am a different man now. My body is not what it was once."

"That is because you are not eating as a man should! When was the last time you had a hot meal?"

Honestly, Emerson did not know the answer to that question, so he kept quiet. It had been a few days since his late-night walk when he had spotted Kate and Lord Reed alone in the garden of Dower House. His mood had overtaken him since then, and Emerson had locked himself away in his bedchamber, claiming an illness to anyone who bothered to ask—which was only Bob, Sparkes, and Francis. One by one, they would knock on his door and ask him to see him, to check on his condition, to deliver a meal for him. And one by one, Emerson would chase them away.

Now it was the night of the Farringdon ball, and no more important was it than today.

As he'd expected, Bob was standing on the other side of Emerson's locked door, trying to cajole him out of the room.

"You will waste away in there, you know," came the earl's booming voice once more. "At least eat something. That way, your body will have what it needs to fight the illness."

"I shall," Emerson said, faking weakness. He had no intention of doing such a thing. Honestly, his last meal might have been the day before yesterday, and Emerson was sure it was nothing more than half a sandwich left outside his door on a platter. He'd taken a few bites and had filled the rest of his stomach with his whiskey, which was now, sadly, coming to an end.

Perhaps later he could sneak out while the house was asleep and take some from the parlor.

He entertained the idea as he stared out the doors of his balcony, the wind drifting past his ankles. He'd watched as the sun went down and the minutes ticked by, the commencement of the Farringdon ball drawing nearer. There was no way he could attend. Not after what he'd seen. Not after confirming with his own two eyes that Miss Kate was soon to be betrothed to the viscount. Otherwise, why else would they do something as scandalous as being alone together?

The thought only soured his mood even more, and when there was another knock on the door, it took all his strength not to snap. A person bedridden with a contagious illness would not do such a thing, after all.

"Your Grace," came Sparkes' voice. "Please, I urge you to come out and have something to eat, at least."

"Leave me be," Emerson growled, loud enough for him to hear across the room.

"I cannot, in good judgment, do such a thing, Your Grace," Sparkes said determinedly. "You have not eaten in quite some time. You cannot exist on only whiskey and brandy for the rest of your days." He paused. "I have with me a bowl of artichoke soup. Will you at least let me in so that I may serve it for you?"

The mention of the soup had Emerson's stomach growling. In that moment, he realized just how hungry he truly was. He glanced back at the door, temptation rising.

Sparkes knocked again. "Lord Wellbourne has left, if that is what you are wondering. He said that he would relay to the guests at the ball that you were unwell and could not attend. Unfortunately, he could not wait for you any longer."

A little more intrigued with the idea now, Emerson mulled it over for a bit before bellowing, "Come."

He kept his back turned, listening as the door opened and someone crept inside. Emerson pointed to the side of him, where the bed stood. "Lay it there."

"And we shall pin you down and feed you by force if we have to."

Emerson whirled at Bob's voice. The three of them—Sparkes, Bob, and Francis—were now in his room, Sparkes gingerly closing the door behind him. Emerson narrowed his eyes at the butler. "You liar."

Sparkes did not seem upset at the slight. "I did what I thought was best for you, Your Grace," he responded with a shrug. "And I do indeed have soup."

The soup was put on the table next to the bed by Francis. The two servants lingered back, as if they did not dare to approach and face the brunt of Emerson's wrath. Bob, however, walked up to Emerson, looking him up and down.

"I cannot tell if you are truly sick or just hungry and pale from lack of sunlight," the earl commented.

"Leave me be!" Emerson stalked over to the unlit fireplace, knowing there was nowhere to run. They'd invaded the only space he could get away from them. "I know you're here to convince me to attend the ball, and I shan't give in to it."

"Firstly, I'm here to make sure you eat," Bob said somberly, holding up a finger. Lifting another, he continued, "Secondly, I won't leave here until you are dressed and ready to leave as well. This ball will be good for you, I know. It will be your first step to finding the old Emerson."

"I do not need to find the old me. There is nothing wrong with who I am now." Even those words sounded wrong to him.

"At least, the Emerson I once knew would not back down from a challenge. Surely you are not afraid of seeing Miss Eve and Miss Kate again."

Emerson clenched his jaw, narrowing his eyes at Bob. "What do you mean by that?"

"They will be in attendance, remember? I thought you would have liked to see them again, but if they have scared you off, then you only need to say the word, and I shall leave you be."

"That isn't working."

"I can tell," Bob conceded. "Then let me speak honestly. You are a gentleman, are you not? You won't want them to think you do not keep your promises."

"I don't recall promising anything to anyone," Emerson accused. "If I remember correctly, that was you."

"Yes, well, they won't know that. And I'd hate to leave a bad impression on them. Wouldn't you?"

That gave Emerson pause, though he would not let it show. A bad impression? After he'd tried his best to clear the air with Kate at the picnic, the last thing he wanted was for her to think any less of him now. If she was expecting him to be at the ball, would she be upset that he did not attend?

Would she be disappointed?

That thought made the idea a little bit more tempting. He thought back on how she'd smiled at him while he'd rambled unknowingly. At that time, Lord Reed would have been courting her. And yet she'd shown him interest, had accepted his apology. Was it possible that she wished to be friends with him?

Silence pervaded the room as Bob and the others stared at Emerson, clearly waiting for him to come to a decision. Emerson's mind raced, sorting through one thought after another, wondering and hoping and believing. The jealousy and anger at what he'd seen a few nights ago began to fade, and the thought of seeing Kate again took its place, filling him with uneasy hope. This emotion felt foreign to him, especially after so much time spent hating himself and the company of others. How could he come to terms with throwing himself into the fire once again, just to see one woman?

Emerson looked back and Bob and saw the pleasure in the man's eyes. The earl clearly knew what Emerson was going to say, and for a moment, Emerson considered lying to him instead. The truth rushed to his lips. "You have convinced me. I shall go."

"Marvelous!" whooped Bob, and then the room was suddenly thrown into a flurry.

An excited Sparkes rushed over to him, guiding Emerson to the bowl of soup. Francis could not contain his joy as he raced towards Emerson's armoire and began to pull out one piece of clothing after another. "I already have something prepared, Your Grace," he announced breathlessly. "Because I hoped that you would change your mind. Please, eat. I shall take care of preparing your clothes."

Emerson hardly had a chance to respond when Sparkes shoved the spoon in his hand. "We don't have much time, Your

Grace," his butler said. "You should hurry. But don't eat too much, lest you upset your stomach."

"The carriage is already waiting," Bob announced, not giving Emerson the chance to respond. "How long do you think it will take to be ready? Ten minutes? Twenty."

"Nay, my lord," Sparkes responded. "His Grace has not been within the public eye for some time. He will have to shave, first of all."

"Ah, yes! He can't show up with such long facial hair. How soon?"

Emerson quietly ate as the three of them went on. It was clear they didn't need his input, and Emerson wasn't inclined to give one. Not right now, at least. He was content to be guided about, his empty bowl taken away from him. His mind was full of thoughts of Miss Kate, his determination growing by the second. By the time he was shaved, dressed, and ready to go, he had made up his mind. He would not let the night end without asking Miss Kate to dance.

"Wonderful!" boomed Bob before they were to go out the door. "I cannot believe my eyes. Is this man I befriended all those years ago?"

"It is I who befriend you," Emerson pointed out, but his voice trailed off when Bob steered him towards a tall mirror. He could not believe his eyes.

The scars ... they were on full display. There was no longer any facial hair to hide the worst of it, and his hair was no longer long enough to hide what the beard could not. Yet, the man he had once been shown underneath. Though he still hated the sight of himself, Emerson was struck speechless at how different he looked now, how much of himself he had hidden away. Would Miss Kate even recognize him?

*Of course, she will. No one will miss these terrible scars.*

*It's too late to back out of the plan now*, he decided, turning away from the mirror. Sparkes and Frances waited by the door, beaming with pride. Emerson tried to ignore them as best as he could, but they both bowed, and the butler said, "We hope you enjoy your night, Your Grace."

Emerson kept quiet, heading into the hallway. Bob chattered ceaselessly all the way out of the house, even as they approached the waiting carriage. Emerson listened with half an ear. His anxiety trembled within him with each step he took, his body longing to return to the safety of his bedchamber. He pushed forward, settling into the comfortable folds of the carriage.

Bob continued, talking about all the things he hoped would happen tonight. He would dance the night away, talk to as many people as he could, and have Emerson by him the entire time. His reclusive friend, the duke, would come out of his shell, and they shall have a grand time. Emerson doubted it would go as he said, but he did not voice his opinion. For now, he focused only on one thing—one person—and let it chase away the fear.

"I don't think I remember how to dance," Emerson said suddenly, cutting into Bob's words.

"Don't worry about that," his friend said easily. "The moment you hear the music and are about to begin, it shall come back to you as if nothing had changed."

Emerson certainly hoped so. Dancing with Miss Kate was the only reason he was in the carriage. All he needed was to remember how to—and keep from punching Lord Reed in the face if he came near.

# Chapter Nineteen

"They're here! They're here!"

Kate giggled at the excitement in Eve's voice. The parson's daughter had been standing at the entrance of the drawing room of Dower House for a while now, tilting her head to the front door. How she even heard that the carriage had arrived was beyond Kate, but she could not help being impressed by both her excitement and her keen hearing.

She could not blame her for being excited, though. Unlike Kate, Eve had nothing to deter her from attending and everything to lure her. She did not have to contend with the overbearing, bothersome attention from a certain viscount. Nor did she have to worry about disappointing those who hoped that they would make a match.

"Is it already time?" Mrs. Bellmore looked up from the book she was reading, her spectacles perched on her nose. She did not partake in the act often, preferring to listen to Kate read to her. But when she did, it was always a sight—pushing her spectacles up, sniffling now and again. She closed the book and set it aside, pulling her spectacles from her face.

"Yes, they're coming up to the door." Eve's excitement could not be tamed. With gloved hands, she grasped the skirt of her primrose ball gown, all but jumping in her joy. "Shall we meet them at the door?"

Eve didn't wait for a response. She picked up her skirts, her pink slippers peeking out from underneath, and hurried off, the tail of the ribbons tied into her hair flying out behind her.

Kate rose and quickly helped Mrs. Bellmore to her feet. "Shall we inform Mr. Bellmore that we are leaving now?" Kate suggested.

"He is more than likely sleeping. You know how tired he gets when his stomach aches. Come, we shouldn't waste another second. I wonder what Lord Reed will think about your dress."

Mrs. Bellmore hummed happily to herself as she took the lead, missing the way Kate's face fell at the mention of the viscount. There was no escaping it, she knew. No matter what, she would be forced to face Mrs. Bellmore's expectations—and the dreaded viscount himself.

He and Lady Reed were already spilling through the front door by the time Kate and Mrs. Bellmore arrived. Lady Reed wore a massive hat trimmed with white ribbon and flowers, which complemented her silver gown. She headed straight for her sister, kissing her on both cheeks before she turned to acknowledge Eve and Kate.

"You two look absolutely beautiful!" Lady Reed gushed. "Heavens, if I walk in with you two in tow, men will be flocking my side for introductions."

"If I do not chase them away myself." Lord Reed slid to the front, grasping Kate's hand before she had the chance to retreat. She held herself completely still as he lifted the back of her hand to his lips. Thankfully, she was already wearing gloves. "You look divine, Miss Kate. A true beauty. I am honoured to attend this ball by your side."

"Thank you, my lord," Kate managed. And then, trying her best to be polite, she added, "You look dashing yourself."

"You will make me blush! But dashing may not be strong enough, I'm afraid. Absolutely breathtaking, instead?"

Kate managed a bland smile. She couldn't tell if he was jesting. She did not care. Turning to the others, she said, "Shall we?"

That spurred them all into action, Eve leading the charge. Kate quickened her steps to her friend's side, slipping her arm through hers in the hopes that Lord Reed would not try to join them. She was given a few short seconds of relief before they all piled into the carriage and she was forced to sit between Eve and Lord Reed, with Mrs. Bellmore and Lady Reed sitting across from them.

"I will get straight to the point, Miss Kate," Lord Reed murmured to her, and Kate's heart sank. "I would be honoured if I could have the first dance. The very first set with the most beautiful woman in attendance would make the envy of every gentleman who sees us."

As well as the duke? Kate didn't quite like the idea of that. The last thing she wanted was for the duke to see Lord Reed sticking by her side for the entire ball. What if that chased him away? What if he was afraid to approach her because of it?

"Is that so?" she said noncommittally, not wanting to accept but not seeing a way out of it.

"Have you danced before?" he asked.

"I have … not."

"Then I shall be your first." He leaned back, beaming. "That makes me proud."

"I'm sure you are a lovely dancer, my lord," Eve joined in. "No doubt you have been to countless balls."

"Oh, certainly." And that led Lord Reed into a long discourse about the many balls he had attended in the past and how popular he had been at every one of them. Kate shot Eve a look of gratitude, though she wasn't sure if the other woman had done that on purpose. For now, though, she was saved from having to answer the viscount.

As he continued on, Kate let her thoughts take over—and they inevitably led to the Duke of Edendale. Emerson. His name whispered through her mind, and her heart began to flutter. She did all she could to hold back her smile, daydreaming about finally seeing him again. In her mind, they would lock eyes from across the room. He would smile—she imagined his smile to be as bright and glorious as the rising sun—and would instantly make his way over to her. Kate would not move, the entire room disappearing until they were the only two in existence. And then he would ask her to dance. They would dance the night away and, when they were tired, they would go for a stroll through the gardens. Perhaps hold hands? He would tell her that he missed her. She would tell him that she was infatuated—

Kate shook her head so suddenly that Lord Reed stopped talking, looking at her with surprise. "You don't think so, Miss Kate?"

"P-pardon?" Her face was on fire. She hoped he didn't think it was because of him. "I did not hear the question."

"It was not a question, my dear," Lady Reed said gently. "Archie was just telling us about how exciting it would be if we had all attended the ball held at Thistledown Manor in London, hosted by Lord and Lady Brokendale."

"It sounds like it was a wonderful time," Eve explained. "I'm almost sad that I missed it, though I stood no chance of being invited in the first place."

"Oh, nonsense, Miss Eve." Lord Reed waved a dismissive hand. "I am quite connected, you know. Once others are aware that we are acquainted, every door you wish to go through shall be opened to you."

Again, the conversation moved on without her, much to Kate's relief. She was in no frame of mind to pretend to care. Her mind had wandered too far, imagining things that would not happen. It was useless thinking about such things with Emerson, especially since they had hardly spent any time with each other.

So why did he fill her every thought like this? Why was she so excited to attend?

Those questions both intrigued and plagued her all the way to Harriet Manor, where the Farringdons resided. The property was enclosed by a tall wall and massive gates opened to reveal a long driveway. Other carriages waited in line, each releasing a few guests before moving on. Kate and Eve took the time to appreciate the surroundings—the massive trees lining the driveway, the brick goliath building washed with the golden glow of candles within. It was a beautiful home and did not fail to show the wealth of the people who lived within.

At last, it was their time to exit. Lord Reed hopped out first and helped both Kate and Eve down while a footman assisted Lady Reed and Mrs. Bellmore. The sisters stayed close together, whispering to each other about all manners of things as they went on ahead. Kate hung back, and, sadly, Lord Reed did the same. Clearly, he was hell-bent on staying by her side.

A footman led them inside, through the hallways, to the ballroom. The closer they came, the louder the music grew—until it was loud enough to inspire genuine excitement within Kate. She could almost forget whose company she was in, remembering once again that this was her first ball ever.

The first thing that caught her eyes were the heavy-looking chandeliers hanging from the ceiling, all filled with dozens of candles. The room was well-lit because of it, but the tall ceilings left enough space for cool air. So many were already in attendance—ladies in their muted greens, blues, and yellows, wearing headdresses and ribbons and feathers, and men in their dark coats and cravats. There was a low hum of chatter in the air, complementing the string of music wafting from the orchestra in the corner. Kate spotted a long table lined with refreshments at the far end of the room and noted that not many gathered in that area.

There were a few archways and doors that undoubtedly led to other parts of the ballroom. She watched, even as they were announced, as the group of men wielding cigars entered a dark room, perhaps a parlor or game room. She idly wondered what might be happening within, but those thoughts were interrupted when a busty woman swept in front of them.

"I cannot believe my eyes." The woman looked between Lady Reed and Mrs. Bellmore in disbelief. "You, Caroline, I understand. But Hester is here as well?"

"It has been a while, Georgina," Mrs. Bellmore said with a smile. "Why are you surprised? Was I not to attend?"

"You have ignored every other invite I have sent before, so why would this time be any different?"

"Not ignored," Mrs. Bellmore pointed out. "Respectfully declined."

"It's the same thing." But the woman did not seem upset. In fact, she seemed delighted to have them there and proved that by pulling the sisters into a tight hug. Then, she seemed to notice that they were not alone. "And these two must be …?"

"Miss Kate Cooper and Miss Eve Dewhurst," Mrs. Bellmore told her. "Kate is my companion, and Eve is the daughter of the parson in the nearby village. Ladies, this is Lady Farringdon, tonight's host."

"It is a pleasure to meet you both. My, you two are lovely. I shall be up to my neck in men trying to be introduced, I'm afraid." She smiled warmly at them both. "I hope you two have a wonderful time. I would love to introduce you to my husband, but he's gone off to do God knows what, and I shan't bother myself to look for him." And then, she was moving on, turning to Mrs.

Bellmore again. "Come, the others must see you. They won't believe their eyes."

Kate watched as Mrs. Bellmore and Lady Reed were whisked away by Lady Farringdon. She felt a bit of relief. At least she wouldn't have to deal with them pressuring her to dance with the viscount.

"Pardon me?" came a voice from behind. Both ladies turned to see a man approaching, stopping at Lord Reed's side. He gave the viscount a simple nod before turning his eyes to Eve. "I don't believe we have been introduced."

"We have not been," Eve said, her cheeks coloring.

He held out his hand, and she slid her palm against his. "My name is Victor Hunter, the Baron Banesfield. And you, my beautiful lady, are …?"

Eve blushed harder. "Miss Eve Dewhurst."

"Miss Eve, may I have the first dance? It will be beginning shortly, and I truly hope I was not bested by another gentleman."

"I'd only just arrived, my lord. You are actually the first."

"A victory," he said with a grin. "Then I shall steal you away for those short moments. Though I hope they will last forever."

How poetic, Kate thought. She took a step back, realizing that the baron was not even aware that she was standing there. Eve was blushing to the roots of her hair, and Lord Banesfield looked pleased with himself. Her heart swelled with happiness with her friend, and she gave her a broad smile as Eve was led away.

"That only leaves you and me, Miss Kate," came Lord Reed's grating voice. "The first set shall begin soon."

"I see." She scanned the room, looking for an escape.

Lord Reed grabbed her hand suddenly, pulling her in the same direction Eve had gone in. "Let us begin then, shall we?"

Shock and anger rushed through her like a roaring volcano. Kate bit her lip, suppressing the overwhelming emotions. She had not accepted his request to dance, so why did he think this was appropriate? Yes, she had not declined either, but that was not the point.

Kate bit the inside of her cheeks, swallowing her furious words. It was only one dance. Perhaps after this, he would leave her be.

Consoling herself with that thought, she forced herself to relax as the first set began. Other dances lined the floor, and, through the corner of her eye, she saw Eve with the baron. Kate was afforded a few seconds to recall to memory the steps to the dance before it began.

Lord Reed stepped on her foot. She nearly yelped in pain. And he did not apologize.

The dance went on, and his energetic steps were stilted and off rhythm. He stepped on her toes twice, and it took all of Kate's strength not to end it right there. It seemed to last forever, the most uncomfortable set she could ever imagine—his hand on her waist, the way he towered over her, the fact that he could not find his rhythm, and her poor toes were suffering because of it. Kate couldn't wait for it to be over.

At long last, it drew to an end. Kate said nothing to him. She only stepped back, remembering a second later to curtsy, and hurried away to the refreshments table.

And he followed her!

Despair sank within her. She couldn't escape him. The only thing she could do now was state plainly that she abhorred his presence and wished that he would leave her alone. Surely that would do the trick. But as she quickly reached for a glass of champagne, Kate knew she wouldn't do it. It wasn't in her nature to be so cold and tactless. But being so nice, trying to spare his feelings, was only causing her to suffer.

Lord Reed began to jabber, and she instantly tuned him out. She didn't even pretend that she was listening. Instead, she scanned the room, looking out for the duke. No matter how hard she looked, he was nowhere to be found.

Her heart began to ache at the realization that she might have attended for no reason. She could have feigned illness, could have thought of an excuse not to come to the ball. But because she thought the duke might be in attendance, she opted to endure the torture that was having Lord Reed by her side.

But where was the duke? Why wasn't he here? Wasn't he coming? Had Eve misheard Lord Wellbourne?

The night began to stretch onwards. Men approached her one by one, and soon enough, her dance card was full. Lord Reed's comments turned petty and jealous, and he wrote his name down again, stating that he could at least dance with her again before it was seen as improper. Kate was already planning to complain about her aching feet when that time came.

She danced a few more sets, hoping to immerse herself in the ball. After all, it was a wonderful time. Eve was enjoying herself, going from dancing with other gentlemen to being in the company of the baron. Mrs. Bellmore could hardly stay still, finding one friend after another. It seemed only Kate could not put her heart into it.

Until he entered. They were late, she noted. That was the first thing she thought as she watched Lord Wellbourne and Emerson stroll through the door.

The second thing was that he looked devastatingly handsome.

The beard was gone, and his hair was shorter, though still long enough to shield some of his face. He was dressed in an impeccable waistcoat and matching heavy coat, his auburn cravat standing out among the sea of black and white. The moment he entered, all eyes were drawn to him, but he focused on none of them, scanning the room instead.

Their eyes met across the room, just like she'd imagined.

What she didn't imagine was the host of butterflies that erupted in her stomach. She didn't expect her entire body to go hot, her tongue to dry, and her heart to race the way it did now.

A group of loud, intoxicated men invaded her space, nearly knocking her over as they threw their arms around Lord Reed. Whatever they shouted at him sounded like incoherent nonsense, but she didn't mind because they whisked him away, leaving her standing blissfully alone.

She turned her attention back to where the duke stood. But he wasn't there anymore.

"Miss Kate."

Kate gasped, whirling. Emerson now stood next to her, his dark eyes intent. They were staring over her shoulder, and she could have sworn she saw a glimmer of irritation before they returned to her.

"Your Grace," she breathed. Could he hear how loudly her heart thumped? Could he tell how nervous she was?

Emerson swallowed and ran his gaze down the length of her. "It is good to see you. You look …." She waited, holding her breath. "Absolutely stunning."

"Thank you, Your Grace." The compliment had her swelling with pride. She'd heard similar variations of the same thing over the course of the night, but only he could make her feel like she was floating on air. "You look rather handsome yourself. I'm happy you're here. I was afraid you would not make it."

"I didn't know you were waiting—"

"Miss Kate!" Bob swept into the space, as loud and exuberant as she remembered him. "My, you are like an angel on earth. I must be given the honour of dancing with you. Must!"

Kate flushed, glancing at Emerson. The duke was staring at Bob intently, an unrecognizable emotion shimmering in his eyes. The earl glanced at Emerson and grinned.

"We apologize for arriving so late," Bob went on. "We ran into a … hitch along the way, but all is well now. May I?" He gestured to Kate's dance card.

Reluctantly, she handed it to him, glancing at Emerson once more. He was quiet, but there was something off about him now.

Bob scribbled his name and then paused, putting his hand to his forehead. "Goodness, I forgot I promised to dance with Miss Alexandria. It wouldn't do to forget her, though her mother was really the one who pressed the issue. Emerson, why don't you dance with Miss Kate in my stead?"

Emerson was already shaking his head. "I don't think she—"

"I would love to dance!" Kate said quickly, a little too excitedly. Emerson looked surprised.

"You would?"

"The next set will be starting soon. Shall we?"

She boldly took a step closer. Emerson seemed unsure at first, and the sight warmed her. Kate waited patiently for him to take her hand, and though he, too, wore gloves, the connection was like being shocked by lightning. Every nerve in her body buzzed with excitement as he led her out among the other dancers.

People were watching them. She studied him. Would he turn his face away from her eyes, try to shield his scars with his hair? Kate expected him to, but Emerson seemed more concerned with figuring out what to do with his hands.

The moment the music began, his shoulder sagged. "It is a waltz," he pointed out.

Kate nodded. "I don't remember the steps," she stated honestly.

"Neither do I."

"We shall look like fools."

"We shall."

She smiled, laughter racing past her lips. "Then I have the perfect partner then, don't I?" And then she held up her hands, waiting for him to take them.

For a moment, she thought he might smile as well. He didn't, but he relaxed and took her hand. That was enough for now.

The waltz began. Their first steps were slow and uneven. They were a pace behind the others, but Kate did not care. She was just happy to be in his arms, and, as if he was energized by her smile, Emerson slowly began gaining more confidence. They both remembered far more than they claimed and, soon enough, they were twirling around the room. She was giddy with joy, this fairytale moment so perfect that she loathed for it to end.

He was not a beast, not a terror of a man. She did not see his scars anymore. All she saw was the handsome, uncertain, hopeful, kind, gentle man underneath. She saw the man who was trying his hardest to dance well, who seemed to wear his heart on his sleeve in those moments when he forgot to cover it up. She saw the man who had been locked away behind a shell, behind the beast everyone claimed that he was.

To think that, not too long ago, she had disliked him. And now, Kate feared she might be falling in love.

## Chapter Twenty

Emerson was floating on a cloud. The sensation felt foreign to him. After spending such a long time wallowing in his anger, regret, and self-hatred, he did not know what to do with these emotions. He could not begin to sort through them himself, much less explain to the person who was causing them just how he felt.

But, from the way Miss Kate stared at him, he thought she might already know.

The waltz came to a slow lull. Her tiny frame was pressed against his, and Emerson suddenly wished he had not neglected to have his meals before. She must think he was bony, nothing like the strapping man Lord Reed was.

But if she did, why was she smiling at him like that? Why did her eyes glow as if she could not be happier?

Confusion mounted within him, warring with his own happiness. The hand he had resting on the base of her back itched with the urge to pull her closer to him, to have that heavenly lavender scent of hers wash over him. It did not make any sense, he decided, for one person to be so beautiful. No sense at all.

The dress she wore was gold and white, perfectly molded to her frame. She looked like an angel, her hair curled around her head and expensive yet simple jewelry adorning her. From the moment he entered, he knew she was the center of attention and could tell that she was not aware of it. Not even him, the spectacle that he's made himself by even showing up, did not overshadow her popularity. Why would she want to dance with him? The monster? Why, when there were so many other men vying to dance with her instead?

"What are you thinking, Emerson?" she asked softly.

Her question caught him off guard. "I am not thinking anything," he responded.

That made her laugh, a breathy sound that made his heart skip a beat. "You are not a good liar. It is clear that there is something on your mind. Won't you share it with me?"

"It is nothing, I assure you."

"I will have to cajole it out of you then. That is quite a dilemma, since I'm not very good at convincing others of doing anything."

"Somehow, I doubt that, Miss Kate."

"Kate," she said gently. "Call me Kate. I call you Emerson, after all. It's only fitting."

Emerson nodded, swallowing. Suddenly she was too close. She could certainly see every groove within each scar, every pock in his face. But if she could, why was she smiling at him like this?

"Do you always do that?" she asked suddenly.

"Do what?" He couldn't look at her, and so he looked over her head, skimming the crowd of guests who whispered about him. It surprised him how little he cared in this moment.

"You do not like to meet eye contact, especially when you are put on the spot about something you'd rather not talk about."

Again, her words caught him by surprise. He willed himself to meet her blue eyes. "I wasn't aware that I did such a cowardly thing."

"Cowardly? I wouldn't say that. Uncomfortable? Perhaps." She continued to peer up at him, this time missing none of the steps. She was a natural, despite what she said. "Do I make you uncomfortable, Emerson?"

*Yes, but not in a bad way.* "You unnerve me," he said instead.

"Is that a good thing?"

Emerson took a moment to respond. "I don't know," he stated honestly.

Kate giggled. "I shall take it as a good thing, then, until you are decided on the matter. I figure, since you have asked me to dance, that you do not abhor my presence too much. Though, it was not you who asked but Lord Wellbourne."

"I wanted to," Emerson told her, a little too quickly. He cleared his throat and tried again. "I was going to but …."

"You did not know how?"

"As I've said, you unnerve me."

"Well, I hope that, in time, you will begin to relax when I am around. It will make things much easier, don't you think?" Her smile widened, and Emerson couldn't help but wonder if there was a hidden meaning in her words. "I'm happy that you came, Emerson."

"Why?" The question left his lips before he could stop it.

Kate grew a little more somber as she said, "Because I believe you needed it. And honestly, so did I. Things are a lot clearer for me now."

"You're confusing me."

"My apologies," she said with a laugh. And she was about to continue when the dance came to an end. They were forced to stand apart, but Kate continued to smile at him, eyes glittering with excitement.

Emerson felt emboldened by her demeanor. She was welcoming, seemingly enjoying having him near her. He could actually believe that she was happy that he'd attended and became even more convinced when she came to his side.

And to think he had nearly chosen to stay cooped up in his bedchamber wallowing in his self-deprecating thoughts.

"Shall we go by the refreshments table?" she suggested. "It is getting a little crowded here."

Emerson gestured for her to lead the way, and she did. From behind, he could admire her and was even more aware of all the other men admiring her as well. Jealousy and pride battled, knowing that those same men must wish to be where he stood right now.

She led him off into a corner occupied by an armchair. It was close enough to the refreshments table that it did not seem like there were trying to be alone but far enough away that they could not be easily overheard. The moment they came to a stop, Kate began talking again.

"The last time we saw each other, you were telling me about the *Travels of England and Wales*," she said.

"I remember."

"Could you tell me more about it? Or better yet, I would love to read it myself so that I can share my thoughts with you next time."

"Will there be a next time?" he asked without thinking.

Kate tilted her head to the side in thought. "There certainly could be. Angelfield House is not very far from Dower House, after all. You are welcome to visit any time you wish. But I will take care not to do the same. I don't want to trespass again."

For a moment, her expression was still. Emerson felt guilt rise up to choke him and had an apology ripe on his lips when her expression broke, and she let out a laugh.

It was so full, so light yet hearty, that Emerson felt himself smile. His face felt unusual, and he realized that he had not smiled since the day of the fire.

"Goodness," Kate gasped suddenly. She looked at him with awe.

"What is it?" he asked, fearing the worst.

And then she grinned again, and it chased away the fear like a flame chasing away the cold. "You look so handsome when you smile. I'm honoured to have brought it out of you." She put a finger to her chin. "Shall I tease you some more, then? I wonder how long it will take for me to make you laugh."

Without warning, Emerson tilted his head back and let out a hearty and genuine chuckle.

Kate clapped her hands happily. "That didn't long at all! My, I am certainly good at this."

"Good at what?" They were joined by Miss Eve, Bob following in her wake. They were both flushed, and Emerson realized that they, too, might have just finished dancing.

"I made the Duke of Edendale laugh," Kate stated proudly. "I shall wear that like a badge of honour."

"You should!" boomed Bob. "I have been trying to do the same thing for some time now, and the stubborn man won't crack."

"Because you are not funny," Emerson stated simply.

"And Miss Kate is?" Bob countered.

Emerson only shrugged. Miss Eve laughed, looking at Bob. "I will have to side with His Grace on this one," she said. "Kate does have a way of warming the hearts of others and has an unusual humour that catches you off guard."

"Why, thank you, Eve!" Kate gushed, blushing.

Bob held up his hands in surrender. "I stand corrected then."

"What's happening here?" Another person came to join the small group. It was a frail-looking woman with eyes as sharp as a hawk's. She looked between the four of them, eyes settling on Emerson.

Kate wasn't the unnerving one. Not anymore, at least. She had quickly been replaced by this tiny old woman.

"Mrs. Bellmore," Kate said, stepping closer to the elderly woman. "Please allow me to introduce you to the Earl of Wellbourne, Lord Bob Cherry, and His Grace Emerson Lake, the Duke of Edendale. They are friends of Eve and me. Your Grace, my lord, this is Mrs. Hester Bellmore."

"My, and to think I could not be charmed by yet another beauty, you have appeared." Bob swept in front of Mrs. Bellmore, taking her papery hand in his. He placed a kiss on the back of it. "It is a pleasure, Mrs. Bellmore."

"You're lucky my husband is not here to give you a good whack over the head for that," Mrs. Bellmore stated, not unkindly. It made Kate and Eve laugh. And Bob drew back, surprised.

"I would not hesitate to brawl for your affections," he stated.

"It would not do you good to flirt," she said, waving her hand at him. "Though I will admit that it is amusing."

"Then that is all that matters to me!"

Humor filled Mrs. Bellmore's eyes, even as she turned her attention to Emerson. Under her direct stare, Emerson straightened his spine. "Your Grace, I have heard much about you."

*Nothing good, I'm sure.* Not knowing what to say, he turned to politeness. "Forgive me, Mrs. Bellmore. I should have paid a visit to Dower House sooner."

"There's no use lamenting on the past," she said. "Though I must say you are much more handsome than they say."

"Mrs. Bellmore!" Kate gasped.

"What?" asked the elderly woman. "I gave him a compliment. Did I say something wrong?"

Emerson was blushing, his face as hot as a furnace. There was no hiding it, especially since Mrs. Bellmore still stared at him with those intense, disconcerting eyes, as if she could see right through to his soul. He tried not to shuffle backwards, to keep her eye contact as a duke would, rather than the man who had avoided all social interactions since that fated night.

He swept into a bow. "It is inexcusable," he said because he couldn't think of anything else.

"I'm certain that there are numerous excuses you could think of. I have heard that you have become a recluse of sorts ever since the fire that occurred two years ago."

"Mrs. Bellmore ..." came Kate's warning voice, gentle but firm. She stepped closer, a little in front of Emerson, as if she wished to shield him from Mrs. Bellmore's blunt words.

"That's true," Emerson said. "And it would do me no good to deny it. Though, I don't doubt that you look more fairly on me because of it."

"Is that what you want? For me to view you fairly? You did not strike me as one to rely on pity, Your Grace."

"Not pity. The truth."

"What is the difference?"

"One cannot be denied, even to the densest of peoples."

Mrs. Bellmore narrowed her eyes, and then he spotted the faintest hint of a smile. In the corner of his eye, he saw Bob lean towards Eve and Kate and whisper, "Are you ladies as lost to the conversation as I am?"

Eve nodded slowly. Kate, however, stared at him with eyes full of pride.

Finally, Mrs. Bellmore smiled fully. "I like you, Your Grace. You are welcome to visit Dower House whenever you have the time. I would be happy to host you for tea one day."

Emerson could only nod in response, letting out a soft breath. Somehow, it felt as if he had passed an unusual test, one only privy to the candid Mrs. Bellmore and Kate.

Mrs. Bellmore looked away, craning her neck to see above the many bodies around her. "Now, where is Caroline? There is something I've been meaning to tell her and—oh! There she is! Excuse me."

She hurried off as fast as her frail little legs could take her, and Emerson felt the pressure on his shoulders lift considerably.

The smell of lavender overcame his senses, and he turned to see that Kate had come to stand a little closer.

"Please forgive her," she said. "Mrs. Bellmore is quite old, you see. She lost the patience for niceties a long time ago. She no longer cares to mince her words for the sake of being polite, which makes her quite brusque sometimes."

"I think she likes you, though," Eve put in.

"I agree," Kate said, and she nodded approvingly. She didn't seem capable of ridding of that smile on her face. "I've never seen her like that. And it's clear that you've impressed her."

"Well, I'm glad," Emerson told them with a sigh. "If I have impressed her, then I doubt there is anyone else who could possibly unsettle me."

"I'm proud of you," Kate said to him, and, in that moment, it was all worth it. And Emerson made a promise to himself.

He would find the man he once was. He could feel him deep inside, begging to come out. Relaxed as he was in this company, the Emerson who would shout at children and forbade all trespassers was slowly disappearing. He wanted to make sure that he left completely.

Suddenly, Bob asked Kate to dance. She seemed surprised at the request and even looked up at Emerson as if to ask if that was all right. Emerson said nothing, tremors of envy curling within him as Kate shyly accepted. He watched as they walked away, heading towards the other dancing couples. Eve was also whisked away by an admiring gentleman, and he was left standing alone.

He did not take his eyes off Kate and Bob. He couldn't understand Bob's intentions. Was he truly interested in Kate? Certainly, any man with eyes would be delighted to be by her side. Did he want to court her as well?

Emerson's hands curled into tight fists at the thought. He didn't think he could bear seeing Kate with another man. Whatever uncertainty, whatever confusion he had suffered from before, had now been cleared from his befuddled mind. He was smitten with her. He was falling in love with her. And she had no idea the impact she had on him.

She might never know. Emerson tore his eyes away from the sight of her dancing with Bob and caught Lord Reed emerging from a dark, cloudy room from across the wide space. He was surrounded by a few of his similarly empty-headed friends, laughing cheerily with each other. Emerson wouldn't be surprised if he was deep in his cups.

He couldn't bear the sight of it. All it did was remind him of the fact that Kate was already spoken for. No matter her kind words, her gentle smile, and the way she made him feel as if he could truly belong again, that remained a fact. He could not deny what he had seen with his own eyes—that she was involved with the viscount.

Emerson watched as Lord Reed visibly tried to bring himself together. The viscount was looking through the guests, scanning each dancing couple. Clearly, he was searching for Kate. And when he spotted her, his eyes narrowed, and Emerson saw a man in a similar situation as himself—overridden with jealousy.

How would he be able to handle this? Emerson knew his strengths; he knew that he was powerless against those cornflower blue eyes that stared at him as if he was as vibrant as the sun. But how could he stop his heart from falling?

Despite the hopelessness of his situation, Emerson was certain of one thing. Kate had changed him—and for that, he would forever be grateful to her.

## Chapter Twenty-One

Kate could not concentrate. She'd flipped absently through the pages of her book for the past few minutes and could not recall a single thing she had read. Her mind still remained on that night last week, her heart still fluttering as she recalled the Farringdon ball.

It went more splendidly than she'd imagined it. While the first half of the night was spent with her vying for the duke's presence, looking out for him with every second that clocked by, the second half duly made up for it. She did not leave Emerson's side, save for the one time she'd shared a dance with Bob. From the moment they arrived until Kate had to leave a few hours later, she stood with Emerson, Bob, and Eve and they talked the night away.

Of course, Bob had kept up most of the conversation. But now and again, he and Eve would become occupied with something else, leaving her alone with Emerson. And they would talk about everything and nothing. She'd found the kind spirit she knew that lingered underneath, had found a man who knew how to jest and tease like any other.

Oh, and his smile! Goodness, his smile had made Kate's heart melt.

She felt her own smile tug at her lips as she remembered how often she'd seen it. He had even laughed a few times, and the sound was like music to her ears. Despite the fact that others were whispering about him, Kate truly believed that Emerson had enjoyed his time at the ball, and that fact filled her with pride.

She flipped another page, humming a tune under her breath. She was so caught up in her thoughts that when Mary came rushing into the room, it startled her.

"Kate! You wouldn't believe who—" Mary paused, frowning. "Were you humming just then?"

Kate blinked at her. "Yes."

Mary's frown deepened, and it looked as if she was going to press for more when she shook her head, clearly deciding that it didn't matter. Her excitement returned with full force. "We have a guest," she announced, wagging her eyebrows.

Kate knew what that meant. And her heart sank. "Lord and Lady Reed are here?"

Mary shook her head, brimming with enthusiasm. "Only Lord Reed. He arrived not too long ago."

Kate sighed. "Well, I suppose I should prepare to meet with him then."

"Oh, no, he wished to speak with the Major alone," she explained. "And it sounded serious."

"Mr. Bellmore?" Kate frowned. "Do you know what about?"

"If I did, I would have said it a long time ago. Do you know? You are so close with Mr. and Mrs. Bellmore that I'm sure you know about all their affairs."

"You overestimate me, Mary." Kate was still mulling over what Mary had said. Lord Reed had come straight to Mr. Bellmore? About what?

"Are you certain you don't know?" Mary pestered.

Kate shook her head, coming to a stand. She didn't know, and she wouldn't stay around here to find out. She needed to escape to her room before it was too late.

Mary trailed behind her, hoping to garner more information she stood no hope of getting. But she quickly gave up, and Kate could retreat successfully to her room, left alone to ponder why the viscount was here. She found it odd that he would come to Dower House without attempting to see her first, especially after the way he had behaved last night.

After he'd disappeared with his friends, Kate had not seen him again until Mrs. Bellmore had grown tired, and it was time for them to return home. Only then did he show up, clearly drunken and looking quite vexed. He hadn't said a word to her, and Eve had sat between them in the carriage, which Kate was certain he had done on purpose. But why? Kate had felt immense relief to know that he was not bothering her like before, but the behavior *was* unusual. And now this?

It made her uneasy. His quick change in demeanor would have been welcoming if it had been preceded by something else, something that could account for why he was doing this. This was too sudden, and she had an uncomfortable feeling that she wasn't going to like the reason for it.

Perhaps she could take a nap. Kate entertained the thought as she went to sit on her bed, her book still in her hands. They wouldn't rouse her from her sleep just to see the viscount, after all. Was she that determined to escape him?

Kate decided that she was. Especially now that she understood her feelings for Emerson, she wanted absolutely nothing to do with Lord Reed.

Those hopes were quickly dashed when Mary returned, beaming. "You've been summoned to the drawing room."

Kate didn't bother to sigh. She resigned herself to the task, knowing that it was too late to stop it. Mary trailed eagerly behind, though this time, she remained quiet.

Kate braced herself before she entered the drawing room. There she saw Lord Reed sitting in a chaise lounge close to the door. By the hearth, in the two armchairs that bordered it, was Mr. and Mrs. Bellmore, who looked as pleased as two cats who'd caught mice. Kate could tell she was walking into something she wouldn't like.

Still, her noble upbringing came over, and she paused by the door to give a polite curtsy to Lord Reed before she made her way over to the furthest seat away from him. His eyes watched her go by.

"Kate, Lord Reed was nearby and decided to pay us a visit," Mr. Bellmore explained.

"Is Lady Reed here as well?" Kate asked, even though she knew the answer to that question.

"No," Lord Reed replied. His voice was steady, calmer than usual. He seemed serious today. "She was otherwise occupied."

"I see." She tried her best not to fidget anxiously with her dress. "Then would you like for me to bring tea?"

Kate shot to her feet, but Mrs. Bellmore quickly waved at her to sit. "There's no need, Kate. You needn't bother yourself."

"It is no bother at all, I assure you. It wouldn't do to have a guest without something to drink."

Lord Reed let out a long sigh, and all eyes turned to him. "Ah, no matter the situation you find yourself in, I see you are still a lady at heart. It is one of the things I love most about you, Miss Kate."

Her heart thudded in her chest, pumping fear into every crevice of her body. Love. She didn't like the sound of that word coming past his lips.

"Goodness, I am feeling a bit tired," Mrs. Bellmore stated. She looked over at her husband. "Aren't you?"

"Why, I think that I am indeed. Would you like to go for a walk through the garden?" It would wake us up some, I think."

"Yes," Mrs. Bellmore agreed eagerly. "That is a wonderful idea."

Kate watched, sensing that this situation was about to get worse, as Mr. Bellmore struggled to his feet and held out his hand to his wife. As soon as she was on her feet, Mrs. Bellmore gave Kate a knowing look. Kate blanched.

They were trying to leave her alone with Lord Reed on purpose. And she couldn't do anything about it. She was helpless, knowing that they would carry out their plan with determination. Nothing Kate said or did would deter them.

Which certainly meant that there was meaning behind the viscount's visit today.

Lord Reed remained quiet long after the elderly couple was gone. Kate didn't feel comfortable with being alone with him, but she supposed the distance made it a little more bearable. She didn't plan on breaking the silence, not wanting Lord Reed to believe that she *wanted* to be here.

"I will get straight to the point, Miss Kate," he said suddenly. He leaned forward, sandy hair falling into his eyes. He didn't bother to move it out of the way, his gaze intent.

"Yes?" she breathed, barely audible.

"I am absolutely smitten with you, Miss Kate. As a matter of fact, I know that I have been falling in love with you since the very moment I laid eyes on your angelic face. You have proven time and again that you are worthy of being my wife."'

Worthy of being his wife? Kate felt ill. She couldn't move, hardly breathing out of fear that he might take that as an acceptance of his affection.

"At last night's ball, I realised that I could not allow another gentleman to claim what I believe is mine. I wish to court you, Miss Kate, and officially announce to the world that you are spoken for."

"Court me …." She could only repeat him in disbelief. Deep down, she knew that was what he would say. And somehow, she was not surprised by the way he said it, claiming her to be his as if she was a prized mare.

A pleased look came over his face, and he leaned back, propping his ankle on top of his knee. "If you are unsure as to whether or not Mr. Bellmore would approve, you needn't worry. I have already spoken with him, and he has already approved of our marriage."

*Marriage?* The world spun around her, and it was all she could do to keep from swooning. Somehow, she managed to say, "Mr. Bellmore is not my father."

"But he is acting in his capacity now that you are an orphan, is he not?" Lord Reed waved a dismissive hand. "In any case, it does not matter. What matters is that we will be able to court for a few weeks before we can announce our betrothal."

She couldn't allow this to happen. She just couldn't! Kate knew she felt nothing for Lord Reed. Not even a sliver of affection, and she would not be able to fake it if she tried.

The thought of spending extended lengths of time with Lord Reed was detestable. But Kate couldn't think of a single way to tell him that she would rather spend the rest of her life alone. She did not want to be mean, did not want to step all over the hopes of those who wanted the best for her. She couldn't forget the look Mrs. Bellmore had given her before she'd left. Kate knew, more than anything, that they would be happy to see her and married to the viscount.

But *she* would not be happy. She could not see herself smiling at Lord Reed the way she smiled at Emerson. She did not want to be near him, did not vie for his attention, to have intellectual conversations about all the books they'd read and their thoughts on recent happenings. As a matter of act, Kate didn't think Lord Reed was capable of such a thing. No, she couldn't shackle herself to a man like him.

And she was in love with someone else.

A duke, a man who she loved not for his title but for the sweet, wise man he truly was. He was more handsome than anyone she'd ever met, with a noble heart that led him to shut himself away. She loved him dearly—she could admit that to herself, even if she was not bold enough to say that to Emerson.

"I ..." she began, her heart racing. It was not in her to be mean, but she knew she had no choice.

"We should begin right now, shouldn't we?" Lord Reed hopped to his feet. She doubted he'd even realized that she'd started talking. He made his way over to her, grinning from ear to ear. "I have a horse waiting outside as we speak. Why don't we go for a ride?"

"No!" she exclaimed. Kate shot to her feet, backing away as her face colored with embarrassment. Lord Reed's grin fell.

"Why not?" he pressed.

"I ... I am not feeling very well," she lied, suppressing the guilt she felt at doing so.

"Ah, is that so? Then perhaps a walk, then. I could tell you all about the plans I have for us."

"No, I'm all right, thank you. I need some space. And some time. To think about everything you've just said."

"To think about it?" He seemed genuinely confused. Kate wondered if he'd ever been rejected before. "What is there to think about?"

"You claim that you are in love with me, my lord. A woman needs some time to think about those grand feelings before she does something she might regret." His frown only deepened, so she took another approach. "Please, give me some time to think about the courtship."

"Ah, I see." Lord Reed's shoulders fell. He took a step back, and Kate felt like she could breathe a little easier. "Very well then. If time is what you need, then by all means, you should have it. Just please don't leave me waiting too long. I cannot wait to bring you on a horse ride."

And Kate couldn't wait until she could muster up the courage to reject him outright. For now, she just nodded. She'd bought herself more time. That was all that mattered.

"I'll take my leave then. But rest assured, my love, I will return soon. I don't think I can be away from you for too long."

Kate kept quiet as he backed out of the room, sweeping into an elegant bow before he left.

The pressure felt too much to handle. Kate's legs gave out from under her, and she sank back into her chair with a thud, her breath whooshing from her lungs.

How could she get out of this?

Everything had already been decided for her, it seemed. She loved Mr. Bellmore, adored the fact that he treated her as if she were his own daughter. The last thing Kate wanted to do was to disappoint him and Mrs. Bellmore.

Yet she had no choice. She could not marry Lord Reed.

When she thought of Emerson, her despair deepened. A part of her believed that he might feel the same for her, but she could not be certain until he said so himself. The night of the ball felt so far now, so different. She'd been so happy, and whatever joy lingered over these past few days now simmered away to nothing but sadness.

Tears pricked her eyes. Not wanting to be caught crying in the drawing room, she rushed out, heading straight to the back door. It wasn't until she was already outside that she remembered that Mr. and Mrs. Bellmore had decided to go for a walk in the gardens. Thankfully, they didn't seem to be around.

A sob caught in her throat. She could hardly see anything, barely able to make it to her favorite stone bench. She sank onto the cool surface and covered her face with her hands, tears wetting the stone. At this point, there was nothing she could do to keep from bawling. Her heart seemed to tear from within, and it bled with every beat, with every tear that fell from her eyes.

What should she do now? She had come to love working for the wonderful couple, but the pressure was too much for her to handle. Would she have to leave them behind just to avoid marrying Lord Reed?

Would she have to leave behind Mary, Eve, and the other friends she'd made while being here?

Emerson?

Kate cried and cried until there was nothing left for her to give. Then she just lay there, numb, shaking, and not feeling any better at all.

# Chapter Twenty-Two

It had been a week. A full seven days of Bob pestering him to go riding, or to go fishing, or to go visit the small, quaint teahouse by the lake. One suggestion after another came at Emerson like a raging bull, and he didn't know how he managed to ward the determined earl off.

The truth was, however, that Emerson was not turned off by the suggestions. Once, he even gave in to the notion of going for a stroll through the village center. The thought was not as aversive to him as it once was when he would lock himself away at the very mention of such a thing.

"I've changed." He said those words to nothing but cold, still air.

He received no response. Nothing but the chilly atmosphere of death hung over him. But it was a comfort he had not felt in a long while. Standing here, a good distance away from the charred remains of the main house, were three large tombs. The stones still shone as if they had been laid today, though lines of creeping foliage were slowly crawling up the sides. The servants made sure to keep the tombs clean, an honor to the people who laid six feet underneath.

The largest tomb housed George Lake, the fifth Duke of Edendale, and the man Emerson had looked up to the most. He had been a bear of a man who seemed impervious to life and all it had to throw at him. Emerson once believed that his father was a god who walked among men, and though he had grown up to view his father through more realistic eyes, the shock of his death had not yet died down in all this time. To think that it would be an illness that took him from this world—not an act of bravery or through the wear and tear of time, but a fever. It was cruel and unfair. Emerson had still not forgiven himself for it, but he could at least accept what had happened after all this time.

Next to him was his wife, the beautiful Duchess, Lucy Lake. Where her husband was a hard man, she was gentle ... unless you upset her. Only then did her true wrath show through the beautiful, polite veil she always wore. She was a nurturer, who loved deeply, and worried just as strongly. Emerson felt a wave of wistfulness as he thought of how often his mother would try to talk to him about settling down soon, about thinking about his responsibilities. So often he would tell her that he was the second son, with nothing to tie him down like his brother. He would tell her that he did not intend on marrying until he was completely bored with life, and she would shake her head in disappointment. Emerson missed her smile, missed hearing her laugh, and knowing that his mother—despite all the things he'd done wrong—truly loved him.

And then there was Jeremy, the sixth Duke of Edendale. From the moment his future responsibilities as heir became known to him, Jeremy had duly turned into the responsible young lord he was expected to be. While Emerson would spend all day outdoors, participating in whatever caught his fancy, Jeremy was studying, reading, and working. If he had time to himself, he would spend it fencing or horse racing, not because he liked it but because those activities were socially accepted sports expected of a duke. He had adapted perfectly, had not even shed a tear—in public, at least—when they'd learned of their father's death through Lucy's letter. Emerson wondered if he had cried for his father as he had or if his duties as duke had made him completely impassive.

Even so, Emerson loved his brother and knew how much he loved him. It pained him, even now, to know that he was gone. Jeremy had still been young. He had been planning on participating in the London Season that year to find himself a wife to take care of the family who would one day carry on the dukedom.

Now it all rested on Emerson's shoulders, and all he could do was stare at the lifeless tombs and pretend that their spirits were here with him.

"I don't know when," he continued, a little breathless. The sun shone brightly overhead, and with the coat he wore, the heat was beginning to seep in. Even so, Emerson felt a chill go through his body as he imagined that they were there, listening. "It might have been Bob. He is very insistent and a little more persuasive than I remembered him to be. He won't stop until he sees the man I used to be, though I don't think that man will ever come back."

Emerson paused. If they were alive, his father would say how much he liked Bob and thought that Emerson should emulate some of his discipline. Jeremy would agree. Emerson would say that they didn't know Bob like he did and that Bob was exactly like him. And his mother would tell him that he was perfect the way that he was.

A shadow of a smile came over his face as he thought about it.

"But while his presence here has certainly made an impact, I don't think he is the reason I've been different lately. It's *her*."

The beauty who lived so close, yet so far. The angel who cared for an elderly couple and would be returning to London once the Season was over. Miss Kate Cooper, who he had shouted at like the monster others claim him to be, and she forgave him for it.

Emerson sighed. He shifted his gaze to the left, where the remains of the burnt-out house stood, and watched as Lily and Liam pranced around, treading on the fresh grass that had sprung up over time.

"I do not understand why I feel like this," he explained. "She is beautiful; there is absolutely no doubt about that. And she makes me feel *wanted*. But when we are apart, I cannot stop thinking about her. When she is near me, I feel like the luckiest man alive. I had even attended a ball a week prior to today where nearly every guest in attendance whispered about me, yet I did not care. As long as she stood next to me, I was happy. Content."

Emerson let out a long, loud sigh. Lily looked up at the sound and then trotted over, sitting quietly by his side. Emerson absently reached out and scratched the top of her head.

"How could she have such a heavy effect on me in such a short time?" he wondered aloud. "Even now, all I want to do is go to see her."

Lily barked. Emerson looked down at her. "Is that what you want to do, Lily?" She began to pant.

Emerson smiled a little. He looked back at the tombs. "I wish you were alive to meet her. You would have loved her."

And they wouldn't care, he knew, that she was not born a noble. His father might be uncertain at first, but Emerson was sure that once he got to know Kate, he, like everyone else, would come to love her. His family would accept her easily, and the fact that Emerson could not see that happening pained his heart a little.

Lily barked again. Emerson looked down into her earnest eyes.

"Shall we go see her then?" he asked. And she began wagging her tail.

Taking that as enough convincing, Emerson gave the tombs one last look before he turned and walked off. Liam rushed over, as excited as ever. The dogs ran ahead as if they knew exactly where they were headed, and Emerson watched them, his heart fluttering with excitement.

Mrs. Bellmore had invited him to visit any time he wished, after all. It would be rude not to. Surely he could come up with an excuse as to why he'd allowed an entire week to go by without paying them a visit. Emerson felt a tremor of nervousness at seeing Mrs. Bellmore again, after just barely escaping her overbearing and outright personality. At the same time, he was excited. The elderly woman fascinated him, and he was just as eager to meet the husband she'd spoken about.

Above all, though, his steps were spurred on by the thought of seeing Kate again. Perhaps they could go for a stroll through the woods. He could show her all the areas he fancied, all the places he would find himself when on a path of contemplation. Perhaps he could even open up to her a little more, explaining why he had treated her that way when they'd first met. His nervousness grew at the thought, but for some reason, he was no longer afraid. He believed that Kate would accept him for who he truly was.

A noble heart, she'd said. When he was still a stranger to her, who had left such a bad impression, she'd still spoken about him in such a caring manner. Emerson smiled to himself. How could he not fall for such a wonderful being?

But there was another reason he wanted to see her, to get to the bottom of a question that had been plaguing him since the night of the Farringdon ball.

Why hadn't Lord Reed escorted her if they were betrothed?

He could not get the image of them out in the Dower gardens from his mind. Emerson knew what he saw but what if he had assumed wrong? If they truly were betrothed, Lord Reed should have been by her side. They should have danced. They should have made it clear to everyone who came near to her that she was spoken for. But, other than a few glances his way, Kate didn't seem to care that he was in attendance.

They had arrived together, Emerson knew. He'd watched them leave with all the envy in the world. But Miss Eve, Mrs. Bellmore, and Lady Reed had also climbed into the carriage. It would be torturous to assume that there was anything more to it than that.

He needed to get to the bottom of it. This question plagued him at night, and if he were to learn that all his assumptions had been wrongly made ... well, that certainly changed everything.

He quickened his steps, and he caught up with Lily and Liam. Before long, the clearing that led to Dower House came into view. Emerson kept to the cover of the woods as far as he could, then headed straight for the back of the house. The hedges that barred most of the backyard swayed under the gust of the wind, the same wind that tugged on his coat. He pulled it tighter as he skirted around the house towards the front.

And then came to a sudden stop.

His heart sank to the pits of his stomach as he watched Lord Reed amble down the steps from the front door, heading to his waiting horse. He could not see the expression on the viscount's face, but he had a pep in his step, and Emerson could not ignore it. Not to mention the fact that he'd come alone. If Lady Reed had been by his side, perhaps Emerson could write it off as her paying her sister a visit and the viscount just tagging along. But alone? He'd come with a purpose in mind.

That purpose was most certainly Kate.

Emerson took a few steps back, unable to take his eyes off the man as he swung onto his horse. Lord Reed didn't move off immediately. He stayed there for a few seconds, his back turned to Emerson. His shoulders lifted and fell in an obvious sigh. And then he looked back at the house. Emerson caught the edge of a smile.

A wave of despondency washed over him as he watched the viscount take off, a plume of dust in his wake.

*I'm too late ….*

Lord Reed came here to see Kate. And judging by the pleased look on his face when he left, it was clear that he'd gotten what he came for. Anyone with eyes could tell that Lord Reed fancied Kate. Had he asked for her hand in marriage? Had they finally decided to set a date for when they would be married? Had Emerson run out of time?

Despair sinking within him like heavy stones, Emerson turned back the way he'd come. The dogs were oblivious to his pain, still prancing about behind him. His feet felt leaden, his body haggard. Suddenly, it felt as if he could no longer breathe, his chest caving in.

Was this heartache? Had he fallen so deeply for her that his body could not handle this agony?

Something moved deep within him, something akin to that feeling two years ago. Emerson could feel himself sinking back into that dark place, and with every step he took, it felt as if all the progress he'd made was disappearing.

He made it a few steps, near the hedges at the back of the house, before he came to a stop, unable to move any further. He ran a hand down his face, letting out a shuddering breath.

This beautiful, though contemplative, day was already turning sour. Now, Emerson wanted nothing more than to shut himself away in his bedchamber and nurse a decanter of whiskey until he was too far into his cups to think straight.

He continued, intending to do just that, when a sound caught his ear. Sobbing.

Emerson paused. Someone was crying nearby, and when he listened a little closer, he realized that it was the sound of a woman. He inched closer to the hedge, peering through the cracks between the leaves.

And then he saw her. Kate, lying on a stone bench, her arms wrapped around her head. Her body racked with the force of her sobbing, the pain clear in her voice.

Emerson wanted to scale the hedge to get to her. At that moment, he felt nothing but panic and desperation, forgetting his earlier misery. He wanted to pull her into his arms and comfort her. Even if she must cry, he wanted her to do so on his shoulder and find peace in his presence.

He couldn't do anything but stand there. She didn't notice his presence, and so she continued to cry as if her heart was breaking and she was powerless to stop it. The sight and sound tore through him, broke him into a million pieces. Emerson clenched his jaw, his hands curling into fists, feeling a wave of anger at whoever made her cry like this.

Was it Lord Reed? What had he said to her? If he truly had proposed marriage, then why was she so upset? Shouldn't she be happier?

He didn't move, not until her crying died down. He stared through the cracks in the hedge and waited for her to lift her head. She didn't. She continued to lay there as if she was too exhausted to move.

Eventually, Emerson found the strength to walk away. As his steps brought him closer to home, it felt as if he had left a part of himself standing by the house. A myriad of emotions swirled within him, but the very strongest was his bemusement. He didn't know what to make of this situation, didn't know how to approach Kate with all these questions. He didn't know if he could.

All he knew for certain was that he was left more confused than before.

## Chapter Twenty-Three

"Kate? Kate, are you all right?"

Kate straightened at the sound of Mrs. Henry's voice. She kept her back to the cook, wiping at the dried tears on her cheek. Kate knew her cheeks were red and puffy, her eyes swollen. She didn't want Mrs. Henry to see her in this state.

It was too little too late, though. Mrs. Henry approached from the side, bearing a large basket filled with vegetables on her hip. Kate discreetly tried to turn her head away from her as she said, "Good day, Mrs. Henry. Are you about to get started on supper?"

"Yes, just about." Mrs. Henry's voice was somber. "And what of you? Enjoying the afternoon breeze?"

"I was." She didn't have the strength to keep up with her lie. Kate pulled her shoulders back, trying to muster up a smile and failing.

"Kate, were you crying just now?"

"No, I wasn't."

"You shouldn't lie to me, Kate. Especially since you're not particularly good at it." Her tone was gentle, and she shifted closer until she was sitting on the edge of the bench. Kate, embarrassed beyond words, could not face her. "Do you want to talk about it?"

"There's nothing to talk about," Kate continued to lie, wincing as the fib rolled off her tongue. "I was just … overwhelmed. That's all."

"All right. If you say so." But she didn't move. Instead, she set the basket down by the bench and got comfortable, drawing in a slow breath. "Since you don't want to talk about it, then allow me to do the talking."

Kate kept quiet. She appreciated Mrs. Henry's concern, but she doubted anything she said right now would make Kate feel any better.

"Life doesn't always work out the way you wish it would," the cook started somberly. "I recall the plans I had for myself when I first came of age. I lived in a small fishing village near the border, and as I grew older, I would help my father at the wharf. Men would come and go on those large ships. Dukes, earls, and noblemen who did not look my way. Businessmen who came from the colonies, who had the riches though they might not have the social status. I would long for the day to be noticed by one of them so that I could live a happy and comfortable life."

Mrs. Henry chuckled, a sound that was not entirely happy. "As you can see, none of my wishes came true. Instead, a man with a stunted leg decided to fall in love with me and would not stop until he'd pursued me to the ends of the earth. I couldn't help but fall for him as well, though he was nothing like the man I had hoped I would marry. He was neither handsome nor wealthy nor established. He was just the apprentice of a blacksmith who wouldn't begin to make money for himself until years after."

Kate glanced at the older woman, intrigued now. Mrs. Henry stared up into the peaceful sky above them, her eyes lost in her memories. Kate wondered if she knew what was truly going on, if she was aware of the fact that her heart was being pulled in opposite directions—towards the man she loved and the man who everyone wanted her to marry.

Mrs. Henry noticed her staring and gave her a warm smile. "Somehow, I fell in love with him. I don't know how it happened or when. All I know is that I was determined to build a life with him. Before I knew it, I had built a family with this man, who I would not look twice on before."

Kate couldn't help but stare. Her story ... it felt so personal, as if Mrs. Henry had heard her thoughts aloud and had felt her pain. Kate, not knowing what to do with herself, stood and paced away. Mrs. Henry's eyes watched her steadily.

"I don't know what has gotten you so upset, Kate," the cook said gently. "And honestly, I don't need to know. I don't even know if this story of mine helps you in any way. The point I'm truly trying to bring across, however, is that nothing is set in stone. Your life is ultimately in your hands, no matter how impossible that may seem right now."

It did feel impossible. Kate hugged herself, keeping her back to Mrs. Henry so that she would not see the fresh tears running down her face.

She heard shuffling behind her and then a gentle hand on her shoulder. "You're a strong woman," Mrs. Henry said to her. "Though you might not feel that way right now, find that inner strength of yours and continue to push through. Follow your heart, Kate. No matter what. You will be happy that you did."

Now, she could not hold back her sobs. Kate's shoulders shook from the force of them, and she hunched into herself, not realizing that she was digging her nails into her skin.

"I'll leave you alone, Kate," Mrs. Henry told her from behind, and Kate could hear her retreat. "I want to pull you into a tight hug, but I can tell that you want to be alone. Please, you can come and talk with me any time you wish. Sharing the burden has always helped with bearing it, you know."

Kate wanted to turn and run into Mrs. Henry's warm arms. Right now, she wanted nothing more than to bury her face into the chest of someone else and cry her heart out. She wanted to unload her worries onto anyone who was willing to listen.

But she could not. Instead, she had introspecting to do.

Kate sniffled and forced her crying to come to a halt. She could tell that Mrs. Henry was lingering, as if waiting for her to turn and tell her everything that bothered her. Instead of turning, horrified at the thought of Mrs. Henry seeing her red, swollen face, Kate gave her a small glance and the barest of smiles she could manage.

"Thank you, Mrs. Henry," she said softly. "Your words, they really helped. It's given me a lot to think about."

"Then I've done my job." Mrs. Henry sounded pleased. "You should go for a walk to clear your head. I can hear Mary buzzing around inside, and I'm sure you don't want her to see you like this. That is if you want to avoid her bothering you with questions."

Kate let out a soft, genuine laugh. "That would be a good idea. Bless her heart, but she does not know when to hold back that incredible curiosity of hers."

"She has her virtues, I'm certain," Mrs. Henry said, but her tone was playful and lighthearted.

Kate let out a sigh, looking wistfully in the direction of the woods that lingered in the distance. She thought of the pond hidden within, of the man she'd met that fated day, and felt her heart twist in her chest. She yearned to go there now, though she wondered if it would help clear her troubled mind or only make things worse.

"Could you tell Mr. and Mrs.—"

"You needn't worry about them," Mrs. Henry quickly said. "They won't even miss you."

Kate felt a wave of gratitude for the cook, and her throat clogged with the urge to cry again. Mrs. Henry waved her away, edging closer to the back door. "Go on," she encouraged. "Before it grows any later."

Kate nodded and then set off down the path leading towards the back fence that would take her out of the garden. Crying did not make her thoughts any clearer, but her steps felt lighter, as if she had truly shed pounds of weight in tears. Mrs. Henry's words echoed in her mind as she walked. Kate could sense the wisdom in the cook's advice. Choosing herself, her heart, should be the first and only option.

But Kate could not bear disappointing Mr. and Mrs. Bellmore. She could not bring herself to reject Lord Reed, no matter how much she wanted to. She did not care for riches or status the way others in her position might. She cared about spending her life with someone whose company she could enjoy and who shared the same interests as her. And without that, Kate did not mind being alone.

Yet, she was young. Did she truly want to risk becoming a spinster? She only had a few more years being at a marriageable age, so did she want to risk never being asked to be courted again?

Perhaps a few weeks ago, she would have said yes without hesitation. But now, with all the uncertainty swirling within her, Kate was not sure.

If she rejected Lord Reed, was she throwing away her only chance? Did she truly want to place all her hopes and dreams on the man she loved, who would rather lock himself away in his massive house rather than engage with others?

Oh goodness, she didn't know what to think. Her mind had never been this unsettled, not even when her father passed away. At that time, only one option had been open to her. Her father's death had only solidified her decision. She would have to work to survive. By any means. But now ….

Kate let out a loud, long sigh that seemed to echo around her as she slipped within the cover of the trees. Now, she didn't have to think as she made her way to the pond. Her legs simply moved, as if she had traversed this path a thousand times before.

Would Emerson be there?

The chance of that was slim, but Kate's heart skipped a beat nonetheless. She wanted to see him. Perhaps that would make things clearer for her. Or perhaps it would only make her more confused. Either way, she longed to be near him. If she could wrap her arms around him, bury her face in his chest, and breathe in deep as she let his warmth envelop her, Kate felt as if all her stress would melt away. For a moment, she convinced herself that she would do just that if she really did come upon him. When the second passed, though, she came to her senses.

Seeing Emerson might make things worse, or it might make things clearer. She might take one look at him and be reminded of exactly what she wanted. Or perhaps she would become even more befuddled once she remembered how vastly different they were.

She sighed again.

It wasn't long before she came upon the beautiful pond, sunlight glinting above its smooth, serene surface. Ducks waded near the center, and she spotted a few squirrels scurrying away upon her approach. Kate came to a stop near the bank and paused a moment before she chose to sit on an uneven stump.

Soon, only one person occupied her thoughts.

"Emerson," she murmured after a long while of staring blankly at the water. "I want to see you."

# Chapter Twenty-Four

Something brought him to the woods. Emerson moved without thinking and realized where he was only when he was finally immersed within the close cluster of trees. He didn't realize where he was going until he was nearly there, and he quickened his steps, wanting to get there faster.

In truth, he had been lost in thought this entire time. After leaving Dower House, his mind plagued him, a range of debilitating emotions tearing through his mental defenses. Emerson could not make sense of anything. He did not know what to believe anymore. His heart wanted one thing, but his mind told him that it was best to stay away, to save himself from any more heartache.

After losing his entire family, Emerson did not want to risk an attack on his already fragile sensibilities.

But his legs continued to move on their own, and soon enough, his mind caught up. He was headed to the pond.

It made sense. It was the first place he'd met Kate. Ever since that day, her presence had followed him, even into his sleep. He wondered if he had begun to fall in love with her from then. From the moment he laid eyes on her, he knew that she was different. He hadn't wanted to admit it at the time, but in hindsight, he should have known. Her breathtaking beauty was one thing. But the way in which she looked at him, as if she saw the man beneath the scars and was not frightened by his physical appearance, Emerson should have realized just how quickly his heart would fall for her.

But was it meant to be? Was he only setting his heart up for failure?

He needed to know the truth about what was happening between Kate and Lord Reed. But how could he ask her? He couldn't think of a single way to do so without confessing his feelings for her, and the thought of doing such a thing both terrified him and made him eager. This was unlike anything he'd felt before.

Soon enough, the clearing came into view. Lily and Liam, his constant shadows, trotted closely behind. He could all but feel their enthusiasm as they neared the ponds, and the quacking of ducks grew louder. Liam, unable to contain himself any longer, raced forward, and Lily was right on his heels.

Emerson smiled ruefully at the sight. It was so similar to that fateful day that it felt almost unfair to see. In his turmoil, nearly everything reminded him of Kate. And he didn't think time would aid him. Time, Emerson had sadly learned, was not his friend. He did not heal as it passed. His wounds would only dig deeper.

*But perhaps it is different this time*, he thought to himself as he watched Lily and Liam break through the shrubbery and disappear on the other end. *Perhaps I am truly meant to be happy this time. With her. I know that my eyes did not deceive me. She truly had been crying. Which meant that there must be more to this story than I could decipher by watching from afar.*

All he needed to do was find the courage to face her with his questions. The possible rejection ... it turned him away from the thought.

When he'd returned to the house, Emerson had instantly gone in search of Bob. No matter how exuberant and loud he could be, Bob was well known for his sound advice—especially when it involved the opposite sex. Emerson never had to ask him for advice because he'd never felt this way about anyone before. But after looking for him for a while, Emerson learned from Sparkes that Bob had left not too long ago.

And Emerson certainly did not want to approach his butler nor his valet about this matter. They would not understand. They would only believe that he was becoming the man he once was, when that man had died alongside his family two years ago.

"Goodness!"

The sharp feminine voice brought him to a sharp halt. A few seconds later, he would have pushed through the bushes to where the pond stood. But the sound of her voice—her beautiful, angelic voice laced with surprise—made his body go still, his heart racing in his chest.

Only then did he realize just how much he had been hoping to see her here. Only then did it hit him that he had come here because a part of him felt like he was being led here by an unknown force—perhaps the beckoning power of his love.

The thought crossed his mind and brought a wry smile to his face. Who knew he could have such poetic feelings?

Emerson licked his lips. Kate was there. Why? He hadn't a clue, but it didn't matter. She was there and now was his chance to ask her everything that weighed on his mind, to get the pressure off his chest. Even though he knew that her response could break him, Emerson decided then and there that there was no use hiding away like he'd grown accustomed to.

So he pushed through the bushes and out into the clearing surrounding the beautiful pond, his gaze fixed on the lovely woman on the other end.

# Chapter Twenty-Five

Lily and Liam were here, which could only mean one thing. Emerson was not far behind. Kate quickly got to her feet, staring in the direction the dogs had come from while she absentmindedly held her hand out for a half-hearted petting. The dogs seemed content to bump into her legs and her hands, not noticing that her attention was elsewhere.

Her heart began to race. She counted the seconds, peering between the leaves that shielded much of her view. He shouldn't be very far behind, but with every moment that went by, Kate began to lose hope that he was really coming.

Disappointment hit her like a crashing wave. Kate let out a sigh, her gaze dropping to the dogs, who were already losing interest in her. The two muddy hounds rushed off to bother the ducks, leaving Kate with an empty feeling.

She supposed it was too good to be true. What would she even say to him if he did show up? Kate hadn't finished sorting through her befuddled mind as yet to know exactly what she would say. A confession of her love? An admission that she would go against her heart and do what everyone expected of her? She'd come here to clear her mind so she could figure out her next step, and she knew that seeing Emerson would only make it more difficult.

The moment she came to terms with that, tucking her disappointment aside, Emerson emerged.

It was almost like that fated day weeks ago, yet so different. This time, she didn't see an angry man hellbent on keeping the rest of the world at arm's length. He was not wearing an old shirt and worn boots. The man who appeared as the Duke of Edendale—handsome, endearing, and appearing much softer than he had been the first time she met him.

Kate's heart thudded in her chest. The sight of him stole her breath away, her nerves now on edge. She held his gaze, unable to think of a single thing to say to break the quiet. Emerson said nothing either. He simply stood there, staring at her, hands moving at his side with agitated energy.

*Is he angry with me?*

Kate couldn't tell. His expression was still, save for the slightest frown on his face. A twinge of fear whispered through her. Had he heard about her and Lord Reed?

"Emerson—"

"Kate—" he said at the same time. He started forward, but at the sound of her voice, he stopped, his frown deepening. Again, they said nothing to each other, but an unknown language seemed to pass between them at that moment.

"I didn't expect to find you here," he said after a while.

"Neither did. I-I thought that I would be alone." Realizing how her words might be construed, she quickly added, "But I welcome the company, as always."

Emerson's lips twitched, but Kate couldn't tell if it was meant to be a smile or a grimace. "We really should stop running into each other like this," he tried to joke.

Kate forced a smile onto her face, gesturing to the dogs who were sniffing around nearby. "Thanks to them, I don't think that will be possible."

"Yes, well, they seem quite determined to sniff you out wherever you are." He rubbed the back of his head awkwardly. Kate watched him, sensing that there was something he wanted to say. "Kate—"

Emerson started forward. But, just like that day, he missed his step and went plummeting into the pond. Water splashed all over him, soaking him from head to toe. The ducks flew off in fright, and Liam leaped into the water, obviously thinking that it was a game.

"Oh, goodness!" Again, Kate didn't hesitate. She hurried into the water, not minding the fact that her slippers were now soaked and that water was steadily creeping up her dress. She held her hand out to him. "Are you all right?"

Emerson peered up at her, water sparkling on the tips of his eyelashes. "Somehow, it feels as if this happened before."

His innocent tone had her smile, and a grin broke out on his face. "At this point, I must wonder if you'd like to make a habit of tripping into ponds."

"Only when you are nearby, it seems."

Laughter bubbled up her throat, and the giggle slipped out without warning. But this time, it was fine that she was laughing. Emerson was chuckling right alongside her.

The tension in the air dissipated within a second. Kate felt the weight lift from her shoulders, and she reached down to grasp his hand. "Come, up you go. I'd hate for you to get sick."

"After all the times I've lied about that very thing hoping to be left alone, it would be rather ironic, I suppose."

"Ironic, perhaps. Worrying, definitely."

He chuckled again, letting her heave him to his feet. She was unprepared for his weight, however, and so when he was upright, she stumbled back a little. Emerson gripped her hand tighter and pulled her in to keep her from falling back herself.

Their chests came close, their faces closer. Kate felt her heart thud painfully in her chest, butterflies filling her stomach. She could not stop her gaze from wandering away from his dark eyes down to the gentle swell of his beautiful lips. Startled by the direction of her thoughts—and the resulting flush creeping over her face—she looked down, realizing that their hands were still clasped together.

He was not wearing any gloves. The scars were as clear as day, and Kate realized that this was her first time seeing them up close. She studied the way they twisted his skin and how much character they gave him. Kate glanced back up at him and noticed that he was watching her intently.

*He's waiting for my reaction.*

She nearly smiled a little at that. She had no reaction. His hands were as beautiful as the rest of him, but clearly, he expected her to spurn him in some way. Kate brushed her other hand over the scars, studying them with the tips of her fingers. The silence felt intense, as if he had put himself on the judgment block and was waiting for the axe to come down.

"Kate …." His voice was soft, as if he didn't dare to break the moment. He gripped her hand a little tighter and began leading them out of the water. "There is something I would like to ask you. And I'm not sure—"

"Emerson!"

He'd moved a little too quickly in a patch of mud, and it slid under his foot. Emerson went crashing, and, holding on to Kate as he was, she fell with him. He twisted around, falling onto his back, and Kate fell right on his chest, the breath knocked out of her lungs.

Emerson's arms instantly banded around her, keeping her away from the mud. "Are you all right?" he asked worriedly.

A few tendrils of her hair fell into her face, and she pushed them away. "A ... little breathless ..." she managed.

He paused. And then chuckled. Kate laughed as well, but she wasn't lost on the fact that they were so close! Her body grew hot, her laughter false to her ears as she tried not to focus on the fact that her lips were so close to his that she was quite literally pressed against his body.

*Kiss me.*

She hoped he would hear her thoughts, that he would somehow know what she wanted. But as Emerson's laughter faded, she saw realization dawn in his eyes, and he quickly helped her to her feet, raking a hand through his hair to compose himself.

Kate simply stared at him, a little amused by how flustered he seemed. It was so clear to her now that she could not believe that she had doubted herself earlier. Emerson was the man she loved. She could not share her life with a man like Lord Reed when she held such deep feelings for the man standing across from her.

She tilted her head to the side. With her disappointment that he had not kissed her, Kate felt a tremor of relief that her feelings now felt much clearer.

"Emerson?" she called to him. "Did you say you had something you would like to ask me?"

Emerson still seemed a little rattled by their close encounter, but he nodded. "Yes, I do. Though, I'm not sure how best to ask it."

"Say it plainly," she suggested. She felt no anxiety, no nervousness, no tense feelings of apprehension at what he might say. She was only certain, and with that certainty came a clarity that eluded her for so long.

## Chapter Twenty-Six

"Are you being courted by the Viscount Reed?"

The question burst from his lips without warning. Emerson tried thinking of another way to say it, but nothing else seemed right. And the longer Kate stared at him, the more pressure he felt to fill the silence.

Kate tilted her head to the side, her lips thinning just a little. She took a moment to respond, busying herself by twisting the end of her dress. They'd returned to the rock she had been sitting on, Emerson standing a few feet away while Kate chose to resume the makeshift seat as she wrung the water from her dress. Rivulets ran down her hand, dripping silently into the earth. Kate let go of her dress and flicked idly at the wet ends of her hair.

"I ...."

"Perhaps it is best that you do not answer." Anxiety was eating away at him, forcing him to look away from her. "It is none of my business. You are free to do whatever you wish without having to explain yourself to me."

"Emerson, look at me."

Emerson braced himself, expecting the worse. He turned back to look at her, and his heart skipped a beat when he realized how close she was. Without warning, she took his scarred hand in both of hers, tears shimmering in her eyes. She sniffled, and a tear ran down her cheek.

"Kate—" he began, but she shook her head, forcing him to stop.

"I am not being courted by Lord Reed. I promise this to you. Honestly, he is a nice man in his own way, but nothing would make me more unhappy."

"Then, all those times I saw you two together—" Emerson broke off, coloring. He didn't need Kate to know that he'd wandered to Dower House on more than one occasion and had espied them when they thought they were alone.

"Those occasions were woefully out of my control. I do not want to be courted by Lord Reed. There is only one gentleman I care for."

Emerson swallowed hard. At this point, he was afraid to ask, afraid of the rejection that might follow. Even though he so desperately wanted it to be true, he understood that no matter how kind and perfect she was, he could not expect her to love a man who had been scarred inside and out.

"Lord Reed came to me earlier," she explained. "And he did ask me to court him. At the time, I was unsure of what to do, so I told him that I would think about it and give him a response another time. I know Mr. and Mrs. Bellmore would love to see us matched, which left me so conflicted. Should I follow my heart or my mind? It brought me to such bitter tears."

"Kate ...." He wiped away the tears streaming down her face, his heart skipping a beat when she smiled for just a second. It was like the sun shining through dark, rain-swollen clouds.

"I do not want to be courted by him," she pressed. "I do not fancy that man in the slightest."

"Don't cry." Emerson framed her face with his hands.

"It is happy tears," she said. "Because I finally understand what I do want. Though I am a little afraid to say it."

"Then allow me to speak first. Though you are crying while you speak, I have never felt such relief to hear those words. To know that you are not already promised to another makes me feel as if perhaps I have a chance at your heart."

"Emerson, you have my heart."

"As you have mine." He felt lighter than he's ever been in years. He brought his face so close to hers that he could not stop himself from dipping towards her lips, longing to feel them.

The kiss was gentle yet enough to make him heady with happiness. He'd longed for this moment, had laid awake at night imagining them in a position like this. Her words echoed in his mind as she gripped his waistcoat and leaned into the kiss.

*Emerson, you have my heart.*

It was all he had been hoping to hear. His heart swelled with such happiness that he grew heady from it, his trembling with the need to pull her close and never let her go.

When he finally pulled away, Emerson could not let go of her. He kept her in his arms, gazing down into her bright blue eyes.

"Allow me to court you then." Again, the words rolled off his tongue, and he didn't give her the chance to respond just yet. "As long as you're certain that you can stomach the thought of being courted by someone with such horrifying—"

"Don't even say it," she cut in. "Your scars are something to be proud of, Emerson. You are a hero, and I have the utmost admiration for you because of them. They do not mar you in the slightest. As a matter of fact, I believe you to be the most handsome man I have ever met."

Emerson blushed furiously. "Then are you telling me you will?"

A smile stretched across her face, slow and languid. "I would love nothing more, Emerson."

Emerson thought his heart might burst from happiness. He wanted to scoop her into his arms and twirl her around. Kate, as if she sensed the direction of her thoughts, stepped out of his embrace while still holding tightly onto his hand.

"There is something I am curious about, though," she said to him.

"And that is?"

"Why do you blame yourself for what happened? I heard about the fire, but I do not understand why you thought it fit to punish yourself for two years if you were not the one who started it."

Emerson expected his good mood to flee in light of her serious question. He'd never spoken about the past before. While it hung over his head, that was a topic that no one dared broach with him, and Emerson was not keen on starting a discussion on it. With Kate, however, he felt the truth rush to his lips without warning.

"It is because I was the only one who survived." He wanted to leave it at that, but Kate stayed quiet, waiting patiently for him to continue. Emerson felt his chest cave a little as he thought back on the death of the people he loved. "My father passed away first from an illness while traveling. He was a strong and sturdy man, so to have learned of his sudden death when he was so far from home was ... painful."

"You could not have been blamed for that."

"He'd asked me to come, to put aside my life of entertaining myself with anything that caught my fancy to spend time with my family. I thought he wanted me to become more exposed to the world around me in an effort to satiate my constant need for adventure. Or perhaps he wished for me to grow more responsible once I've gotten a taste of other cultures. He may have only wanted to spend some time with me since the only time I was home was when I was resting for another day and night of entertainment."

Kate squeezed his hand. "It wasn't your fault," she said, as if she knew exactly where he was going with this.

But now that he had begun, Emerson could not stop himself. Kate had opened a wound he'd long since tried to sew close himself, and now all his pain was bleeding out.

"I should have been there," he explained, his voice low and raw. The dogs frolicking in the pond nearby seemed so distant now. "Even if I would not be able to be there to stop him from becoming ill, I could have at least been there for him in his final days. He longed for my presence, and I'd spurned him for months to suit my own selfish needs."

"Emerson ...."

"The fire was unconnected, but that is truly what broke me. I had been away from home for days, gallivanting in London. Mother had wished for me to stay for dinner, but I told her I had more interesting things to do. I saw the flames reaching far into the sky before I'd even gotten close to the house. The sound and smell came after."

Tears burned his eyes. He couldn't tell when last he'd cried about that day, but now it felt as if a dry dam was being filled once more, and the gates could not hold back the flood.

"I did not stop to think about what I was doing. The servants were outside, desperately trying to kill the flames. My butler was going mad with desperation, asking anyone who could hear him if they had seen the Duke and the Dowager Duchess.

Many of them had escaped, but the moment I arrived, I knew that they were still trapped inside."

He touched the scars on his hands, and Kate touched the ones on his face. They seemed to burn in the memory of that night.

"I raced into the fire to save them, but … but I couldn't do it. They'd already inhaled too much of the smoke. By the time I brought them outside, burnt and in pain, they were gone—" His voice broke in a sob. Kate was crying as well, her bottom lip quivering as she tried her best to hold it in. "I was the only one who survived."

"That isn't your fault, Emerson. You could not have known what would happen on both occasions."

"But—"

"No 'buts'." She shook her head, wiped her tears, and gave him a determined look. "You did all that you could to save them, and the scars you bear are your brand of honour. And you cannot blame yourself for things that happened when you were not even present."

"How could I be the only survivor?" Desperation rushed through him at those words. He wanted to know the truth, even though he was well aware that there might not be an answer to his question.

"Because you were meant to." She gazed into his eyes as she spoke, willing him to listen to her. "You would not be here, standing with me, if you hadn't."

The words struck a chord in him. It felt as if she had put her hand against that wound and it sealed under her touch. As he stared into her eyes, he felt at ease, the worries and pain that had born down on him gently lifting.

"Where were you all my life, Kate?" he whispered.

Kate smiled. "I was living a life on borrowed time."

That made him frown. "What do you mean?"

Her smile slipped a bit. "I have not been entirely honest with you, Emerson."

"Nothing you say will turn my heart against you, Kate."

"I hope so." She drew in a breath. "I am not who I say that I am."

"You are not Kate Cooper?"

"I am, but I am also Lady Kate Cooper, daughter of the late Earl of Cookham."

"The Earl of Cookham?" The name rang a bell, but Emerson could not recall where he'd heard it from. "You mean to say that you are the daughter of a noble?"

She nodded, biting her lip as she looked hopelessly up at him. "My father was the sixth earl before he perished, leaving me with all his debt. I had not even debuted as yet, and I had no close male relatives who would help me secure my future, so I had no choice but to take on work for myself. I began as a lady companion to a Mrs. King first, and when she passed away, I began to work for the Bellmores." She lowered her eyes, looking uncertain. "I understand if you feel as if I have deceived you, but—"

Emerson caught her hand, putting his own against her cheek. "In truth, Kate, I am not surprised to learn that you are the daughter of an earl."

Her eyes went wide. "You aren't?"

"You have the most graceful demeanor I have ever seen in a lady. If you had not told me that you are the daughter of an earl, I would have easily believed that you are the Queen herself."

Kate giggled, and Emerson was delighted to see the uncertainty clear from her eyes, filling with happiness instead. "I could hardly compare, Emerson, but thank you."

"Earl's daughter or no, it feels almost wrong for me to ask this of you, but …." He pulled her closer. "And since Mr. Bellmore is the only father figure in your life, I believe it would be fit to ask for his blessings."

"Then, shall we?"

"Right now?" he asked, surprised.

Kate gave him a cheeky grin. "No better time than the present, I believe."

She tugged on his arm, pulling him away from the pond. Emerson allowed himself to be steered, knowing that the dogs would fall in step eventually. Knowing that they were on their way to Dower House made him nervous all of a sudden. It was one thing to be accepted by Kate for all that he was, but it was another thing entirely to ask someone else to accept him.

But as he clutched her hand, staring at her from behind, Emerson decided that he would no longer hide from the world. For Kate, he would do anything.

## Chapter Twenty-Seven

Major Thomas Bellmore, despite all his current ailments, was a rather intimidating man. He sat in the high back chair of his study with this cane between his legs, and both hands rested firmly on top. Emerson sat across from him in one of the armchairs in front of his wide, mahogany desk. The desk was empty, save for a pot of ink and a quill and a few decorative paperweights.

Emerson kept his back straight, even though he was floundering under Mr. Bellmore's steady gaze. When he had shown up at the house alongside Kate, the Bellmores had seemed surprised. That surprise cleared quickly when Emerson asked to speak to Mr. Bellmore in private. It was as if the older man knew exactly what he was going to say and was not going to make it easy.

Emerson braced himself. He was a duke. It was a reminder that bolstered his courage.

Even so, before Mr. Bellmore, Emerson was yet another gentleman who vied for Kate's hand.

"Forgive the silence, Mr. Bellmore," Emerson began. "I am wondering whether to begin with pleasantries or to get straight to the point."

Mr. Bellmore tilted his head to the side. "You do not strike me as the type who cares for pleasantries, Your Grace. Then again, I hardly know anything about you."

"That is my fault." He paused, but Mr. Bellmore offered no consolation. Clearing his throat, he continued, "I understand that I have not been very welcoming since you and Mrs. Bellmore arrived at Dower House. I deeply regret that and wish to rectify it as soon as possible."

"I see." Mr. Bellmore shifted at last, and Emerson braced himself for whatever was to come. "You have gone through quite a lot, Your Grace. I understand that as well. Though I cannot say it is any excuse for how you have conducted yourself as of late."

Emerson tried not to hang his head in shame. He knew the rumors that went around about him—how he was nothing but a monster inside and out.

"I deeply regret my actions," Emerson said humbly. "I want to change, to become a better duke and, more importantly, a better person. For her."

"Kate?"

Emerson nodded, not breaking eye contact for a second. "She has shown me how to be a better person. She is the reason I am able to put aside all my self-hatred and misdirected anger. At least, she makes me want to try."

"I was not aware that you two had grown close."

Mr. Bellmore's expression didn't lift. Unimpressed. He wasn't going to make this easy, even though Emerson was certain the major knew exactly where this was going.

"Our meetings happened by chance at first. And I believe I fell in love with her at first sight, even though I was not yet aware of it." Those words had Mr. Bellmore's eyebrows shooting toward his eyebrows. Emerson raised his chin. "That is the reason I am here right now. I have confessed my affection to Kate herself, and now I wish to ask you for your blessing to court her."

"Court or marry?"

That took him by surprise. Emerson opened his mouth to respond and then, realizing that he'd thought of nothing, closed it right after. Mr. Bellmore chuckled.

"The moment you two walked in, I could tell that there was something special between the two of you. You wishing to speak with me only solidified my assumption."

"Ah." Emerson felt his cheeks grow warm. "I didn't know it was so obvious."

"There are hearts in your eyes, Your Grace," Mr. Bellmore said with a chuckle. "You cannot hide it even if you tried."

"Then is that a yes? Will you give us your blessing?"

"You have not answered the question, Your Grace. Do you simply wish to court Kate, or do you want to marry her?"

"I would like nothing more than to make her my wife. But—" Emerson broke off when Mr. Bellmore began to struggle to his feet. He rose as well, rounding the desk to help the older man as he gripped the cane for dear life.

Mr. Bellmore waved away Emerson's attempt to help. Once he'd caught his breath, he waddled his way over to the door and opened it. Emerson caught a flash of dark hair and felt a smile on his lips when he saw that it was Kate, caught in the act of pressing her ear against the door.

"Come in," Mr. Bellmore said to her, his voice tinged with amusement.

Kate flushed furiously, but she did as she was told, slipping into the study with her head bowed slightly. She caught Emerson's eyes and quickly made her way over to him. "What did he say?" she whispered.

"I'm not sure," he whispered back, hoping that Mr. Bellmore—who was making his way back to his chair—did not hear them. "He has not responded as yet."

"Have a seat, you two," said Mr. Bellmore, and both Emerson and Kate were quick to comply.

Emerson resisted the urge to reach over and take Kate's hand. He braced himself for what was to come, unable to gauge the major's reaction. Kate had a slight frown on her face as well, as if she two could not tell what he was about to say.

Mr. Bellmore paused, eyes sliding between the two of them. Then he cleared his throat and said, "Firstly, I am honored that you would think to approach me about this matter. I know very well that I did not sire Kate myself, but she has quickly become the daughter I never had."

"Mr. Bellmore ..." Kate murmured.

Mr. Bellmore held up his hand, warding Kate off from saying anything further. "Now that I have gotten that out of the way, there is something I wish to ask you, Kate."

"Yes." She straightened. "Go ahead."

"Do you love the Duke of Edendale?"

"I do." She responded with no hesitation, her voice firm and sure. Even Mr. Bellmore seemed surprised by it. Emerson, however, was trying his hardest to keep the smile from his face, his chest growing warm with happiness. He didn't think he would ever tire of hearing that.

"Good." Mr. Bellmore's surprise melted into delight. "Then that should make answering my next question easier. Do you wish to marry—"

"Nothing would make me happier," Kate said hurriedly, her cheeks as red as a tomato. Emerson stared into the side of her face, but even though she must have felt the weight of his gaze, she did not take her eyes off Mr. Bellmore, her eyes fierce.

"Lovely! Then it is settled, isn't it? I give my blessing for you two to be married."

"Oh, thank you so much!" Kate squealed.

Emerson got to his feet and made his way around the desk in two quick strides. He stuck his hand out to the major and then gripped him by the elbow as well when Mr. Bellmore took it. "Thank you," he breathed, relief flooding him. "Thank you so much. I could not be happier to hear those words."

"Take care of her, Your Grace. Kate has been through quite a lot. After all her hardships, she deserves an easy life full of love."

"And I shall do all that I can to do that for her. Thank you."

Then he straightened, turning to his future wife. Kate was standing as well, her eyes glittering with unshed tears. Slowly, Emerson made his way over to her, taking her hand in his. He wanted to kiss her then and there, to pull her into a tight embrace and breathe her in. But because he wished to be respectful, he kept it at that simple touch, even though he could see the same longing shining in her eyes.

"We should tell Mrs. Bellmore," Kate said after a long moment, finally looking away from Emerson to Mr. Bellmore. "I'm sure she is simply dying to know what all of this is about."

"I am." As if summoned, Mrs. Bellmore appeared at the door. She waved her hand at their surprised faces. "Oh, don't be silly; I only happened to be walking by when I heard what Kate said. I was not lingering in the shadows waiting for my moment to appear."

"Though I would not put it past you," Mr. Bellmore mumbled.

"What did you say?"

"Nothing, my dear, beautiful wife." He flashed her a broad grin as Mrs. Bellmore narrowed her eyes at him. Emerson held back the urge to chuckle. "Now, now, don't look at me like that," Mr. Bellmore chided lightly. "Today is a day of celebration. His Grace has come to ask for Kate's hand in marriage, and I have given my blessing."

"Truly?" Like a flame coming to life, Mrs. Bellmore lit up, her eyes bright and happy. "Oh, heavens, that is wonderful news! We should celebrate! Your Grace, we must have you for dinner this evening."

"It would be an honour, Mrs. Bellmore," Emerson began, but the elderly woman was already shaking her head, tutting at him.

"Now, now, there is no need for the formalities," she chided lightly. "Kate is our family, and now so will you. Oh, goodness, I am so happy for you!"

Emerson went awkwardly still when Mrs. Bellmore enveloped him in a tight embrace. He could not tell when last he had felt such a warm, motherly touch, and he felt the tension slip from his body, more relaxed than he'd felt in years. When she pulled away, Emerson felt a slight chill in her absence.

But then Kate was by his side. She didn't take his hand, but it brushed his own, a reminder that she was there with him. Always and forever. Emerson didn't need to hear the words anymore. Right now, in this study, while Mr. and Mrs. Bellmore bickered about what they should have prepared for dinner and Kate shook her head at them, Emerson felt as if he'd finally found the place he belonged.

No one could replace the family he'd once had. But with Kate, he could begin to build his own.

***

Kate could hardly believe all that had happened.

Emerson had left to get dressed for the dinner, and the moment he exited the house, Mrs. Bellmore began with the preparation—which meant that Mrs. Henry had all the kitchen maids running to and fro to ensure that Mrs. Bellmore's precise instructions were carried out perfectly.

Kate could not contain her excitement. She looked at herself in the mirror of her vanity table, untwisting her hair from the tight chignon she'd spun it in. Her heart still fluttered incessantly, a smile fixed on her face. No matter how many times she thought about what happened at the pond—and then earlier in the study—Kate felt as if she was sleeping and it had all been a dream.

*Am I really engaged to the Duke of Edendale?*

No matter how many times she asked herself that question, she still could not believe that it was true. After all this time, with all the tears that she had shed, did she truly have the man she'd yearned for all this time?

Kate let out a chuckle. How foolish she had been.

She rose, running her fingers through her hair since she was far too exhausted to brush it. It had been a long day, and she believed that tomorrow would be even longer. Mr. and Mrs. Bellmore wanted the wedding to take place as soon as possible, and Kate could not deny to herself that she, too, longed for it to happen as quickly as it could. If she could marry him tomorrow, she would.

But this was the wedding of a duke. Preparations had to be made. It would arguably be the most exciting day of her life, and she could not wait to put everything together.

Just as she was about to get into bed, there was a knock on the door. Kate didn't think who might possibly be standing on the other end this late at night until she'd already opened it and caught Mary's bright eyes.

The maid didn't wait for Kate to say anything. She grabbed Kate's hand as she bustled into the room, pulling her to the table and chair under the window. "Tell me everything," she demanded.

Kate feigned confusion. As dinner was being prepared, Kate had skillfully avoided Mary as best as she could, knowing that the girl would ask her what was going on. But Kate knew that she could not escape her forever.

"What do you mean?" Kate asked innocently.

Mary stomped her leg impatiently. "Oh, don't play dumb with me! You know exactly what I'm talking about. What was happening today with the Duke of Edendale?"

"I'm not sure what you're asking me, Mary. Clearly, he came to have dinner."

Frustration flashed in Mary's eyes, and Kate tried her best to hold in her laughter. "Look at you being coy. You know more than I that there is something under the surface. It seemed like a celebration. What exactly were we celebrating? And with the duke, no less."

Kate thought about it for a moment, unable to keep the smile off her face. "He has been betrothed."

"Betrothed?" Mary gasped. "That monster of a man?"

"He is not a monster."

Mary blinked at the force in Kate's voice. Slowly, she leaned back, eyes going wide. "Is he betrothed to you?" Mary whispered in disbelief. When Kate didn't answer fast enough, Mary shot to her feet with a loud gasp, hand flying to her mouth. "He is! You're betrothed to the Duke of Edendale!"

"Hush now!" Kate said quickly. "There's no need to let the entire house know."

"But they should know. Better yet, I should climb onto the roof and shout it into the night sky."

Kate let out a laugh as she pulled Mary back into her chair. "There is no need to do that. But I understand your surprise—"

"Surprise?" Mary's expressions were exaggerated, with wide eyes and a gaping mouth as if she could not figure out what to say. "Kate, I can hardly fathom the thought of the reclusive duke wanting to marry in the first place, let alone to you. And, of course, I mean that you are so beautiful and kind and wonderful that I did not think you would want to marry someone like the duke either."

"He is much more than he appears, I assure you," Kate said to her. She leaned back in her chair, eyes drifting out the window as her handsome betrothed's face came before her mind's eye. "He's caring, gentle, and knows exactly how to make me laugh. Not to mention that he can sometimes be so adorably clueless that it's hard to believe that he's the same man everyone speaks about so harshly. And I find him to be the most handsome man I have ever met."

"Oh, goodness, you love him."

Her cheeks warmed at Mary's observation, but she couldn't help but nod. "I do. I love him very much."

"Oh, Kate, I'm so happy for you!" Without warning, Mary threw her arms around Kate, forcing her to a stand so that they didn't topple over from the force of the embrace. With her own arms pinned at her side, Kate tried her best to return the hug.

"Thank you, Mary," she wheezed. "Now, please, I cannot breathe."

"Oh, I'm sorry." Just as quickly, Mary released her and took a step back. But her hearty grin was still fixed on her face. "How did I not see this sooner? You are absolutely radiating your love for him. I hope he loves you just as dearly."

Kate's face grew even hotter as she nodded. "I believe that he does."

"Oh my, my heart cannot take this." Mary fell dramatically into her chair. Then she sat up straight. "What about Lord Reed?"

The mention of the viscount had Kate's heart sinking in her chest. The truth was that she hadn't given a single thought as to what she would do about Lord Reed. He was surely still waiting for her response.

Perhaps he will come by tomorrow. I shall tell him then.

As soon as the thought crossed her mind, she dismissed it. Kate couldn't count on that possibility. And the last thing she wanted was for the viscount to believe he still had a chance when she was fated to marry someone else.

"I shall write him a letter," Kate decided. "And I shall have it delivered first thing tomorrow. He should know that I am meant for another."

"Aha! So that means there was something happening between you and Lord Reed!"

Kate giggled, rolling her eyes playfully. "Well, now that it is over, there is no need to deny it."

"Well, I had already figured as much. It was only up to you to confirm my suspicions." Then she let out a wistful sigh, reaching over to squeeze Kate's hand. "Oh, Kate, I'm so happy for you. Perhaps now His Grace will desist from shouting at the village children."

"I assure you, he won't do that again."

"I trust your word." Mary rose, stretching her arms high above her head. "It's already so late, so we should be going to bed now. I'm sure you have a long day ahead of you tomorrow. Goodnight, Kate."

"Goodnight, Mary."

Kate watched as the maid slipped through the door, but not before she gave Kate another excited wag of her brows paired with a broad grin. Kate shook her head, letting out a giggle. It felt nice telling Mary everything. The idea of shouting her betrothal from the rooftop did not seem so horrifying now.

With a happy sigh, she rose and made her way to the bed, slipping under the cool covers. In the morning, the first thing she would do was write the letter to Lord Reed. For now, though, the viscount was the last thing Kate wanted to think about as she drifted to sleep. She closed her eyes, a soft smile still on her face, and let all thoughts of Emerson lull her unconscious.

## Chapter Twenty-Eight

The day was still young, with the fog of dawn still clearing from the air. Emerson rocked back and forth on his heels, his hands tucked in the pockets of his breeches. He could not keep himself still, his eyes fixed on the door of Dower House.

"He is quite charged with energy, isn't he?" Emerson heard Bob say. "He cannot keep himself still."

"Yes," came Sparkes' steady tone. "I don't think I have ever seen His Grace act this way before."

"That is what happens when you find someone that you love," Francis' whisper joined the conversation. "He won't be able to hide it no matter how hard he tries."

"I didn't think I would ever live to see the day." Sparkes sniffled, and Emerson was alarmed at the very thought of the older man crying. That would certainly be a sight to see, but he did not take his eyes off the front door, nor did he make it clear to the three men that he could overhear their conversation.

"It was only a matter of time," Bob said. Unlike the other two, he was not trying that hard to keep his voice low. "He is a man, after all. And when a man finds a woman who can make an honest person out of him, there is not a thing he can do about it."

"Are you included in that generalization, Bob?" Emerson asked, finally looking over at them.

Francis jumped and cowered a little behind Sparkes at having been caught. Sparkes didn't move, though he did see a little surprised that they had been caught. And, of course, Bob did not seem to care in the slightest, a broad grin stretching across his face.

"Well, of course!" he boomed. "I may be a marvelous bachelor, but I do think I would make a good husband as well."

"Then why don't you make a lady lucky and be married to her?" Emerson drawled, eyes returning to the door. It was steadily growing hotter, and he was becoming more and more anxious with every second that went by.

"That is because I have not yet found the love of my life as you have, my good friend." Unprepared for it, Emerson staggered under the weight of Bob's arms when it was slung over his shoulder. "Don't worry about me, Emerson. Married or not, I am simply content to see that my dear friend has returned."

Emerson brushed Bob's hand off, but the other man was not perturbed by it in the slightest. "I won't ever be the man I once was."

"That is true. But you are no longer the man I returned from England to see. That alone is enough for me."

At that moment, the door opened, and Kate stepped through. Emerson's heart thundered in his chest at the sight of her. Her hair was pinned to the back of her head, with a few dark tendrils falling down around her face. She wore a lovely primrose-colored dress that, though Emerson could tell that it was out of fashion, framed her body perfectly and brought out the blush of her cheeks. Her eyes roved over the lot of them, and when they rested on Emerson, Kate gave him a warm smile. Emerson's knees went weak.

He still could not believe it. This woman—this beautiful, kind, clever woman—had agreed to marry him. No matter how many times she said it, Emerson was still finding it hard to see the beauty himself. But, with the way she looked at him now, Emerson could believe that she meant it. He could see the love in her eyes, could see the genuine happiness that lay there.

He was so caught up in the sight of her that he did not notice that Miss Eve had exited the house behind her until Bob boomed, "Ah, the ladies have arrived at last!"

Emerson followed Bob as the earl sauntered past the gate with his arms spread wide. "What a sight for sore eyes," he greeted loudly. "I was already growing bored of the current company."

Without thinking, Emerson smacked Bob lightly on the back of his head. Both Kate and Miss Eve giggled. "I hope we did not keep you waiting for too long," Kate said.

"You did not, dear Kate," Bob responded as he ruefully rubbed the back of his head. "Though I cannot say the same for this one here. I'm sure he would have gone charging in the house out of his longing to see you."

"Bob ..." Emerson growled warningly.

"I feel the same way," Kate said. Emerson's heart skipped a beat. She smiled warmly at him, and in that moment, it felt as if only the two of them existed. "I was counting the seconds until I saw you again, Emerson."

There was so much he wanted to say then and there. He nearly reached out to take her hand, nearly gave into the urge to pull her close to him and wrap his arms around her. Had it not been for the fact that silence had followed her words, as if everyone was waiting to hear what he would say in response, Emerson might just have.

Instead, he cleared his throat, rubbing the back of his head as his cheeks grew warm. "Let us proceed, shall we?"

Kate giggled behind her hand, clearly not offended by his lack of response. If anything, it seemed as if she was intrigued by it. He gestured for her to go ahead with a sweep of his arm, but she simply came closer and slid her arm through his. Emerson didn't know what to do with his body.

"Relax," she whispered to him. "There's no need to be nervous."

The gentle command had the tension flowing from his body. Her touch was enough to set him on fire, and, with others around, Emerson didn't know what to do with it.

"I suppose I was more excited to see you than I thought," he whispered back as they began making their way to the waiting carriage. Bob and Miss Eve were walking ahead, talking among themselves. Sparkes and Francis were still by the carriage, waiting patiently.

"As was I. I've been thinking about you all night."

"It could not possibly be more than I have been."

Kate raised a brow at him, a smile on her lips. "Are we competing with each other, Emerson?"

"Certainly not. But if we were, I would win."

"Is that so? I did not think you to be so competitive."

"There is so much you still don't know about me, Kate. So much I am so eager for you to learn."

"I'm looking forward to it."

"But there is one thing you must know." He put his hand over hers, pausing to gaze into her eyes. "I will cherish you until I take my last breath. I plan to make you happy for the rest of your life."

Kate's cheeks went red, her eyes widening just a bit. But the words seem to rush quickly to her tongue. "How odd, Emerson. You took the words right from my lips."

Emerson grinned at that. He wished they could stay there forever, but he became suddenly aware of the fact that Bob and Miss Eve had already boarded the carriage, and they were all still waiting for them.

"Well, Kate," he said. "Shall we?"

"Certainly, Your Grace," Kate said easily, laughing as she climbed into the carriage.

As Emerson went in behind her, he felt lighter than air. The world seemed brighter somehow, the sound around him far more musical. Only a few weeks ago, he had been filled with turmoil at the thought of Lord Reed courting Kate. And now, he was on his way into town to make purchases for the wedding that would be happening only next week.

*After all that has happened, perhaps I can truly say that I am blessed.*

Emerson wanted everything to be new. He told Kate that she need not spare any expense, wanting to ensure that she enjoyed her day as much as possible. She would want for nothing, not on his watch.

The conversation flowed easily as they ventured into London, and when it came time for the men to part ways, Emerson suddenly felt sick. He handed Kate a reticule full of banknotes for her to spend, saying, "I hope this is enough. If not, then—"

"I'm sure it will be fine," she cut in with a laugh. She put her hand on top of his, and Emerson knew that it would be even harder for him to leave. "Go ahead. We cannot be here all day."

"I know." Yet tearing himself away from her was one of the hardest things he had to do. Emerson alighted from the carriage, standing next to Bob, who was observing everything on the side of the street—wearing a broad smile—and Francis, who seemed to be trying to hide his own. Emerson ignored the look his friend was giving, very much aware of how smitten he appeared right now. But he didn't care—because Kate seemed just as reluctant to leave him behind. She gave him a sad smile even as Francis closed the carriage doors. He told himself he would see her again shortly, but that did not make parting ways any easier. Though he supposed it would make meeting again that much sweeter.

\*\*\*

"This one!"

Eve rushed over to a shimmering cerulean fabric that was sitting in the back of the modiste's shop, eyes bright with eagerness. Kate slowly made her way over, observing as many of the fabrics and colors as she could. She wanted to ensure that she made the right choice, even though Emerson had given her more than enough money to make a few mistakes.

"I like it!" the modiste, Mrs. Jameson, gushed. Her thick Irish accent was as charming as it was difficult to understand, but Kate took her enthusiastic nod as an agreement with Eve's words.

"As do I," Kate said. "But perhaps we should look around a little more before we decide on something."

"We?" Eve was quick to come to her side, sliding her arm through Kate's as they began to wander around the shop once more, Mrs. Jameson their constant shadow. "You are the one making the decision here, so if you are not certain, don't let us persuade you."

"It is my wedding, but you're as much a part of this as I am," Kate said with a smile, resting her hand on top of Eve's. She enjoyed the fabrics and liked the bespoke dresses hung up. She admired a sparkling moss-green gown as Eve answered her.

"How do you feel?"

"About marrying Emerson?" Kate couldn't take the smile off her face. "It feels as if it is a dream. This morning, I woke up and still could not believe that I have found someone to love, someone who loves me just as dearly."

"There is certainly no doubt about that," Eve said, sighing happily. "And soon, it will be my turn."

Kate looked curiously at Eve. "Is that so?"

A faint blush colored her cheeks, and Eve wouldn't meet her eyes. It seemed as if she was going to say something but then decided against it, clearing her throat instead. "What do you think about this?" she asked, breaking away from Kate to point to a lavender-colored fabric.

Kate didn't bother to press her for more information. Eve would tell her what was going on in due time. For now, she only needed to focus on one thing.

And focus she did—even when they made their way to other shops along the street. By the time they were done, Kate had spent nearly everything in her reticule, hands heavy with a maid of honor dress for Eve, a bridesmaid's gown for Mary, and an assortment of other gowns and accessories. And, of course, her wedding dress.

\*\*\*

Gunter's was nearly full by the time Kate and Eve arrived, but they found Emerson and Bob sitting in the corner, speaking with each other. The air was a little chillier inside the shop, but Kate welcomed it, not thinking about anything else than the fact that she'd missed Emerson dearly. She'd left her purchases in the carriage outside and so moved quickly and unburdened to their side, smiling the moment Emerson spotted her.

His eyes sparkled with love. She slid into the chair next to him, and he instantly grasped her hand before letting it go, a quick and beautiful display of his affection.

"How did it fare?" he asked her, his voice low.

"I think this will speak for itself," Kate responded, showing him the almost empty reticule.

Emerson seemed pleased by it, but it was Bob who spoke next, his voice cutting through the air. "Ah, she has no problem spending your money, Emerson. She is certainly the one for you since you have far more than you can deal with."

"Oh, I am not a spend-thrift, if that is what you're thinking," Kate protested quickly. "There were just so many lovely things ...."

"And I was the devil on her shoulder urging her to get everything her heart desired," Eve said with a laugh. She sat between Kate and Bob, and her smile widened when the ice the men had clearly ordered before their arrival was put down before them. She instantly dug in with her spoon.

Emerson grasped Kate's hand under the table once more and didn't let go this time. Kate's heart fluttered in her chest, her face turning red.

Bob, though he may not have seen their hands, did not miss the blush on Kate's cheeks. He grinned. "Ah, to be in the presence of love." Then he looked at Eve. "Shall we tell them?"

Eve's face fell, face turning as red as a tomato. "N-now?" she stammered.

"If you do not mind."

Kate raised a brow, sharing a look of curiosity with Emerson. She'd never heard Bob sound so gentle before. Quietly, she watched the silent conversation between Bob and Eve, who looked at him with questions in her eyes. Slowly, a smile stretched across Eve's face, and she let out a giggle.

"I think we might have already revealed the secret, Bob," she said.

Bob grinned back and then looked at Kate and Emerson. "Then I shall come right out and say it. Miss Eve has given me the honor of courting her."

"Truly?" Kate gasped. She reached over the table to grab Eve's hand, and her friend smiled back at her with true happiness in her eyes.

"It happened so quickly," Eve tried to explain. "I did not have the chance to tell you."

"Oh, you don't have to explain yourself to me. I'm so happy for you!"

"As am I, dear friend," Emerson said to Bob, a look of admiration on his face. "Though for someone who meddled so much in my affairs, I am a bit upset that you did not tell me."

Bob waved it away, laughing. "I shall make it up to you later this evening. But I must thank you, Emerson. If it was not for you—and Miss Kate—I never would have met my Eve."

The tender endearment nearly set poor Eve on fire from the way she flushed. She giggled, hiding her face as she scooped a bit of ice in her mouth. Bob grinned as he watched her, clearly smitten. Kate could not believe her eyes. Watching them now, how had they hidden this so easily?

She supposed she had been too caught up in her own issues to see what was happening around her. But now that the truth was out, the air felt lighter, the day considerably brighter. Kate didn't think she'd ever felt this happy, but as she looked at Emerson and saw the promise in his eyes, she couldn't wait to be proven wrong.

# Chapter Twenty-Nine

"Do you think it should go there?"

"I am certain."

Kate laughed at Eve's sure tone. She was a great contrast to Mary, who was so excited that she didn't seem to know how to keep herself still. She'd gone from laying out Kate's accessories for the wedding, to assisting her with dressing, to walking back and forth in Kate's room as she thought about how best to do her hair, and now she was back to helping her dress, constantly hovering over Eve's shoulder.

Kate glanced at Mrs. Bellmore, who sat in the chair by the window, watching everything with tears shimmering in her eyes. As soon as the other woman caught her looking, she hid her face with her hand and used her other hand to wave Kate's gaze away. "Stop looking at me," she protested. "I am quite emotional, as you know, and I do not want you to see me crying."

"You have been crying all day, Mrs. Bellmore," Eve pointed out. She didn't look at Mrs. Bellmore when she spoke. All of her focus went to pinning and tying the various layers of the dress on Kate's body. It was, by far, the most fashionable, most intricate gown Kate had ever worn, and Eve was doing a lovely job of helping her into it.

"And I believe that I will be crying all day at this rate. I cannot believe that this is happening, even though His Grace asked for your hand weeks ago."

"If you cry, I'll cry," Kate said, her voice thick all of a sudden. She'd been keeping it at bay for some time now, but now that the day of her wedding was finally upon her, it felt appropriate to cry.

"Don't you dare," Mary warned, sliding in front of her and pointing a warning finger. "If you do, your cheeks might become splotchy, and your eyes might swell. You must look perfect."

"I agree," Eve said from behind, just as she pulled tightly on the strings of her corset. Kate sucked in a breath and tried to remember how to breathe. "Please save it for when you're walking down the aisle. I'm sure Emerson would love that."

"Very well, I'll stay quiet," Mrs. Bellmore said. "I don't want to tempt you, Kate. But, my dear, you look so beautiful."

Kate smiled, the urge to cry only growing stronger. The day had begun quite early. Mary had insisted that she eat a simple breakfast since she would have to save space for the wedding breakfast. After that, they had begun getting ready, Mary and Mrs. Henry drawing a hot bath for her and scrubbing every inch of her skin. Since Mary was to be a bridesmaid and Eve was to be the maid of honor, Mrs. Henry helped them both in getting ready before all the attention could be focused on the bride. The wedding would begin in short order, and after she was dressed, the only thing she had left to do was her hair, which she intended to leave in Mary's capable hands.

"Do you think he will cry?" Mary asked Kate curiously. Finally, she decided to sit at the vanity table, hands on her knees like an eager child. She looked rather pretty in her primrose-colored gown, which sparkled when she hit the sunlight. Eve was donned in a similar gown, though she'd decided to wear a beautiful rose broach.

Kate thought about it and then shook her head. "I don't think so. He is not as emotional as I am."

"It would be rather romantic if he did cry," Mary went on. "When he sees you walking down the aisle with your bouquet in your hands. Perhaps he will even fall to his knees and thank God for making him so lucky."

"You are far too much of a hopeless romantic for your own good," Mrs. Bellmore said.

Eve and Kate laughed. "I agree," Eve said as she began the cumbersome task of threading and tying the ribbons on the back of Kate's dress. "Far too hopeless, but I suppose it is nice to imagine."

"He is quite romantic in his own way," Kate said.

"How?" Mary probed, leaning closer.

Kate thought about it for a moment. And then she told them—without revealing too much—all about the tender moments between her and Emerson, his gentle, heart-fluttering words, and how often he reassured her of his love for her, even if he did not say the words themselves.

By the time she was done, Mary and Eve were swooning, and Mrs. Bellmore was desperately trying to hold back her tears. It sparked a conversation that had Mary at the helm, talking about how happy she was for Kate and how much she wanted her turn to come one day. Once she was finally dressed, Kate claimed the chair at the vanity table and listened to Mary go on as she began her hair.

Her urge to cry was gone nearly completely. Soon enough, they were listening to Mrs. Bellmore tell them all about how Mr. Bellmore had pursued her, even when he had left home to be a part of the army. She still had the letters, and had it not been for the fact that she'd gotten quite comfortable in her chair, she would have gone for them.

Before long, Kate was ready. Mary stood back, arms folded, a look of pride on her face. "I think this may have been my best work yet," she boasted.

Kate had to agree. She studied her reflection, marveling at how beautiful she looked. Mary had pinned most of her dark curls to the top of her head, with a few tendrils falling to the back. The front of her hair had been curled as well, with a few strands pinned away and the rest framing her face. She appeared youthful and lovely and, paired with the cream-colored wedding gown she wore, almost angelic.

Her heart began to pound as she rose. It was time to go to the church.

"Thank you, Mary and Eve," she said, a little breathless with anticipation.

"You're quite welcome, Kate," Eve responded. "Now, let us go. We shouldn't be late."

Kate nodded and allowed them to lead the way. She paused to watch Mrs. Bellmore get to her feet, looking quite lovely herself. The elderly woman reached out to take Kate's hand, and together, they both left the room, making their way downstairs.

Mr. Bellmore was waiting for them at the bottom of the stairs, leaning heavily on his cane.

"Mr. Bellmore, you should be resting," Kate chastised lightly as she came to the bottom.

"And miss this beautiful sight? That would be a crime." Mr. Bellmore took Kate's hand and leaned in to kiss her gently on the cheek. "Congratulations on this beautiful day, my dear."

"Thank you, Mr. Bellmore," Kate murmured, her heart swelling with love. "Now, please, I can see you sweating. You need to sit down."

"I shall soon. First, you should follow me."

He turned and walked away, in the direction of his study, without waiting for her response. Kate indicated to Mary and Eve to wait for her in the carriage before she followed the major, his wife on Kate's heels.

In the study, Mr. Bellmore made his way around the desk and sank heavily into the chair as if his legs had given way beneath him. He reached into one of the upper drawers and put a small ornate box in the center of the desk. Kate came closer, not saying anything, a part of her already guessing what might be inside and her heart racing at the thought.

"What is this?" she whispered as Mrs. Bellmore came to her husband's side.

"It's a family heirloom," she explained. "Passed down from my grandmother to my mother and then to me. I had intended on giving it to my daughter, but since God never blessed me with one, it feels fitting to give it to you, the daughter I've always wanted."

"Mrs. Bellmore ..." Kate trailed off when the elderly lady held up a hand.

"Please don't say that it's too much, Kate. After all the time we've spent together, you've become a part of this family, and this is our gift to you. I only hope that one day you will be able to pass it on to your own daughter."

Mr. Bellmore lifted the box and opened it for Kate to see. Sitting in the center was a necklace bearing a beautiful sapphire gem in the center, diamonds glinting around it. It was certainly the most expensive piece of jewelry Kate had ever laid eyes on, and a part of her was afraid to touch it.

As if he sensed her line of thought, Mr. Bellmore pushed it closer to her, urging her to take it. With trembling hands, Kate picked up the necklace. It was far lighter than she expected it to be, the gem twirling. She put the necklace around her neck and fastened it with ease, almost as if it was meant for her.

"Thank you," she breathed, emotions thick in her voice. "I don't know how best to thank you for all that you've done for me."

"That should be our line, my dear," Mr. Bellmore said gently. "I wish I could be there to walk you down the aisle, but these bad legs of mine chose the worst day to act up."

"I would much rather you rest. We will return soon for you for the wedding breakfast at the Angelfield House."

"Don't forget me now," Mr. Bellmore joked, and Kate laughed through the tears brimming in her eyes.

She came around the desk and enveloped Mrs. Bellmore in a warm hug before leaning down to embrace Mr. Bellmore as well. She wiped at the tears that had escaped her eyelids and brought a smile to her face.

"Let us go, Kate," Mrs. Bellmore said into the silence. "We shouldn't be late."

Kate nodded and followed her out the door, looking back at Mr. Bellmore as she left. The last thing she saw was him staring after them with a happy smile on her face, and it was enough to chase away her own lingering tears, focusing instead on what was ahead of her.

# Chapter Thirty

The house was in a frenzy. Emerson stood on the terrace of his bedchamber, staring down at the grounds below. Sparkes stood nearly directly underneath, pointing at something off to the left as he directed a footman about a mundane detail. The footman nodded and ran off to do as he was told while Sparkes turned to a maid, saying something that Emerson could not hear.

He didn't think he'd ever seen so many servants since … since that night. Yet the memory of the servants dousing the flame-ridden house with water did not sour Emerson's mood. He supposed it was his fault they would go into hiding when, before, Angelfield House had been a warm place where the duke and duchess had treated their help as family.

*Mother, Father, I hope you are proud of me.*

The late duke and duchess would have been the ones directing, he was certain. Though it was more common to leave such things to the head staff, such as the butler, his parents would not be able to contain themselves. His mother especially would take part in the arrangements as best as she could, ecstatic at the very thought of her son finally settling down.

Instead, it was Sparkes who did much of the preparations. From the wedding to the wedding breakfast that would take part after, he had taken care of everything, leaving Emerson with nothing to do. Though he supposed he hadn't a clue where to begin. He'd never gotten married before. Before Kate, he hadn't even considered the thought.

"On such a day like today, you stand out here looking somber?"

Emerson didn't turn at Bob's voice but watched in his peripherals as his friend came to his side, a cigar in one hand and a glass of scotch in the other. "You have nothing but whiskey and brandy in this house, Emerson. Did you know that?"

"I thought it would have deterred you from coming, but I see that it failed."

Bob chuckled at Emerson's sarcastic tone. "You could not have stopped me no matter what you did. Especially not after whom I had seen you'd become." Bob paused to sip his scotch. "You've changed."

"All thanks to Kate."

"Yes, she is the reason you *began* to change, but a part of me feels as if you wanted to do so all along."

"What do you mean?"

"You didn't see it, Emerson, but I did. You hid yourself away because you thought you didn't deserve to live like a normal human being, surrounded by others. Yet, with everything in you, you wanted to return back to normal. And that internal conflict is what was ripping you apart."

Emerson finally turned to look at Bob. "I didn't think my best man would suddenly become so philosophical on my wedding day of all days."

Bob huffed a laugh before he took a long drag of his cigar. "Well, usually, men get a talk from their fathers. But in your case ...."

The casual mention of the late duke did not upset Emerson the way it would have before. It was a fact that he had come to accept. But with the way Bob was studying him, he knew his friend was expecting a fierce reaction.

"And so you thought to stand in the place of my father?" Emerson plucked the glass from Bob's hand and took a sip. "That's a little odd, but I suppose I won't shame you for it."

"Am I doing a bad job?"'

"Horrendous."

Emerson's blandly sarcastic tone had them both chuckling. It felt good to laugh. He'd felt light since the moment he woke, and nothing could ruin his mood.

"Sparkes is over the moon," Bob pointed out. "And Francis is obsessing over your wedding attire."

"That he is." Emerson had forgotten that Francis was in his room. He looked behind him to see his steward picking at the clothes on Emerson's bed, mumbling under his breath. A maid was behind him, running off to do his bidding before returning with whatever he'd sent her for.

Emerson looked back in front. He would have to get dressed soon, but for now, it was comforting to stand here with his friend.

"I didn't think it would ever happen," he said after a long moment. Next to him, Bob continued to smoke his cigar, and Emerson handed him his glass back. "I thought I deserved to die alone. After all that had happened, I deserved nothing short of that."

"Their death was not your fault."

"I know that now. Truth is, I think I knew that all along. But every time the thought crossed my mind, the deep guilt I felt at being the only one to survive tore so violently through me that it felt as if it was eating me alive. I couldn't bring myself to be around anyone else. I didn't think I deserved it. But to think, after all that self-hatred, someone as kind and beautiful as Kate would come into my life ... maybe I did deserve something good. Maybe I deserved to live."

"You truly do love her, do you?"

"Did you ever doubt it?"

"I didn't, but to hear you speak this way is always a surprise."

"Right now, she is the reason I wake in the morning, my reason for living. I love her so much that it feels as if she's become a part of me, and if she is gone, I am not truly whole."

"Save it for the wedding, Emerson," Bob joked, and Emerson broke the somberness with a laugh.

"I shall. For every day of my life, I shall ensure that she knows how much I cherish her."

"Your Grace!"

Emerson turned at Francis' voice, raising his brow at the other man's obvious excitement.

"It is ready," he announced. "And it is time for you to get dressed before you are late."

"I shall see to it that Sparkes does not drive the help insane," Bob said, putting his hand on Emerson's shoulder. Emerson watched as he walked away, stopping by Francis only to say, "Try not to cry, Francis."

Emerson grinned as Francis nodded and made a physical effort to hold his tears at bay. Bob's laughter followed him out the door. Emerson approached and allowed Francis to get to work. And by the time he was finished, and Emerson looked at himself in the tall mirror, he was almost unrecognizable.

*This is the man Kate has fallen in love with.*

Scarred, and yet she called him handsome. And for the first time in what felt like forever, Emerson did not feel disgust when he looked at himself. His hair was brushed away from his face, his waistcoat and breeches black and contrasting the starch white of his shirt. Francis had emblazoned the Edendale crest on his waistcoat, a red brand against the black and white.

Emerson was tempted to pull his gloves off, had it not been for social necessities. He wanted to put his scars on display. Hiding them was something the old Emerson would have done. This new Emerson, who was not entirely the same as the person he'd been before the fire, did not care to hide the thing that now defined him.

He was to be married today. That in itself was enough to make him relax, to fill him with hope for the future. He had lost so much time, but he could make up for now it by building a life with the person he loved most.

They left shortly after and found it difficult to pull up to the church. The street was swarming with people, every single one of them pouring into the church. The moment they spotted the incoming carriage, they stopped to watch, talking eagerly with each other.

Emerson couldn't believe his eyes. These people were here to witness the wedding. They were not here out of ill will; he could see the pure happiness in their eyes as they waited for him to come out. He didn't move, afraid that he was wrong.

"Well?" came Bob's voice. "Your people await you."

Emerson caught his friend's grin but could not bring himself to smile back. He was no king. He could hardly call himself a duke after neglecting these people for so long. But he would not cower any longer.

So he alighted from the carriage, bracing himself for the cold onslaught that would come from them.

Instead, they swarmed him, each of them trying to give him their warm congratulations before the other. The force of it overwhelmed Emerson, and he could barely manage to answer. Bob, realizing this, remained rooted behind him, steering him towards the entrance of the church and up to the pulpit where he would wait for Kate.

"Your Grace," Parson Dewhurst greeted once he approached.

"Mr. Dewhurst," Emerson greeted in return. Bob abandoned him to go talk with a few of the villagers, forcing him to face the parson alone. He hadn't spoken to him since they'd spoken about the upcoming wedding a few days ago, and Emerson was still feeling as uncomfortable now as he had been then.

"It is your wedding day," the parson pointed out. "And yet you look as if you're preparing for war."

Emerson tried not to scratch the back of his head. "It feels as if this is all undeserved," he admitted without thought.

"What is?" The parson glanced back at the slowly filling church. "They have come to give you well wishes for a long marriage, Your Grace. I think many grooms deserve such a thing on a special day like today."

Emerson nodded, though that didn't make him feel any more comfortable with it. It felt as if there were things still left unsaid on his part. "I must apologize, Mr. Dewhurst," he said after a long moment, "for locking myself away and neglecting anyone who came to seek my aid. For my horrible behavior over these past few years."

"Your apology is welcomed but unnecessary, Your Grace. No one blames you. It is time you stop blaming yourself."

Emerson relaxed a little. "You sound so much like Kate."

"Kate is quite wise. She is a great match for you, Your Grace, and I hope you will make her happy."

"I hope so too. What you can be sure of is that I will do whatever I can to ensure that she is."

"And that is all that matters."

Emerson didn't say anything in response. The guests had finally gotten settled, even after a few more chairs had been brought in. Still, so many of them were outside, peering in through the gaping doors and the open windows.

As if on cue, they all turned around. And then many of them rushed away, which made it clear to Emerson that Kate had arrived. He brushed his hands against his waistcoat, straightening his spine. He longed to see her, but he willed himself to be patient, knowing that she would have to make her way through the throng first.

*It is finally time.*

It felt as if so much of the last two years had been leading to this moment. There was much to look forward to and many milestones to hit. But right now, the fact that Kate Cooper would finally become Kate Lake was all he could think about. His heart raced with anticipation, and he opened and closed his hands as he tried to remain calm.

The nightmares, the self-torture, the deprecation … all the horrors he had endured and had put himself through would come to an end. Emerson knew it as certainly as he knew his love for Kate. She brought a light into his life, and when she finally arrived at the door, like an angel straight from heaven, Emerson wanted only to be bathed in it.

## Chapter Thirty-One

The church was so full that there was no longer any space for anyone to sit inside. The entire village was in attendance, along with friends and family who'd heard that the reclusive duke was getting married. As the carriage pulled up to the front, the guests chattered excitedly, a few bold enough to approach the carriage themselves.

Kate could not believe her eyes. She stared through the window of the carriage, her heart pounding in her chest. "So many people."

"I suppose a lot of them are curious about the duke being married," Mrs. Bellmore surmised. She, too, was peering out the window, as surprised as Kate was. "I did not expect this many of them, though."

"I'm starting to feel nervous."

"Don't be," Eve said, reaching over to take Kate's hand. "Today isn't about anyone else but you and His Grace."

"You're right." Kate had been thinking about him the entire ride to the church. She could see his carriage as well, and the very thought that he was already here made her heart flutter. She couldn't wait to see him. The more she thought of him, the more impatient she became waiting for the footman to open the door for them.

He came at last, having pushed his way through the crowd of people who were hoping to see inside the carriage. The doors opened to reveal Mary and Eve first, who alighted gracefully from the carriage with the footman's help. They stood to the side, allowing Mrs. Bellmore to dismount after. And then a small hush went over the crowd of guests as they waited for Kate to come forward.

The tense anticipation that hung in the air made Kate feel as important as the queen herself. She tried to rid the anxiousness that claimed her as she shifted towards the doors and then accepted the footman's hand. The moment she came into view, a cheer went through the crowd. Faces she recognized and did not were shouting for her, showering her with compliments and congratulations. The raw support was overwhelming, but it brought a bright smile to Kate's face.

"This is for you," Mary said as she handed Kate the bouquet of roses she had brought with her from Dower House for Kate to carry down the aisle. Kate accepted it gratefully.

She didn't get to move away from the carriage as two familiar figures approached. Kate blinked in surprise as she took note of how smartly Francis and Sparkes were dressed.

"Miss Kate," Sparkes greeted. "You look beautiful."

"Thank you, Sparkes."

Francis could hardly contain his excitement when he came closer to whisper, "He is waiting for you."

Kate couldn't take the smile off her face. She had no words, could only manage a nod. The two of them looked at her like proud fathers who could not be happier, and it made her more relaxed.

Francis turned to Mrs. Bellmore. "A spot has been saved for you at the front, Mrs. Bellmore. And I have been tasked to escort you."

Mrs. Bellmore appraised him with lifted brows. "Well, I've had far less attractive escorts. Lead the way."

Francis flushed at Mrs. Bellmore's bold statement and offered her his arm. Eve and Mary giggled at the interaction. They gave Kate encouraging smiles before they followed Francis and Mrs. Bellmore up the steps that led into the church.

"Shall we?" Sparkes asked, offering his arm as well. Since Mr. Bellmore was not able to walk her down the aisle, Sparkes had offered to do the honors. She was grateful to him for it.

She had no words. She was so happy that she could not bring herself to speak. Kate only slid her arm through his, clutching her bouquet with her other hand. Together, they made their way through the throng of people, who followed behind so they could watch the procession through the open doors.

The music began as she approached. Kate kept her eyes on the ground, nervous all of a sudden. If she lifted them, she would see him, but she didn't do so until she was crossing over the threshold of the church's entrance.

And the moment her eyes landed on Emerson, everything faded.

A part of her took note of the fact that the church was full, with all the additional seats that had been brought into the church already occupied. But Kate did not pay attention to the faces around her. She only saw him, marveling at how handsome he looked.

Emerson shifted on his feet, his jaw ticking as he watched her approach. Kate moved slowly to the tune of the music, but she didn't feel her feet as she went down the aisle. Even Sparkes walking next to her disappeared. She saw only Emerson, her chest swelling with such sharp love for him that she could hardly contain it, and she could not wait to be by his side.

At long last, Sparkes released her, and she was free to continue the short tip up to the altar. Only then did Kate notice the parson standing between them, Eve's father beaming with happiness. She gave him a small smile of acknowledgment before she finally turned to her future husband.

Up close, Emerson's eyes were bright with love. She felt it radiating off him, could see it trembling in his hands. He moved, hesitated, and then gave in to the urge to take one of her hands in his. Without thinking, Kate stretched her arm to the side, and someone—either Mary or Eve—took the bouquet from her hands, leaving her free to hold both of his.

"Kate, you look ..." Emerson trailed off, his throat throbbing.

Kate's face was starting to hurt from her smiling. "Thank you," she said to his unfinished compliment. "You look as handsome as the day I first met you."

"Covered in pond water?"

"Very well, perhaps a tad more handsome."

Emerson chuckled, squeezing her hands. Kate would have forgotten that there were onlookers had the parson not cleared his throat. "Shall I begin?" he asked.

"Please do," Emerson said to him without looking. He was staring into Kate's eyes instead, as if he never wanted to look away.

Parson Dewhurst began the procession with a prayer from the Book of Common Prayer. Kate heard him with only half an ear. She was falling into a trance, a part of her unable to believe that she was truly standing here. Like she'd said before, it felt like a dream, one she did not want to wake from. A life with Emerson, where she could build a family with him, was now all she ever wanted.

As the parson continued, Kate almost grew impatient. But before she knew it, it was time for her to say her vows. She echoed the parson's words as he recited the words from the Book of Commons. And as Emerson did the same, he felt the force of those words as much as she felt his love for her.

Through sickness and health, until death did them part ….

"Will all of you witnessing these promises do all in your power to uphold these two persons in their marriage?" Parson Dewhurst asked loudly to the guests.

"We will," they echoed.

He grinned. "As it is said, you two are wed. You may kiss your pride, Your Grace."

"At long last," Emerson whispered before he slid his hand around Kate's back and pulled her into him. He captured her lips tenderly, and every bit of her melted in his arms. The cheer that erupted in the church hall was enough to deafen her, but she did not focus on anything but the gentle feel of his lips.

He pulled away a second later and left Kate longing for more. She could see the same need across his face, but he said nothing, holding her hand even though he stepped away from her.

Kate didn't get the chance to say anything. They were led by the parson to the room nearby, where they were meant to sign their marriage papers. It took no more than a few minutes, and then they were free to return to the hall.

The moment they did, they were bombarded by the villagers. The blacksmith and his wife, who smiled broadly at Emerson, clearly harboring no ill will for how he had shouted at his children. The baker. Mrs. Dewhurst, with Mrs. Bellmore at her side, Bob. More and more of them came to offer their personal congratulations, and Emerson remained by her side as they steadily accepted them all, slowly making their way out of the church and to the carriage. The joy of them all was palpable and overwhelming, and Kate could tell that Emerson was not used to it. She could not blame his reaction, though. After all he'd done, it wasn't unreasonable for him to think that no one would give him their well-wishes, let alone everyone.

Finally, they arrived at Emerson's carriage. Somehow, Sparkes had made it to the carriage first, waiting to admit them in. He covered them as much as he could as they climbed inside.

Kate let out her first breath the moment she was settled. "I did not expect so many people to come."

"Neither did I." Emerson studied her. He was sitting on the other side of the carriage and moved to her side. "How do you feel?"

"Happy. So incredibly happy. And you?"

"Words cannot express how elated I am."

"Yet you do it so eloquently." She could not help herself. She leaned in for a kiss, just a gentle peck that would satiate her for the moment. A smile stretched across Emerson as he hummed with pleasure.

"Shall we return for your wedding breakfast, Mrs. Lake? It is a barn dance on the lawn of Angelfield House, just as you requested. Every guest who attended the wedding will be able to eat and drink to their heart's content."

Her new title was like music to her ears. "Our wedding breakfast, my love. And yes, let us. So that it will be over all the sooner so I can spend some time with my husband."

The flush that brushed his cheeks was adorable as it was endearing. Kate rested her cheek on his shoulder as the carriage took off to her new home.

# Epilogue

*Two Years Since the Wedding*

"I do not think we can handle another one, Kate."

Kate ignored Emerson, though she smiled at the false concern in his voice. He was trying to be the voice of reason, she knew, but it wasn't working. He wanted this as much as she did.

Kate lowered to a stoop, watching as the tiny pup tried to lift its overly large head and failed. It toppled over and fell into its brother, who then fell into its sister, and the three puppies dropped on their sides one by one. Their mother, Lily, sniffed at them as if urging them to get to their feet. The wise dog looked up at Kate, and if she did not think better, Kate thought there might have been a bit of embarrassment in the dog's eyes.

Emerson crouched next to her, folding his arms above his knees. "I'm serious, Kate."

"I know you are," she said. "At least, you're trying to be. But what can we do to stop them? Lily will continue to produce more puppies."

"We will have to give them away when she does. This is her third litter and will bring us up to seven dogs in total."

"It is quite miraculous, isn't it?" Kate asked as she rubbed one of the puppies' bellies with her finger. "Her first two pregnancies only produced one puppy each, but with this one, she has a total of three! She must be so proud."

"Don't encourage her."

Kate laughed. "How can I? I have very little say in whether she wishes to mate or not."

Emerson sighed. He said nothing for a while, but then he gave in and began to pet one of the puppies, who was trying its best to crawl towards him. They'd only just opened their eyes, barely aware of the world around them.

Kate watched him, pleased. Emerson was stronger than when she'd first met him, though he still veered on the lanky side. As much as he tried to hide it, he was as happy with the litter as she was. The other puppies were prancing excitedly behind them, locked behind the gate so that they would not disturb the new mother and her children. Only Liam had been allowed on this side, and he seemed completely uninterested in them, trying to play with the older puppies through the fence.

*I wonder how he will react when I finally tell him.*

Many scenarios came to her mind, and Emerson caught her gazing into the distance, raising a brow. "Where have you gone?"

"Nowhere."

"Come." He stood and held out his hand. "Walk with me."

Kate was more than happy to. She rose and took his hand, enjoying the way his fingers threaded between hers. Together, they left Lily to feed her puppies, but Liam, noticing that they were leaving, was quick to join their side.

They fell silent, enjoying the brisk air of the morning. They walked like this often, sometimes with the dogs and sometimes only with each other. Kate enjoyed every moment of it, happy with her tiny slice of heaven at Angelfield House. She didn't go into the village very often, though she did visit Mr. and Mrs. Bellmore often. Ever since they purchased Dower House from the Evans family, they'd been closer than ever, coming to Angelfield House often for dinner or tea.

And when she was not at home, she was at the small school she'd had built on the outskirts of the grounds, where she taught the village children.

As she continued to walk, her mind went back to when they were married. It had already been two years. It felt as if it was just yesterday that she had danced and sang with the villagers during her wedding breakfast. Only the next day, she and Emerson had left for the coast, intending to spend their honeymoon on the Continent. It had been the most enjoyable month she'd ever had, which only set the tone for the rest of her time as the Duchess of Edendale. Though her life was no longer as exciting as it had been on the Continent, Kate was happy, content to spend her days with her husband, who did not go into the village either unless he was taking care of business. They read together, ate together, and walked together. They did almost everything in the company of the other.

"Bob and Eve are visiting," Kate said into the silence. "Eve sent me a letter, and I've only just remembered to tell you."

"Ah, and the peace will now be shattered."

Kate giggled. "You will be surprised to know how calm Eve makes him."

"Only when she is not encouraging his behavior." Emerson shrugged. "I suppose it is why she loves him. And I admit it will be good to see him again."

"Oh, don't act as if you haven't missed him dearly. You mention him every day since he and Eve left for India for their honeymoon."

"Please don't tell him that when he arrives."

Kate laughed again. She couldn't believe it; her days were constantly filled with laughter, happiness, and mundane excitement.

"They will be living at Wellbourne Manor, won't they?" Kate asked. "Didn't you say that it is quite a distance from Angelfield?"

"It is, but I reckon they will make frequent visits since Eve's family still resides here. Not to mention the fact that they wish to be here when Sparkes retires."

The butler would be leaving them soon to live out the rest of his days in the house on the estate that Emerson had gifted them, forever a friend of the family.

"Yes, I believe you're right. I'm so happy for them. I cannot think of a more perfect couple."

Emerson squeezed her hand. "I can."

Kate leaned into him. She stopped, and it forced him to pause, too, looking curiously at her. Kate's heart was swelling with such love that she did not think she could contain the news any longer, though she had been hoping to tell him later during dinner.

"What is it?" he asked.

"I have been wanting to tell you something," she said to him. "I've known for a while, and now I do not know how best to get the words out."

"You're making me nervous."

"Don't be." She framed his face with her hand. "It is good news, I promise. I received confirmation from the physician and ... Emerson, I am with child."

Emerson's legs gave way beneath him, but he righted himself before he fell. His eyes were dazed with shock, his mouth opening. Kate held back her laugh, waiting for him to find his words.

"You're ... you're with child?"

"Perhaps it will be a boy," she said, rubbing her stomach. The mound was barely visible, but when touched, it was quite clear. Emerson looked down at her stomach and then back at her face. "The heir? Or maybe the first time will be a daughter."

"Kate ...." Emerson didn't seem to know what to do with himself. He reached forward uncertainly, and Kate encouraged him with a nod. He put his hand against her rounded belly, and his eyes went as wide as saucers. "It's true," he whispered.

"Did you think I would lie?" she giggled. "I am with child, Emerson, with your firstborn."

He didn't give her a chance to prepare when he scooped her into his arms, spinning her around. As quickly as he did, he released her, allowing her to slide back to the ground. Emerson stepped away quickly, looking frightened. "Did I hurt you?"

"No," she reassured him. "I am not that fragile. Not as yet, at least. For now, you are free to pick me up as often as you'd like before I become too heavy."

"God, I love you." He pulled her closer once more, kissing her fiercely. Kate felt the same emotion stir within her even when he pulled away. "And I love you," he said to her stomach, putting his hand on top once more.

"What do you think, Emerson? Do you think you can handle one more child to care for after the new pups?"

"You don't even have to ask." And then he embraced her again, picking her up once more as he twirled her around. It was a new beginning for them, Kate knew, and Kate could not wait for many, many more.

# Extended Epilogue

*Ten Years Since the Wedding*

"Papa, you must tell us!"

"Yes, Papa, or else we will simply die!"

Emerson resisted the urge to let out a sigh. "You will not die," he said to the children sitting cross-legged before him.

Eight-year-old Henry Lake and six-year-old Victor looked at each other. They were very similar to each other in almost every way—from the dark curls on their heads to the blue eyes they'd adopted from their mother to even the smattering of freckles that covered their faces. And even more so, they seemed to share the same brain at times, and the moment he caught the look they shared, Emerson knew he was not going to like what they did next.

Both boys, as if trying to prove their father wrong, threw themselves back onto the floor with their eyes closed, pretending to be dead.

Emerson didn't know whether to sigh or laugh at the sight. He decided to simply shake his head, coming to a stand. He was far too tired to find humor in his sons' actions, wishing they would simply give in to their exhaustion instead. It was obvious that they were fighting the need to sleep, wanting to be a part of the excitement.

Said excitement had begun just after dinner, and now that it was nearing midnight, Emerson had no more energy left to spare to appease the boys. They refused to return to their bedchambers, insisting that Emerson answer all their questions.

Emerson made his way over to the sideboard, wanting a glass of brandy and a cigar. He stopped, resisting the urge. Not here when the children were awake to see him. His duties as a father—and a husband—came first.

Victor was the first to break. He popped one eye open, spotted Emerson standing nearby, and then shook his brother awake. Henry turned but kept his eyes closed, and this time,

Emerson smiled. Perhaps he'd forgotten that he was supposed to be playing dead, not asleep.

"He's not fooled," Victor whispered to his brother, and Henry sighed like an aging man as he sat up. He hopped to his feet and sank his knees into the couch behind them, leaning over the back of it. Victor joined him.

"Please, Papa," he began again. "When is the baby coming?"

"Will it be a boy or a girl?" Victor pressed.

"And why can't we see Mama?" Henry asked. "Is it because she's in pain? Will we make it worse?"

"I do not know the answers to your questions," Emerson said once again.

"Of course you do!" Henry protested. "You know everything."

Emerson shook his head. He'd given up on trying to distract them. Now he wished sleep would claim them instead. "I cannot tell you if it will be a boy or a girl. We'll have to wait until it comes before we find out. And you will only get in the way if you go see your mother now."

"Is that why you're here?" Victor asked quietly.

Emerson nodded though he hated that fact more than anyone. He wanted to be by her side, to hold her hand as she gave birth to their third child. He would have done just that had the midwife, Mrs. Johnson, not chased him away, not daring that he comes close. Emerson was happy that he'd asked Mrs. Johnson to stay with them as Kate came close to giving birth because he did not want to risk having to send for her and any complications that might happen in the interim. But Mrs. Johnson was a strong-willed woman who thought a man had no place in a birthing room. However, how he could possibly be a hindrance, Emerson didn't know.

The hour was growing later. If they were too quiet, they could hear the faintest echo of Kate's screams, which seemed to go on forever. The longer they waited, the more fearful he became. He was quite aware of the complications that might happen while in labor and the very thought that Kate may not ....

He didn't let himself finish the thought. His sons were staring at him with Kate's same disconcerting eyes as if they could tell what he was thinking.

"Why don't we go for a walk?" Emerson suggested. A walk was his answer for everything, and he thought it would do well to entertain them. "But it will be within the house. We don't want to stray too far from your mother."

"A walk in the house?" Henry said, sounding dubious.

"It will be fun, I'm sure." Emerson was already making his way to the door of the drawing room. He feigned excitement, hoping that the boys would begin to mimic him like they usually did. "Perhaps we'll see something we don't—"

He stopped suddenly. With the door open, the silence in the house was deafening. Emerson strained his ears to hear, wondering if it was over. And then he heard it—the faint cry of a baby.

Emerson took off without a thought. He didn't realize that the boys were right on his heels until he was charging up the steps two by two. He raced down the hallways until he skidded to a halt outside the bedchamber they had carried Kate into.

"Let me by," he ordered to the maids standing by the door. They looked at each other, clearly wondering if they should. Certainly, Mrs. Johnson had given them distinct orders to keep him out, but he was still their master.

Before he could try again, the door opened, and Mrs. Johnson slipped out. She crossed her arms, sweat covering her face. "Not yet," she stated.

"I don't care what you say," Emerson said. He'd already decided to ignore the woman's attempt to keep him away. "The baby is out, isn't it? I want to see her."

"She is still recovering. Allow her to regain her strength before—"

Emerson shouldered past her as gently as he could, walking inside. The air smelled of blood, and the maids within were gathering large sheets into one, hiding the stains. Emerson didn't pay them any mind. He rushed to his wife's side.

"Kate," he breathed as he sank next to her.

Kate looked up at him through heavy lids. She, too, was drenched in sweat, her hair plastered to her face, but the smile she gave him was still so beautiful, albeit tired. She didn't say anything at first, looking instead at her sons, who came quietly to the side of her bed.

Their eyes were on the babe in her arms. It had stopped crying and was now latched onto Kate's bosom. The boys were marveling at the sight, and Emerson could tell that Henry wanted to touch it.

"It's a girl," Kate whispered tiredly, though her smile was still present. "Our first girl."

Emerson could not contain the swell of happiness. He wanted to embrace her, to thank her for pushing through, and to apologize for not having been by her side throughout the worst of it. He wanted to hug the baby to his chest and say to her the same thing he had when Henry and Victor had been born—how he would love them until his dying breath and then beyond that. But Henry and Victor had come easily into this world. This newborn babe suckling with such vigor had made Kate work for it.

"I know you have questions," Kate continued to say to her sons. "But I am too tired to answer them now. I'm sure Mrs. Johnson will be willing, though."

Mrs. Johnson, approaching from behind, stiffened when Henry and Victor turned to her. They began their barrage of questions, and she resigned herself to answering while she went around the room and aided the maids in cleaning up.

Kate turned her attention to Emerson. "I hope they did not drive you too mad."

"It is nothing compared to what you endured here." He kissed her on her sweaty temple. "You did so well."

"I think so too." Kate studied the baby in her arms. "After so many hours trying to push her out, you would not expect her to look so tiny."

"She's beautiful."

"And she looks like you. She will be your spitting image when she grows older."

"The poor girl."

"Oh, stop it," Kate laughed, hitting him playfully on the arm. Emerson grinned. He could not take his eyes off his daughter, who seemed so beautiful and fragile in her mother's arms.

"What shall we name her?" he asked.

"There is a name I have been considering for a while now, which I hope you will be fond of." Kate waited until Emerson looked up at her before she continued. "Lucy, after the late Duchess of Edendale."

Emerson felt tears grow thick in his throat. He nodded. "Lucy is perfect."

Kate smiled a little wider. She closed her eyes, settling into the pillow under her neck. "I love you, Emerson. Thank you."

"That should be my line." He kissed her forehead again. "Thank you for everything."

In this small room, his sons continued to ask questions that Mrs. Johnson struggled to answer. His daughter suckled happily, content. His wife breathed deeply as she sunk into sleep. It was a little chaotic, yet he felt happier than ever.

*Thank you, Kate.*

For love. For family. And for making his life worth living again.

## The End

Printed in Great Britain
by Amazon